Until We Can Forgive

Rosemary Goodacre

hera

First published in the United Kingdom in 2020 by Hera

Hera Books
28b Cricketfield Road
London, E5 8NS
United Kingdom

A CIP catalogue record for this book is available from the British Library.

Print ISBN 978 1 80032 169 4
Ebook ISBN 978 1 912973 34 7

Printed and bound in Great Britain by Clays Ltd, Elcograf S.p.A.

To my husband Ian.

Also to Elaine Everest, tutor at The Write Place Creative Writing School at Hextable, and to my group of writing buddies there. They have given me so much help and encouragement, and together we have enjoyed often hilarious social events.

Also to all the devoted medical workers and front line staff, helping us through the COVID crisis.

Chapter 1

Cambridge, spring 1919

At last, there were flowers opening in their little back garden. Amy Derwent seized the moment while Beth took her afternoon nap; she flung on her tweed coat, picked up her scissors and stepped out into the cool air of early April.

Previous tenants must have planted these, she thought.

She bent down and began to pluck the daffodils from the cool earth. There were traditional yellow trumpets, along with pale narcissi with dark golden centres and a delightful perfume. *How lovely they look together. She* picked all the ones coming into flower and a few leaves to keep them company.

Back in the little house, their modest living room was beginning to warm up, for she had already lit the fire. She hung up her coat and went to the kitchen for her one vase, the pale green china one they had recently bought. She arranged her blooms carefully – there, a little glimpse of spring. The winter had dragged on, and even the fact that the war was finally over had not entirely raised people's spirits. There were too many sombre memories.

She took out her large saucepan, for she had a steak and kidney pudding all ready to boil, and if she started it directly it should be ready by the time Edmond got home. Tonight his friend Dennis would be joining them for dinner. *The meal will be quite plain*, she thought with sudden panic. *Will it do? I get the impression Dennis and Horace are from a well-off family.*

Soon her meal was bubbling away on the stove. Amy hurried upstairs and found Beth stirring, ready to wake from her nap. Her nursery was warm, like their parlour, though Amy and Edmond's bedroom went without a fire now it was less cold than a few weeks earlier, relying on the heat rising from downstairs.

Amy was thankful she could walk almost normally now her ankle had been set successfully at the second attempt. Carefully, she combed Beth's fair curls and carried her fifteen-month-old daughter downstairs.

It was a quiet afternoon, for today was not one of the days when Grace the maid came and helped her with the heaviest chores, and Ellen, the nanny, was no longer employed. Amy had been glad of her help while her ankle healed, but she had always intended to bring up her daughter herself. Beth could walk well now, and there was time for them to play and look at the cloth book Aunt Sophie had given her for her first birthday. Amy fed Beth some mashed up vegetables for her tea.

Ashley Street, where they lived, was quiet, but more traffic began to pass as the university and few local businesses closed for the day, and not quite everyone used bicycles. She peeped outside into the cool dusk; soon it would be time to draw the curtains. A young man's footsteps echoed from the brickwork and she saw a soldier marching past with his kitbag. *Is he finally returning home*, she wondered, *or just on leave?* She knew that, under the terms of the treaty, soldiers would still be posted abroad to enforce the peace, particularly along the Rhine.

Then her spirits rose as she heard the sound of Edmond's motorbike, and saw him swoop towards their house. He alighted from his beloved vehicle, hurried indoors and rushed to embrace the two of them. He was tall and still thin, never having quite recovered his robust appearance from before he had been injured.

Edmond picked up his daughter, now wearing her nightclothes and all prepared for bed. They passed a few minutes together before he took the drowsy child upstairs to the nursery and set her down in her cot.

Almost at once there was a knock at the door. Edmond answered it and she heard him welcoming his friend. 'This is Dennis,' he said, taking his greatcoat to hang up.

She followed him into the hall. 'Lovely to meet you,' she said. She had not met the tall, fair-haired young soldier before. He had studied with Edmond in his first year at university. Back then she had known Edmond only from their encounters as children. They had become reacquainted just before the war had broken out, and by autumn 1914 Edmond had volunteered to become an officer. It had been around a year later that Dennis had joined up to fight.

He's one of our first visitors. I must make him welcome.

'I know your brother, Horace, of course,' she said, leading him through to their tiny dining room, where she had already set the table using the cloth Mother had made with the elaborate, lacy, crocheted border.

She began serving their meal on the Royal Albert Crown china plates from their dinner service. Edmond poured them some wine.

'This is delicious, Amy,' Dennis said.

'So you're not back from France permanently yet?' she asked Dennis. He was in the familiar khaki uniform.

'Only on leave. I gather from Edmond that while he was fighting in France you were working as a nurse.'

'Yes – I joined the Voluntary Aid Detachment.' Her war work had been demanding and she had witnessed some horrifying injuries, but she was thankful she had played her part. They had married while he was on leave. 'When we were both in France, Edmond and I would try to get leave so we could snatch days or a weekend together.' She had scarcely dared to try to plan their future together in those fraught days.

Their time abroad had ended in 1917 when Edmond had been hit by a shell while serving near Ypres. She still sometimes had nightmares about the days when she had not even known if he would survive, and now she was resigned to the fact that his health would never entirely recover. She had been sent home too, as she had been expecting Beth. They had at least been together while they were staying with his family at The Beeches. No longer fit enough to fight, he had been anxious to resume his pre-war studies; anything less would have seemed like allowing the Huns to ruin his life.

Dennis looked at their treasured photograph, hanging from the picture rail in its silver-plated frame. 'And that must be your daughter!'

'That's the lovely picture of the three of us at Beth's christening last summer,' she said.

'So you all moved here last autumn?' Dennis asked.

'Edmond did, and I meant to join him,' she said. She had intended to move with him at the start of Michaelmas term, to cosset him and make sure he did not overexert himself. A succession of illnesses in the family had compelled her to delay moving here with Beth. She looked across at Edmond's contented face. At last they were finally settled together. Edmond was older than some of the undergraduates in his year, and one of the few married ones.

'Edmond's family gave us a home at their fine house, but I always longed for a little place of our own,' she told their visitor.

'I remember how thrilled you looked when you first cooked us Sunday lunch here, and when you arranged the nursery for Beth,' Edmond said, with his captivating smile.

There had been her early visits to see their future home, admiring the little brick-built house with ivy on its façade, and the quaint old town. Finally, in the new year, she had been thrilled to move in with Beth and the last of their possessions. 'Sometimes it still seems a miracle that the three of us are all together, in our own home at last.'

Edmond helped her clear the dishes and there was an aroma of cinnamon and cloves as she served the apple pie for their pudding.

By the time Edmond had been sufficiently recovered from his injury to return to university, Horace, Dennis's younger brother, had started studying there, excused from fighting because of his poor eyesight.

'So you've taken to the academic life again?' Dennis asked him. 'You cope well in spite of your wound?'

'Yes!' Edmond insisted as usual.

'How are your studies going?'

Edmond told him a little about his lectures, and the laboratory work he needed to do for his metallurgy course.

'Any news about you being discharged?' he asked Dennis.

'No sign so far. I may be sent to join the Army of Occupation.'

'You should try to take up your studies again,' Edmond urged. 'I'm glad I returned.'

Soon the men were talking about the war. Dennis had missed most of the Somme campaign, having sustained an injury early on, but he had recovered enough to fight at Ypres. 'If I'd known you were in the hospital there I'd have visited you,' he told Edmond.

'Horace told me you were fighting in tanks!'

'I did for a while, later on.' For a moment Dennis seemed about to launch into an account of the later stages of the war, then he checked himself. 'Those days were horrific, though, I'm thankful to put them behind me.' Perhaps he imagined that Amy would find the topic tedious or upsetting.

When they had finished the meal, Dennis proposed going out.

'Horace suggested we join him in *The Fenman*,' he said. 'I gather you go most Friday evenings for a pint or two, and that Amy sometimes comes too.'

'Have you arranged for Grace to be here with Beth?' Edmond asked her.

'I decided to stay at home tonight,' she said, 'but you two should go.'

'I hope Gerald didn't annoy you last week,' Edmond said. 'He can get argumentative. He might not even come this week.'

She got on well with Horace, but some of the other undergraduates who might be there could be annoying. 'I'll come another week, I promise.' She was glad that he invited her to join them.

'Horace and I are planning to go punting tomorrow,' Dennis said. 'Would you two like to come?'

Punting — she had seen the undergraduates in their punts on the Cam, and thought what fun it must be. All the same... 'I'd rather not take Beth in a punt,' she said, 'but if you're all going I'll come and watch.'

As she gathered up their plates the men put on their outdoor clothes.

'Want to come on the back of my bike?' Edmond asked his friend, and they set out together.

Wearily, Amy began the washing up. There was still some mending to do as well.

Edmond had grown up in a wealthy household, where servants had tackled the hard work. She was anxious he should never suffer hardship for marrying a schoolmaster's daughter, instead of someone of his own class.

—

The public house was dingy, but the beer was cheap to suit students. Edmond felt warm at their table near the fire, except when customers opened the door and a draught blew in. Besides Horace, their friend Gerald was there, who had not met Dennis before. He was a frail-looking, dark-haired student. He had been excused from fighting too, as he had had tuberculosis as a child. Sometimes they would joke ruefully that their year's intake were all weaklings.

Edmond was curious to hear about tank battles, and asked Dennis to tell him more.

'They were a great advance over conventional vehicles,' he said. 'With their caterpillar tracks they could charge ahead across dreadfully churned up terrain, like at Passchendaele.'

'I've heard they hastened our victory.'

'They had disadvantages. They were vulnerable to a direct hit from a shell, or a grenade if you were overrun by the infantry.'

'Overrun?'

'They couldn't go faster than about four miles per hour. At first, I hoped to be transferred to a tank unit, but I didn't get trained until early last year, and I only took part in a few of the later battles in the summer.'

Gerald fetched another round of beer. He and Horace were beginning to look bored, still sensitive about not having been part of the war effort themselves.

'You soon discovered how unpleasant it actually is inside a tank,' Dennis went on. 'The ventilation is very poor. You're exposed to vapour from the engine and cordite fumes from the weapons. It's fiendishly hot inside, especially in summer.'

'I hadn't realised it was so bad,' Edmond said. Was he being morbid, still curious about the grisly battles? 'At least it's all over now,' he said.

'Thank God,' Dennis said. 'I'll be relieved when I can get my discharge.'

'Men are still serving abroad,' his brother Horace complained. He was a thin, fair-haired, young student with glasses.

'Do we really need to occupy the Rhineland, now the Germans have been so thoroughly thrashed?' Gerald asked.

'I believe we do,' Edmond said reluctantly. 'There are some hotheads, apparently, who can't accept defeat.' Amy's pacifist cousin James would have liked to see reconciliation with the enemy, but the conflict had destroyed so many young lives that Edmond was desperate to believe that the Huns could never rise again to challenge them. He liked to hear the great conflict referred to as *the war to end all wars*.

'When will your car be ready?' Horace asked him presently.

'By Monday or Tuesday, I believe,' Edmond said. 'It'll be perfect for visiting my parents over Easter. The motorbike isn't an option for family travel.'

The others looked set to stay till closing time but he left before ten. A chill wind was blowing from the fens. He climbed on the back of his motorbike and set off to cover the short distance home. He turned into his own street just as the bike began to splutter. *Confound it,* he thought, *am I short of petrol?*

The second-hand – or maybe third- or fourth-hand – car he had bought from another undergraduate, had seen some careless driving and little maintenance. The mechanic was replacing various worn parts. The day before, he had discovered the brakes needed urgent attention. Edmond had not wanted to draw out too much of his grandfather's legacy and had skimped on day to day expenses, but it seemed he had been optimistic about how long the petrol in his bike would last. Fifty yards further down the road it came to a halt.

Wearily, he pushed the vehicle the remaining hundred yards or so to their little house. He was soon growing hot and flustered in spite of the cold wind. He paused as he grew short of breath, then continued. However much his health had improved over the past year and a half, he was deluding himself if he pretended he would ever be totally fit. His right lung would never fully recover from that shell blast near Ypres.

He drew the deepest breath he could and made one last effort which brought him to his house.

'Hello, darling! Have a nice evening?' Amy called as he stepped inside.

He was too out of breath to reply straight away. She came to meet him in the hall, a pink woolly shawl around her shoulders. 'Are you all right?'

'A little out of breath, that's all.' As he recovered he told her what had happened.

Her eyes widened with concern. 'Come and sit down by the fire – I'll bring you some cocoa. You must try not to overdo things.'

Soon she was sitting next to him as they drank their nightcaps. The sofa was the one they had had in their room at The Beeches, upholstered in dark green fabric. The parlour fire was dying down but still throwing out some heat.

'We must go out together, just the two of us,' he said. 'Grace can stay with Beth for the evening. I'll have the car soon, so you needn't go on the back of the bike. Let's look out for a play or concert you'd enjoy. Or we could go for a meal in a restaurant.'

'That would be lovely.'

Their budget was small, but they should be able to manage an outing once a month or so.

–

'It's about time to join the others down by the Cam,' Edmond said the next afternoon.

'I'll get Beth ready,' Amy said.

'I'll deal with the washing up from lunch.' How thoughtful he was. For years she had longed to set up home with Edmond, and she loved looking after him, but now she was at home every day she looked forward to the occasional outing. It was Saturday, so he had not had any lectures, and she had tried to complete all today's chores before lunch.

She went upstairs, roused their daughter and got her ready to go out. Soon they were setting off with Beth in her pram. There was sunshine today but they still needed coats.

They turned off in the direction of the river, enjoying the view of the willows and the Colleges across the Cam.

'You don't mind spending the afternoon with my friends?' he asked her.

'No – it's a lovely day for a walk by the river.'

The area was busy today, and sunshine bright on the surface of the water. Young men were crowding into punts.

'There are Dennis and Horace!' Edmond cried, and they went to join the two fair-haired brothers.

'Are you coming punting with us?' Horace asked Amy.

'I'd rather not, with Beth,' Amy said, for the narrow waterways were crowded and she was anxious that her daughter might wriggle out of her arms.

There was a long queue of undergraduates waiting for a punt. Amy and Edmond sat on the bank with their friends. Gerald soon arrived too.

As often happened, Amy found the young men involved in an argument.

'We must make the Huns pay the price for all the years of fighting!' Dennis was asserting.

'It is time to call a halt,' Gerald cried angrily.

There was a tendency to demand a rapid conclusion to the years of fighting. Even young men who had escaped conscription, usually for a good reason, were ready to criticise the political leaders for their latest decisions.

Undergraduates surged forward now to claim punts. Gerald joined a heavily built, young boatman and the two of them hired a punt and pushed away into the river. Dennis and Horace were shouting, prolonging the argument as they followed them in a second punt.

Amy looked after them in exasperation.

'They're always debating what course the Peace Treaty should take,' Edmond said. As his friends punted further downstream their voices carried and Beth went on staring in their direction. Amy sat by the riverside, trying to relax.

'Now they're turning it into a fight,' she said uneasily. The opponents in the two punts were aiming their poles at each other's vessels. Other punters were shouting at them to take care.

'It's like a dogfight, when airmen fought each other over France,' he said, with a mixture of shock and amusement.

He went in search of ice creams, then they wandered along the bank for a while, enjoying their first glimpses of butterflies that year.

Before long, they could hear his friends returning. 'I need to get back,' called Gerald's friend. 'Do you want to take my place in the punt, Edmond?'

'You go for a quick trip,' Amy urged him, knowing he was longing to join his friends. He climbed in with Gerald and they punted off while she and Beth watched. Edmond and his friend wove through the water, dodging other young men, as far as the nearest bridge and back again.

'Let's get the peace settled,' Gerald was crying now as they came back into earshot.

They're still quarrelsome, she thought.

'Nonsense! We must make absolutely certain of seizing reparations from the Germans!' Horace said from the other punt.

'Take care!' Dennis cried as Horace thrust his punt angrily towards the one Gerald was steering. The water was still teeming with activity.

Amy watched with alarm as Gerald and Horace aimed poles at each other's punts.

'Stop the horseplay!' someone called loudly from a nearby punt.

Just then Gerald thrust Horace's punt across the river, whirling through the water. Edmond, in the back of Gerald's punt, looked apprehensive for a moment. Horace brought his boat under control, punted back at top speed and thrust his pole fiercely at the other one. It jerked across the river and Gerald was hurled out of it into the water with a giant splash. He screamed loudly.

Edmond stood up, alarmed. 'He can't swim! And he's not very fit.' He looked around and realised that their pole had ended up with Gerald in the Cam. 'I haven't got a pole!'

Dennis and Horace hurriedly propelled their punt in Gerald's direction. One of their friends on a nearby punt leapt on to Edmond's one, carrying a pole, and steered him to the bank. He jumped off, landing awkwardly on the steep slope, and leant down in an attempt to reach Gerald.

Beth began to cry in sympathy. 'Take care!' Amy shouted. 'You're far from fit yourself, Edmond!'

Soon half a dozen young men were rushing to the edge of the river, while others punted towards the man in difficulties. Gerald was near the bank and Edmond extended his arm towards his struggling friend. Amy rushed towards them, but she needed to hang on to Beth. Edmond slipped on the muddy bank and soon he was thrashing in the water.

Dennis leapt from his punt, landing heavily on the bank, and pulled Gerald from the water, well on to the grass. Edmond pulled himself out with a great effort and flopped down next to them. Amy felt a surge of relief.

Dennis was looking angrily at Horace. 'You're very foolish. Gerald isn't strong and neither is Edmond.' He began practising artificial respiration on Gerald, water pouring from his clothes. Soon it was clear that Gerald was breathing almost normally.

Amy was reassuring herself Edmond was unharmed. She settled Beth in her pram.

'It's all right,' Edmond said with an almighty cough, 'I'm not in any danger.' His teeth were chattering and his clothes were thoroughly saturated and slimy from the water.

'I'm taking you all home in my car,' Dennis said.

'Are you taking Gerald?'

'He can squash in as well. You'll have to walk, Horace.'

'Don't cry, sweetheart,' Edmond told Beth gently. 'Everyone is all right.'

Though they hardly deserve to be, Amy thought. As they walked across the grass towards the road the sun went in. Gerald was showing signs of a good recovery as he clung on to Dennis.

'It's what happens every year,' Horace said. 'Men are always falling in.'

'I know,' Dennis admitted reluctantly.

'But I should have known better than to take chances,' he conceded finally.

'I'll push the pram,' Amy insisted as Edmond tried to take it. She did not know what Dennis's car looked like or how far they might need to walk. A cold wind was beginning to blow. Edmond paused as he grew short of breath, then continued.

'Are you all right, darling?'

He struggled to reply. 'A little out of breath, that's all.'

Dennis stopped by a fairly basic car and let in Edmond and Gerald.

'I'll never get the pram in there!' Amy cried with sudden realisation.

'You and Beth get in the car, Amy,' Dennis said. 'Horace can push your pram home for you!'

A look of horror appeared on his face.

'Get on with it!' Dennis demanded. 'It will serve you right.'

Reluctantly he set off across the grass with the basket-work perambulator, while other undergraduates stared at him. Dennis drove the rest of them towards Ashley Street. There was a smell of muddy river water.

'Is there anything else I can do?' asked Dennis.

'When you've taken us home, go and call on my maid, Grace, and ask her if she can come to help this evening,' Amy said. 'Then if Edmond is at all ill she can go for a doctor.'

'I'll be all right,' Edmond said.

'I'll do it anyway,' Dennis said, 'then I'll take you to a doctor too, Gerald.'

'When are you going back to France?' Edmond asked him.

'Next week... but as soon as I can get discharged I'll take up my education again, I promise you. Then I can keep an eye on all you maniacs!'

Half an hour later their fire was lit and Edmond was wearing dry clothes and warming up as he drank his second cup of tea.

'You really mustn't take chances with your health,' Amy said.

'Sorry, darling – I had to help Gerald, didn't I?'

Grace, their middle-aged maid who normally only worked there two days a week, began preparing them a meal. 'You young men are always messing about in those punts,' she reproached him. 'No sooner do some of you get back from the war than you're running risks again.'

'You're right,' Edmond said, to Amy's surprise. 'As a father I should take more care.'

They sat in their small dining room and Amy helped Beth eat her portion of the mince Grace had cooked quickly.

After the meal Amy put Beth to bed. Grace went home and Amy lounged next to Edmond on the sofa.

'How lovely you look in the lamplight,' he said, stroking her long blonde curls. He put his arm about her and kissed her.

Chapter 2

'Is this car all right?' Amy asked as they set off for The Beeches for Easter.

'It's in good order,' he assured her. 'Don't worry, darling! It's all fixed and we can travel properly, with Beth and some luggage!'

'You won't need the motorbike any longer.'

'Perhaps I should keep it for a while longer, just for emergencies.' He had first ridden a motorbike in France, and she knew how he loved it.

There were around a hundred miles to travel, so they stopped the car at a modest inn just north of London for lunch. They continued, skirting the capital to the east and crossing the Thames by the Woolwich ferry before continuing into Sussex.

By late afternoon they were driving into Larchbury. *Now we're back we'll be staying with Edmond's family, but we'll be able to visit my parents too,* Amy thought.

Soon Edmond was driving up the avenue of great beeches towards his family's imposing stone house. On the hill ahead was the forest, mainly of pines, from which the family made their business.

Back to The Beeches, Amy thought. *How I used to long for us to leave there and get a home of our own!* For much of her married life Edmond's mother and sister had been distant towards her. Not only was she not of Edmond's class, but they disapproved of her pre-war involvement with the Suffragettes. She did not regret demanding the vote for women, but wished she had stopped short of joining friends in a provocative prank. They had broken into the cricket pavilion and scrawled slogans there, which had led to her having to serve a week in prison.

As Edmond parked the car in front of the house, Pa came out to greet them. Mr Derwent had encouraged Amy to call him Pa, and his wife Ma. He had been the first one of Edmond's family to accept her, and she greeted him warmly as he said a smiling hello to Beth and looked over Edmond's Ford car a little dubiously. It was clear that the bodywork had been patched up here and there, in some workshop where the mechanic was prepared to make a quick but adequate repair to keep costs down.

In the hall, Ma greeted them brightly.

'You're looking much better now,' Amy said. She was no longer thin and drawn, as she had been after the influenza. However, her face still looked a little pasty.

'I believe I'm almost recovered now.'

Beatrice, Edmond's sister, smartly dressed as usual in a blouse and skirt which showed off her good figure, also hurried to greet them.

'Auntie Bee-trice!' cried Beth, happy to receive a cuddle from her.

Before long they were sitting in the wooden-panelled dining room and Cook was serving vegetable soup. In the middle of the table was a splendid arrangement of pink tulips, which could only be the handiwork of Beatrice.

'Beth has grown so much since I last saw her,' Ma said, smiling at the plump-faced little girl.

It's as though Ma's pleased to see us, Amy thought as she helped Beth, seated beside her in a highchair, spoon up her soup.

'Mrs Johnson is here today,' Beatrice told her. 'I sent her to unpack your cases.'

'Thank you.' She was the middle-aged woman who acted as maid to her own parents one day a week and to Edmond's family twice weekly since the war had left them short-staffed.

'But she's embarrassed about her daughter, Elsie. It's best not to mention her.'

What's all that about?

'Are you happy with your domestic staff now?' Amy asked Ma, remembering her panic when one of the servants had left the previous year and could not at first be replaced.

'Daisy works well, I'm glad to say. But we haven't got as many staff as we had before the war.' Ma was fretful now.

'Cook is as wonderful as ever,' Amy said, once the plump, grey-haired woman had served them roast pork. After all the chores connected with their move to Cambridge, Amy could not help looking forward to some weeks of having her meals prepared for her. *And I'm almost happy to be staying with Edmond's family,* she thought. *I've missed them more than I expected.*

'Ma has largely recovered, but she still tires easily,' Beatrice explained.

'As soon as summer arrives we must take a holiday,' Pa promised. He looked a little less weary than he had done during the war, when he had struggled to keep up with the demand for timber, with his workforce depleted.

'Oh – if only we could go to the south of France again! We should go soon, before it gets too hot. Is that possible, do you think?' Ma asked.

'You'd have to travel through all the ravaged area in the north to get there,' Edmond told her patiently. 'I'm afraid Europe is in turmoil now.'

'There's surely somewhere we can go!'

'Holland, maybe – the Dutch were neutral.'

Ma's expression showed she had no interest in going there.

'I'm afraid it's all been ruined across the Channel,' Beatrice said. 'Remember what Peter has told us about it. I've longed for peace too, but I'm beginning to realise that nothing will ever be the same. We need to move on.' Her pretty features revealed resignation.

It was the first time Amy had heard her speak so calmly of accepting the changes.

'I promise you we'll find somewhere lovely to stay on the south coast,' Pa told them. 'They'll have removed the barbed wire from the beaches at last.'

'Is Peter still in France?' Edmond asked his parents for news of his older brother.

'He's continuing at High Command,' Pa said brightly. 'They're planning details for the occupation of the Rhineland. It's easier for him to get leave now there's no more fighting, but we don't know when he'll next be home.'

'And Caleb is in France still too, but he tells me he'll manage to get leave soon,' Beatrice said, a dreamy expression in her greenish eyes. Her gleaming chestnut hair had tiny curls at the front, and was drawn loosely into a bun at the back of her head. Fashions were more casual than they had once been.

Amy had wondered if Beatrice was still seeing Caleb. She herself had only met the American once or twice at the beginning of the year, and although he and Beatrice had seemed absorbed in each other, she had not imagined the attachment lasting for long.

Beth was growing sleepy. 'Remember your first nursery?' Amy asked her. 'You'll be sleeping there again tonight.'

The little girl settled readily in her old cot. Beatrice came up to the nursery to sing her a lullaby. Then they joined the others in the drawing room.

Amy settled on the sofa next to Edmond. The room had a Turkish carpet and deep blue, velvet curtains. Though she was content enough with her little house in Cambridge, she could not help realising that the parlour there was half the size. She looked around at the comfortable furniture and the piano, wondering if they would ever afford one.

Ma seemed to read her thoughts. 'How are you settling in?' she asked Amy.

'We're very comfortable, thank you.' Thank goodness Ma was not planning to visit them.

'We'll be getting some new curtains for the parlour soon,' Edmond said.

It was true that the ones provided by their landlord were unattractively dark. 'Yes, I plan to make some,' Amy said quickly, wondering where they were to find the money for the fabric, and how she could make time to sew them.

'Haven't we got some spare curtains here?' Pa asked. 'We've got more visitors' rooms than we use, not counting the attic room that's available if we ever have an extra live-in servant. We could surely spare a set of curtains? But only if there's some that Amy and Edmond really like, of course.'

How kind he is, Amy thought. *And he's seen our house, and knows it's quite basic, but I'm sure he'll have given a good account of it to Ma.*

'I daresay we might manage with one less set of curtains,' Ma said.

'That's very generous, Ma, and Pa,' Edmond said.

Amy echoed his sentiments.

'Only not the rose-pink satin ones in the corner room,' Beatrice begged. 'That's such a lovely room for when Vicky stays the night, or one of my friends.'

'They sound beautiful, but more for a young lady's bedroom than our parlour,' Amy said. *She did not want fancy ones with frills and draping.*

They had made an early start that morning so went upstairs soon. Their large bedroom, overlooking the azaleas in the garden, had served for a while as their private sitting room as well, but now some of the furniture and their books and records were in Cambridge.

'I feel as though your mother and sister have finally accepted me,' she told Edmond as they prepared for bed.

'I should think so! After all, you nursed Ma back to health when she had the Spanish influenza!'

That had been a terrible time, last autumn, when Amy had wondered if Ma would survive, and whether others of them would succumb to the often fatal disease. She had needed all her nursing skills, but Ma had recovered, and Amy had prevented the infection from spreading. She felt she deserved their gratitude.

Beatrice had also called upon her sympathy, when she had confided the details of an unfortunate incident which she felt unable to mention to anyone else. Amy suspected her sister-in-law was still traumatised by what had taken place.

Edmond climbed into bed. 'Never doubt it, you're a valued member of the family!' he said, holding out his arms. She hurried contentedly into his embrace.

–

Easter Sunday was mild and sunny, and the service, led by Amy's uncle Arthur, was an inspiring one. They were well into April and the spring weather had raised the spirits of most of the congregation. Amy held Beth's hand as they left St Stephen's, the old, stone church, and hovered near the porch to chat to their friends. They had already called on Amy's parents, but there were many others she had not seen since leaving for Cambridge.

Soon her old friend Florence rushed to greet her. She was a good correspondent but as yet she had not visited them in their new home. Then Florence was joined by James, her fiancé. He was Amy's cousin, the vicar's son, and they had announced their engagement on New Year's Day, at the party for Beth's first birthday.

'I haven't even seen your ring yet,' Amy said.

Florence had described it in one of her letters, and now her face dimpled as she removed her glove to reveal the modest gold band with two small diamonds. Once Florence had been engaged to Amy's brother Bertie, but he had been killed in the fighting on the Somme. Although she and her parents were pleased to see Florence making a fresh life with James, grief would suddenly sweep over her when she remembered Bertie.

'I was lucky, I got leave for Easter,' James told them, 'but I need to return afterwards. There are still many invalids in

France who aren't ready yet to be sent home.' James served as a medical orderly. Seeing him always affected Amy, for with his grey eyes he reminded her of Bertie.

'But you'll be back in three weeks for our wedding!' Florence cried, her hazel eyes bright, and James grinned and nodded.

'You will be able to come, won't you?' Florence urged Amy.

'Yes – we don't need to be back in Cambridge till just afterwards.'

She had been close friends with Florence since they had started school together. In the far-off days before the war they had joined the local band of Suffragettes, with their slightly older friend Lavinia, who had been an early enthusiast for the organisation. Lavinia was also engaged now, to Captain Charles Shenwood, and planning to marry later in the summer.

'Now, tell me, Edmond, is your health still improving?' James asked. 'You look well.'

'I don't think of myself as an invalid anymore!' He smiled broadly, always positive about his fitness.

'You had a check-up in February, didn't you?' James persisted.

'Yes, we went to the London hospital, and the surgeon there was very impressed with my progress.'

Only Amy realised quite how tired he could become if he overexerted himself.

As they gossiped, they broke off to nod to other friends going past. Mrs Johnson, the charlady, was one of the last to leave the church. She was supporting a young, fair-haired woman on her arm, and Amy gasped when she realised it was her daughter Elsie, who was clearly expecting a child – sometime in the next couple of months, by the look of her.

'I didn't know Elsie was expecting,' Amy said quietly to Florence. She remembered now that Beatrice had mentioned her as though there was some element of scandal.

'She's not married,' Florence whispered.

Amy nodded to Mrs Johnson and her daughter as they passed. Now was not an appropriate time to ask them any probing questions. Elsie smiled back at her. She had always given the impression of being a little simple, and she was only seventeen, young to be with child.

'I don't suppose… has there been any news of Henry Smith?' Along with his brothers he had worked at The Beeches as a gardener before he had joined up. He had gone missing just before the end of the war.

'No,' James said regretfully. Men who went missing in action were seldom found alive. 'I understand he was involved in one of our last serious battles in the war.'

'I know he was Elsie's sweetheart last summer,' Amy said, remembering seeing them together.

'Everyone thinks he's the father but she claims she had another admirer,' Florence said.

Edmond seemed to be listening, intrigued.

'No one believes her, but she claims Philip Brownlee, the airman, is the father.' Philip had died just after the end of the war from injuries sustained in a crash.

Amy gasped. So far as she knew there had not been any attachment between the handsome young airman and Elsie.

No wonder there's scandal surrounding her, she thought. As the young girl made her way past the yew trees and slowly out of the churchyard, still clinging to her mother, curious eyes followed her and parishioners bent their heads to discuss her situation.

–

When Amy visited her parents' little house in Sebastopol Terrace, Mrs Johnson was there tackling the weekly wash. She and Amy chatted as they usually did. The kindly charlady commented on Beth's confident walking and gradually improving speech.

'You'll soon have another grandchild,' Amy remarked. Mrs Johnson had an older daughter, who was settled, with several young children and a devoted husband who was fortunate to have survived the war.

'Elsie is such an embarrassment,' Mrs Johnson admitted. 'Of course, we'll stand by her if Henry's family won't support her. Or the Brownlees – that's very unlikely.'

'I'm relieved Elsie won't need to resort to leaving her baby at the orphanage,' Amy's mother told her, while Mrs Johnson was hanging the washing outside.

Mother had once had fair hair, like Amy's, but it was greyer now. She had started working twice a week in a voluntary capacity in the orphanage, which was growing in importance as a local institution. Two other young girls, left in the family way after their soldier followers had died abroad, had already left their babies there.

'I'm sure the staff are glad to have your help,' Amy said. 'Do you enjoy working there?'

'Yes – there's plenty to do and I enjoy looking after young ones again.'

Amy took tea with her parents in their parlour. Beth settled on her grandmother's lap.

'Is there any chance we'll have another grandchild soon?' Mother asked, not for the first time.

Amy smiled. 'Someday, not too far away, I hope.' At present there was quite enough to do with Beth, and settling into the house, but one day they hoped to have another child or two.

From the mantelpiece an old photograph of Bertie in his lieutenant's uniform smiled down on them. She would never forget his merry face, with fair hair and a moustache.

'There's still unfinished business from the war,' she said to her parents. 'Until the fallen are settled in worthy graves we can't know real peace.'

Ever since Bertie's memorial service in 1916 they had wanted to know where he lay, and had begged for a photograph of his grave. Like most bereaved relatives wanting these details, they had been further distressed at the limited information available, and had had to resign themselves to waiting for well laid-out cemeteries to be completed after the war. Now they were impatient for more action by the National Committee for the Care of Soldiers' Graves, presided over by Edward, Prince of Wales.

'It was a dreadful shock to hear that they won't be repatriating the bodies,' Mother said.

Amy was almost equally upset that Bertie's remains would stay abroad, though she realised what an undertaking it would have been to bring all the fallen soldiers home. 'They've arranged to buy land in France and Belgium now,' she said, 'and the Committee will be responsible for the upkeep.'

'At least they've decided on standard memorials being used, to avoid class distinctions,' Father said. As a schoolteacher he was not yet back at work after the Easter holidays. 'One of the only bearable memories of the war is the brotherhood that developed between the different ranks.'

—

By late afternoon Amy was walking back towards The Beeches with Beth in her pram. How liberating it was to be able to walk well, now her broken ankle was finally almost back to normal.

As she turned into the lane she saw Elsie Johnson coming towards her, with a large bunch of bluebells. 'Hello, Mrs Derwent.'

'Hello, Elsie. I'd almost forgotten the bluebells are coming out now. I must take Beth there to pick some one day.' They grew prolifically each spring at the edge of the forest, just outside the Derwents' land. If it had not been a little late, she might have taken her daughter there now.

Elsie hovered, as though eager to talk. Her skirt was strained across her stomach. 'I'm going to have my own little one,' she said brightly, as though Amy might not have realised her condition.

'Yes – is your baby due quite soon?' she asked.

'By about June, the doctor said.' Elsie stooped and sat down wearily on a tree stump.

That's the correct time for the birth if Henry Smith is the father, Amy thought, remembering seeing the young couple canoodling when Henry had last been on leave in September.

So far as she could remember, Philip had not been on leave from the Royal Flying Corps then. She seemed to remember Elsie once passing him in the street, a handsome young man, in his uniform. She had stopped and stared at him, but Amy did not believe he encouraged her in any way.

Amy leant against a stile. *Should I say something to her?* she wondered. *She's still very young.* She remembered Elsie's slapdash attempts to help with the laundry and chop vegetables for Cook at The Beeches. *She needs some guidance. There's bound to be gossip about her pregnancy, but if Elsie is careful what she says she might limit the censure. I believe Edmond said that George, Henry's elder brother, is expected back in Larchbury soon, discharged from the army.*

'If only Philip knew he was going to have a son!' Elsie said, a dreamy expression in her blue eyes.

'Listen, Elsie, are you sure he might be the father?' Amy asked. 'Everyone saw you with Henry Smith last summer.'

'No, Philip's the father. We were in love, him and me.'

Amy laid her hand on the younger girl's arm. 'Listen, if you're in any doubt it would be best not to claim that Philip is the father,' she said. 'Village people saw you spending time with Henry, and if you were sharing your time between two young men it would appear... well, a little scandalous. People might imagine you were trying to get the Brownlee family to support you because they're wealthy.'

Elsie's jaw dropped open. Her eyes were wide, but Amy suspected she still did not grasp all the implications of her claim.

'We were in love, Philip and me,' she repeated.

The sun was sinking lower and it was becoming chilly.

'I must hurry back to The Beeches,' Amy said. 'I shouldn't keep Beth out too late. Think about what I said, Elsie.'

–

One day Edmond's cousin Vicky came to visit. Amy had liked her since first meeting her as a fourteen-year-old, but now she was eighteen and much more grown up, her abundant auburn hair held at the nape of her neck. When Amy went into the drawing room she looked up from talking to Edmond and greeted Amy and Beth.

'I'm starting nursing soon,' Vicky said proudly.

'I'm so pleased,' Amy said. 'It's not an easy occupation, but I'm sure you realise that.' Vicky had often talked of following Amy's choice of work. 'Was it easy to find a place, now the war's over?'

There was talk that, providing the influenza cases continued to decline, they might release some of the VAD nurses from their duties. The lucky ones had some prospect of sweethearts returning from the Front, but many did not, after all the losses suffered, and some planned to remain in the profession.

'I had quite a tough interview,' Vicky admitted. 'But it turns out they are taking on some girls for training near here, at Wealdham Hospital, and they've offered me a place.'

'Good news, isn't it?' said Edmond, who had already heard. 'You'll be able to visit often.'

'They've got a Resident Medical Officer there, so they can offer basic training. They may send us elsewhere for a few weeks – maybe to the Mothers' Home in the East End of London to learn midwifery.'

Beth was wandering the room, fiddling with cushions. Vicky reached out and pulled her up on to her lap. 'You know what my parents are like,' she said. 'They have ideas about young women staying at home till they marry. They are quite dreadfully old-fashioned.'

Amy smiled, remembering meeting Vicky's father, Edmond's Uncle Eustace. How dismayed he had been at Beth's christening when Vicky had mentioned her plans to nurse! 'Most people used to think that,' Amy said. 'Edmond's mother was scandalised when I planned to work after we were married. But the war brought such a shortage of labour that they had to include more women in the workforce.'

'They're a little happier about the prospect now they know I'll be living near Aunt Mabel and Uncle Hugh. Not that I expect your parents to look after me, Edmond. I'm going to live in the nurses' hostel near the hospital.'

'You're lucky there's a hostel now. Wealdham is where I did my initial training,' Amy told her. 'I used to come back to Larchbury each night, but other girls had to sleep in the poky attics.' She wondered if the same stern matron was still there. 'They almost threw me out on my first day, as they'd heard about my Suffragette activity,' she recalled.

'I know I should be relieved that the war's over,' Vicky said, 'but I sometimes think that women your age enjoyed travel and adventure that I won't experience. Sorry, Edmond, I don't mean to be insensitive. I know how badly you were wounded.'

Amy was a little shocked but could understand her envy. She was concerned for Edmond's feelings, and made a point of taking Vicky upstairs to show her the new pale pink, silk dress she would wear to be matron of honour at Florence's wedding.

'That's beautiful, Amy.'

'All I need now is a lovely hat in a similar shade. Beatrice is the person to help me choose one.'

'The hats this year are smaller and less showy,' Beatrice complained as they came out of the milliner's shop that afternoon.

'I'm very pleased with what we chose,' Amy said. 'You're so good at selecting one which will suit me.'

'It looks lovely, with those silk flowers,' Vicky said.

They're right, Beatrice thought, *the one I picked out for her to try has an asymmetric brim, flattering to Amy's round face.*

The afternoon had turned out mild. 'Let's stop for tea,' she said, indicating the smart teashop. 'I believe it's warm enough to sit outside.'

They sat down and ordered tea and scones.

Beatrice took out the feathery concoction she had bought herself. 'I believe this will do quite well,' she said. 'Didn't you want a new hat for spring, Vicky?'

The younger girl shook her auburn curls. 'I shall be wearing uniform most of the time,' she said, sounding regretful.

The waitress poured their tea.

'I daresay you miss Caleb,' Vicky said suddenly. She had seen her cousin receive his letter that morning, and had insisted on seeing his photograph.

Beatrice did not welcome her curiosity. 'I'd hoped we'd have the young men home by now, but many are still abroad,' she said. 'And in Caleb's case it's different, because he comes from America.'

'But are you in love?' Vicky pursued eagerly. 'Would you want to marry him and go to live there?'

Why can't she mind her own business? 'I've only known him a few months, and most of that time he's been in France,' she said, wishing she knew the answer herself. 'How should I know if I'd like to live in America? I

33

haven't any idea what it's like there. You don't know any Americans, do you, Amy?'

Her sister-in-law shook her head.

'I can't imagine leaving everyone I know here and going to a country so far away. I gather Caleb's family are farmers.'

'Is he a cowboy?' Vicky asked curiously.

'No, they work their land. I don't believe they're great landowners. Whatever would Ma think if I married a humble farmer?'

The others exchanged glances.

'And don't tell Ma, but Caleb has only a low rank – he's just a warrant officer.'

They were subdued as they walked back to The Beeches. Beatrice had the feeling Amy was anxious she should not set her hopes too much on a future with Caleb, and perhaps her impetuous young cousin had finally realised she was being far too inquisitive. Beatrice was thankful Vicky was not staying the night this time.

Before the war I used to love going to parties to meet young men, she thought, *and I imagined they'd eventually return from war and I'd carry on as before. Mother expects me to do so, afraid I might otherwise miss the chance to get married. But it's not the same now, with so many fine young men lost.*

She still loved dressing smartly, but she had to face reality: her horizons had narrowed. And she must take care. Occasionally she could not help remembering her ordeal that autumn at the hands of the officer who had behaved improperly in a taxi.

The only one I care for is Caleb, but I simply can't see my way ahead to resolve the situation. If I can't have him I don't plan to settle for second best.

Chapter 3

Larchbury, spring 1919

James was back in Larchbury the week before his wedding, in time to hear his father read the banns in St Stephen's church for the final time. Florence stood beside him in her lightweight suit. *This time next week we'll be married*, she thought, scarcely able to believe the day would finally come.

They would be living in the vicarage, where two rooms had been set aside for them. James would need to return to France to complete his duties as a medical orderly, until he was discharged. *She would be living with her in-laws, just like Amy had to at first – though at least hers were more congenial than Mrs Derwent and Beatrice!*

After the service they went to talk to Amy and Edmond. His brother Peter was accompanying them today, on leave from his position with High Command. He looked like an older, fitter version of Edmond. She did not know him well, because before the war he had held a position in India, and had only returned when young men there began to feel the necessity to fight for king and country.

Today there was another young man with him, who she imagined was one of his army comrades, though he was not wearing uniform.

'Good morning, Florence and James,' Peter said. He was tall and walked confidently, the way Edmond had done before he was injured. 'Congratulations on your wedding next week.'

'Thank you.'

The others in the Derwent family greeted her. 'May I introduce Maxim Duclos?' Peter went on, indicating his friend. The young man shook their hands warmly, and greeted them with some kind of continental accent. His skin had an olive tone, and his hair was black, though his eyes were blue.

'Maxim comes from France,' Peter said. 'He's a chef. I've got to know him while I've been out there. He's looking for work, and is going to apply for the vacancy at the inn. He's staying with us until he finds lodgings.'

'You're not remaining in your country to help rebuild it after the war?' James asked him.

'I always meant to work abroad,' he said, in English that was competent but had a noticeable accent. 'I want to improve my English. At last there is more chance to travel.'

'Have you said hello to my father?' James smiled encouragingly. 'He's keen to make friends with people from abroad. He wants to make contact with Germans, but Frenchmen too. There's talk of a League of Nations now, isn't there, to help preserve the peace.'

'Yes, I spoke with him,' Maxim said. 'He has asked me to call on him.'

Mr Derwent helped Amy and Beth into his car, with his wife and Beatrice.

'The rest of us are walking back,' Peter said. 'Every good wish for next week.'

Amy liked Peter's friend. Maxim seemed reluctant to talk much about France but eager to find work. Already by the Friday he was moving on. 'Your family have welcomed me,' the young man told her and Edmond, 'but now I have work at the inn.'

'Well done!'

'I will only be the junior chef and will need to work as a waiter too. I have taken lodgings with a Miss Miller, in Sebastopol Terrace.' His pronunciation was approximate.

'She lives next door to my parents!' Amy exclaimed. She refrained from telling Maxim what a gossip she was. *How she watched us when Edmond was first courting me!* she recalled.

'She is renting me quite a small room, but it is all I need.'

The spinster sometimes let out one of her bedrooms when she was short of money. Amy had heard her roof needed attention.

Later that afternoon Amy set off to walk to Florence's house, to check that everything was prepared for the following day. As she reached the end of the drive, Maxim caught her up; he was on his way to Miss Miller's house with a few belongings in a suitcase. 'I plan to do a last-minute check if there's anything else I need,' he said.

'I'm sure Edmond would give you a lift,' she told him. 'He offered to drive me, but it's a sunny day so I decided to walk.'

'Mr Derwent has already taken most of my belongings there,' he told her, as they set off for the High Street. He walked quickly and she had difficulty keeping up. Before being shelled at Ypres Edmond had walked fast, though not quite at Maxim's speed.

They had just passed the first shops and were crossing the road when she saw a familiar figure. 'Madame Rousseau!' she called. She had not expected to see her Belgian friend here in Larchbury, for she lived in Wealdham.

The middle-aged lady was pleased to see her. 'I'm on my way to see Florence,' she said. 'I've made her lace veil and I'm just delivering it.'

'How wonderful!' Amy wished she had got further with the lacemaking lessons Mrs Rousseau had started giving her. 'This is Maxim Duclos,' she said, remembering her companion. 'He's come from France and he's going to work at the inn.'

'People here are very kind,' the Belgian lady told him. 'I came over with the refugees in 1914 and they made us welcome in Wealdham.'

'They've been taking care of me at The Beeches, since I arrived,' he told her.

'I am shortly returning to Belgium. Yolande and I will rejoin our family there... You did not want to help peacetime France to recover, Monsieur Duclos?'

'The situation there is confused at present,' he said vaguely. 'I always intended to work in England, but it was not possible during the war.'

'Like you, I'm going to see Florence,' Amy told Madame Rousseau. 'You walk fast, Maxim – do you want to go on ahead?'

'Yes, I will, if you'll excuse me. It was lovely meeting you, Madame.'

As he strode on, Madame Rousseau watched him curiously. 'Is he really French?' she asked. 'He has a bizarre accent.'

'My brother-in-law knew him out there.'

'Well – perhaps he could be from eastern France.'

Soon they were walking up the drive to Florence's house. School had started again, but it was late enough for her to be back from her teaching day. She had permission to take three days off the following week for her honeymoon.

'I've brought your veil!' Madame Rousseau said.

Florence clapped her hands excitedly. They followed her up to her room, where her white lacy dress was hanging ready for the following morning.

Madame Rousseau took the parcel from her basket and unwrapped it. They both exclaimed over the veil, with its scalloped edge and pretty floral pattern.

'I'm lucky to have such a beautiful outfit!' Florence exclaimed.

They went downstairs and chatted to Madame Rousseau over a cup of tea, before she said she must leave to get back to Wealdham.

'I hope you're soon back in your old routine in Liège,' Amy said.

Madame Rousseau paused halfway through pulling on her glove. 'Listen, Amy, if you and Edmond ever come to Belgium, you must be sure and visit me. We may live with my father again. I will write and tell you my address as soon as I am certain.'

'Oh – that's very kind.' Amy could not imagine why they would wish to return there – Ypres held only bad memories. 'Liège is in eastern Belgium, isn't it?'

'Yes, it's near the Ardennes, a hilly region. It's an attractive area to visit. You too, Florence, you and James should come to see me. You made us so welcome when we took refuge here.'

Florence smiled. 'I'd like to visit one day, if we get the chance.'

'Edmond says we can go and visit Bertie's grave in the Somme area,' Amy said. She was determined to make the trip when the war cemeteries were ready. 'But that's a long way from Liège: I'm not sure we'll have time to visit there as well.'

'Do your best to come. I've always longed to go back, but now the time is arriving I know I'm going to miss all my British friends.' She shook hands with them and set off towards the station.

Amy checked with Florence what time she should arrive next morning. She followed her back to her room and made sure her suitcase was packed for her honeymoon.

As Florence hung up the veil with her gown, Amy could sense her excitement.

She made her way back to The Beeches. As she approached the drive, someone caught up with her: it was Peter, returning from calling on a friend.

'I've been wanting to tell you about our progress with bringing Wilfrid Fairlawn to justice,' he said.

Amy winced as he mentioned the name, though earlier she had wondered how she might find a moment to bring up the subject. The Fairlawns lived nearby in Alderbank. Wilfrid's father was Colonel Fairlawn, who, near the start of the war, had pressed for Amy to be sent to jail for her Suffragette action. One night in 1917 when Amy had been on her way to the nurses' hostel in Ypres, Wilfrid, who was serving nearby, had tried to force his attentions on her, and in escaping his clutches she had fallen and broken her ankle. At the time Edmond had been fighting for his life after his chest injury. Because of his frailty she had not told him of Wilfrid's behaviour, and she still had not found the occasion to relate to him the nightmare of that evening.

'It's taken a long time for Robert Lambert to assemble the evidence,' Peter said. Robert was his friend who was dealing with her complaint about Wilfrid. 'He felt that someone was trying to delay matters: Colonel Fairlawn, I shouldn't wonder. But now the case is scheduled for a few weeks' time.'

'Thank goodness,' she said. While the war had lasted, Wilfrid had seemed unassailable because of his impressive war record. How glad she was that she herself would not be one of the young women giving evidence, for it still upset her to review those events.

'I believe we'll be successful,' Peter said.

Relief surged through her.

—

On Saturday St Stephen's was decked out with tulips, and packed with well-wishers, James being the vicar's son. Once he had been disliked for becoming a medical orderly in the war instead of fighting, but when it became known how he had risked his own life, and sustained an injury, in rescuing Captain Charles Shenwood, he had gained a reputation for bravery and become accepted again.

Mr Clifford took Florence's arm to lead her up the aisle. How lovely she looked, in her bridal gown, Amy thought as she followed them.

James was wearing his uniform, less impressive than that of an officer, but asserting the part he played. As Florence took her place beside him the couple seemed to inhabit an enchanted world of their own. Amy's thoughts drifted contentedly to her own wedding to Edmond, in his smart lieutenant's uniform, in the uncertain days of 1915.

James's father led his son and Florence through the service. Then the newlyweds were signing the register.

As they processed back down the aisle Amy smiled at Lavinia, standing next to Charles. He was making consistent progress with his artificial legs. He had been wounded, around a year earlier, during the Germans' spring offensive. He had lost part of his right leg, and some of his left foot. He and Lavinia had set a date in early August for their own wedding.

Florence's parents, the Cliffords, had booked a large room at *The Farmers,* the main inn in Larchbury, for the reception. The guests hovered in the garden outside until everyone was assembled.

Mrs Clifford looked impatient as she waited. She was elegant in a light grey spring suit. Her hair, always held rigidly in a bun, was largely concealed by her elaborate feathered hat. Amy had been in awe of her as a child, and later had lost the woman's approval after her escapade with the Suffragettes had led to her brief term in jail. She had only recovered her standing with Florence's mother when the value of her nursing had become appreciated.

'I'm so thrilled at seeing Florence married,' Amy said. They had all accepted that Bertie, her first choice, would have wanted her to find someone else after his death. 'If only James can get released from the army soon.'

'Florence told me he'll almost certainly be too late to find a place at university this year,' her mother said.

'If only he had settled employment,' said Florence's elder sister Sarah, plump but smart in her blue outfit. She was several years older than Florence, and her husband Geoffrey was a shopkeeper in Wealdham.

'Aren't you just thankful he'll be back?' Amy faltered. Returning safely from the terrible conflict was an achievement, for he had faced danger, even as a medical orderly. She experienced a pang of grief whenever she allowed herself to realise how their hopes and expectations had changed over the past five years.

'I believe we should go inside now,' Mrs Clifford said. She took the arm of her husband, who worked as a solicitor.

Amy and Edmond sat down on gilt chairs at the top table, with the bridal couple, and both families. As uncle and aunt of the groom, Amy's parents were there. This afternoon it was the responsibility of Cook at The Beeches to look after Beth, a task which she would relish, she had told them.

Amy noticed that Peter's young French friend Maxim was helping to serve the soup, apparently a useful member of staff already. The array of cutlery and glassware promised a lavish reception.

Besides Florence's parents, Sarah, her husband and their school-aged boys were sitting with them at the top table. Amy's parents were in high spirits, Mother in a pretty floral dress and Father in his new suit. Edmond's family were not present, as the Derwents were not close friends of the Cliffords, but Amy was confident that any reports that reached them would give a good account of her family.

'So you're off to Brighton for the honeymoon?' Mother asked the bridal couple.

'Yes — we've only got five days till I have to rejoin my unit,' James said.

'Make sure you're not late back, like I was!' Edmond said.

'Oh, goodness, how they punished you for going AWOL!' Amy remembered. Edmond had received a telegram instructing him to return to France sooner than originally arranged, and had deliberately ignored it so he and Amy could spend their wedding night together.

'It wouldn't be so bad now, when we're no longer at war,' Edmond said.

'Don't worry, I haven't received any telegram recalling me early!' James said.

'Are you enjoying your stay at The Beeches?' Uncle Arthur asked Amy, as the roast beef was served. Florence looked concerned at the question, knowing the difficulties Amy had had with her in-laws.

'I'm happy to be visiting Edmond's family – they accept me more than they did at first,' she said truthfully. 'Edmond's parents have given us some curtains for our house,' she told them. 'They're in a lovely William Morris pattern. They'll go well with our green sofa.' With their graceful flowery pattern they had no fussy extra adornment. She would need to shorten them a little, but otherwise they were ideal.

'How kind of your in-laws!' her mother said.

Eventually the cake was cut and the speeches were started. Amy sat contentedly, looking forward to their return to Cambridge in the near future, taking little notice of the fairly predictable contributions from Mr Clifford and the best man, Edmond's cousin on Aunt Sophie's side of the family.

James was more eloquent, speaking of coming through the war and his delight at the prospect of discharge. He was more confident than the clumsy youth he had been at the start of the war. 'And how very fortunate I am to have such a wonderful bride to help me move on,' he said, as

Florence dimpled. 'And now the fighting is over we need to take the Christian step of seeking reconciliation,' he added. At this there was murmuring among the guests.

'What! Do you really expect us to forgive the Huns?' exclaimed Mr Clifford, as James sat down.

Then Uncle Arthur rose to his feet. As vicar, besides being father of the groom, Mr Clifford had invited him to speak too.

He pursued James's views. 'Perhaps it's early for us to be talking like this, but I believe we should all consider reconciliation with the Germans,' he said.

Mr Clifford looked shocked, and there were more mutterings.

'The occupation of their Rhineland may be regarded as excessive,' Amy's uncle was continuing, 'and the level of reparations is liable to cause great poverty to German civilians.' His eyes were clear and determined in his broad face.

Florence turned to James. He nodded to her as though in agreement with his father.

'What is the vicar thinking?' Florence's father muttered. 'Has he forgotten so quickly how many families have lost their young men?' He looked as though he would have liked to thrust the vicar back into his seat.

Amy exchanged glances with Edmond. She had a good deal of sympathy for her uncle's views, and suspected that he did too, but the controversial subject was at odds with the initially merry atmosphere of her friend's wedding.

The vicar looked about him. 'But perhaps these are themes for a future sermon,' he allowed. 'May I just extend my hearty congratulations to my son for his war effort, and wish him and my kind-hearted new daughter-in-law every happiness in their life together.'

To Amy's relief he sat down. Aunt Sophie, quietly dressed in a cream-coloured suit, took his arm supportively. The guests were more settled now, after his good wishes.

The best man beckoned to Maxim, who had been standing, expressionless, listening to the speech. He began replenishing the well-wishers' glasses.

James put his arm around his new bride.

'It's very soon to talk of reconciliation with the Germans,' Amy heard him say. 'I'm sorry if it's embarrassing for you, as you join my family.'

'No, darling, he's right, you both are,' Florence said. 'I saw some Germans at Lavinia's hospital and they looked so like our soldiers – I can't believe the average German is a monster.'

Amy's father spoke up in his best schoolmasterly voice. 'I stand by my brother,' he asserted. 'I believe he's right.'

Florence's father was looking at him disapprovingly through his thick glasses. 'Did you Fletchers always plan to disrupt Florence's wedding like this?'

'I didn't plan it,' James said wretchedly. 'It's a view we've discussed at home.'

'I'm sorry for raising a contentious subject,' the vicar said, dismayed.

The glasses were now charged with champagne and the best man stood up hastily. 'It's time to drink a toast to the bride and groom,' he announced.

Guests rose to their feet. 'To Florence and James!' they cried. As they sat down again the talk became light-hearted. Now the formalities were complete, the guests began to circulate.

Amy stuck close to Florence, hoping her day was not spoilt.

Mr Clifford seized his daughter's arm. 'You might find yourself becoming unpopular, now you're joining this family,' he said in a low voice.

'Somehow we have to move forward,' she said.

'Surely you haven't forgotten Bertie?' Mrs Clifford said. 'The Huns killed him.'

Florence looked as though she might cry. 'I believe he'd want us to make a fresh start,' she told them.

Her father shook his head at her. 'If the vicar starts preaching sermons like that I'll be driving to Wealdham to attend church with Sarah and Geoffrey.'

Amy took Florence's other arm. 'Let's go and talk to Lavinia and Charles,' she said. Florence broke away from her parents. She and James went with Amy and Edmond to speak to their old friends.

Amy had seen Charles arrive at the inn, using a stick but moving with confidence.

'You two are next up the aisle,' Amy said, though they would be married at the church in Alderbank. She and Edmond sat beside them, near the door open to the garden. The fragrance of lilac wafted in. Florence and James looked glad to join them and avoid any further fraught discussion about the Germans.

'Charles has almost completed his rehabilitation at Roehampton,' Lavinia said, looking splendid in her new yellow gown. 'I'm sorry now that we've got to wait till August to marry.'

'I need to look around to find a suitable occupation,' Charles said. 'I'd like to have plans for the future before we wed.'

'Oh, but I'm impatient to be your wife – can't we just elope?' she continued mischievously.

They all smiled. 'Better respect all the wedding plans your parents are making,' he chided her gently.

Across the room they could see Florence's family forming a group with friends who had lost loved ones in the war, looking disgruntled as they talked.

Lavinia beamed at the prospect of her own happy day. During the war she had seemed indefatigable as she nursed the wounded. Other VAD recruits had said she was especially quick to grasp the skills. Her father, Mr Westholme, was the distinguished surgeon who had operated on Edmond and brought about his recovery when his chances had looked slender. Colleagues said that Lavinia had nursing in her blood. Lately, though, she had devoted most of her leave to helping Charles in his recovery. There was a sweet, soft look in her dark eyes which had only appeared as she had grown close to him.

'I can't imagine how I'd manage without her,' Charles said. There was less pain in his expression now and his face was handsome once more.

'Just now we were talking about Elsie Johnson,' Lavinia told them. 'Another unsuitable topic, I fear, but it diverted everyone's attention from the intricacies of the Peace Treaty.'

'I didn't know you'd heard of Elsie's predicament,' Amy said.

'I'm afraid we have.' Charles looked concerned. 'My younger sister, Alice, was writing to Philip Brownlee, before he died. They were close – he was only young but they were sweethearts. Imagine how she feels now that foolish girl is claiming he fathered her child!'

'I don't know what to think,' Amy said. 'There's at least one army officer, acclaimed for his leadership in action, who's a menace to young nurses.'

'Yes, I know who you mean.' Lavinia's large features formed a sympathetic expression. 'I suppose we can't be certain. One hears of young men taking advantage of lower-class girls, particularly ones who are a little foolish, and shamefully not concerning themselves much with what happens to them.'

'Might he have neglected her in favour of a girl of his own class?' Amy speculated.

'That would be shocking behaviour,' Lavinia said.

Florence gasped. 'I don't believe Philip Brownlee would behave like that!' she said. 'When I visited James in the convalescent hospital in Flanders, Philip was there too, recovering from his first accident. He was a charming young fellow and seemed very honourable. I daresay Elsie would like to have a wealthy family feeling an obligation to support her, instead of the Smiths, who are poor, though perfectly decent.'

'I don't believe Elsie is grasping,' Amy said. 'She's more likely to be fixated on Philip because he was such a dashing young man.'

Mr Clifford arrived at their table with a bottle of champagne and topped up their glasses. He still looked ill at ease. 'Edmond, you're a war veteran who was badly injured,' he demanded. 'What do you make of the vicar's Forgive and Forget attitude?'

'I can't imagine forgetting the war, not for many years,' he said. 'But forgiveness – I believe that has to come.'

'You could cheerfully meet those young men who tried to kill you... and very nearly succeeded?'

'I'm afraid there was a time when I went to war, believing I was doing my duty, and scarcely aware of the cost, to start with. I've almost certainly killed Germans,

49

even if I didn't aim shells at anyone in particular. I'm sure it was the same for them.'

Mr Clifford seemed unprepared for this reply. 'What about you, Captain Shenwood?'

'I agree with Edmond. The League of Nations is intended to maintain peace. We need to make sure this kind of madness never happens again.'

'I completely agree with Charles,' Lavinia asserted.

Mr Clifford glanced at her dismissively, not having asked for her views.

Florence was looking restless. *It was almost time for her to leave with James,* Amy realised, getting to her feet. She followed her friend to the room upstairs which had been reserved for her to change her clothes.

'I'm sorry about all the arguing,' Amy said. 'Don't let it spoil your day.' She helped her friend out of her bridal gown.

Florence shivered. 'I always feel I should respect my parents,' she faltered, 'but at times my views conflict with theirs. Before the war they were angry about my membership of the Suffragette movement.'

'Last year you defied them to visit France to see James,' Amy said, fastening Florence's deep pink dress for going away. She brushed her gleaming, light brown curls.

'I don't like defying them,' Florence said, 'but I need to stick to my principles. Oh, but it seems ungrateful, when they've arranged this lovely wedding for us...'

'They should still respect your views. Now try and put that all behind you and remember how blissful you both looked in church today. It's wonderful to see you two so happy.'

Florence's smile and dimples returned as Amy helped her position her new hat.

'We're going to follow the example of you and Edmond,' she said. 'We won't allow anything to come between us.'

Amy followed her downstairs, and after brief farewells to the guests, James took Florence's hand and helped her into his father's pony trap. They waved as they set off merrily for the station to begin their honeymoon.

Chapter 4

Larchbury, spring and summer 1919

Amy and Edmond were spending their final evening at The Beeches before returning to Cambridge, when Chambers, the grey-haired butler, admitted a tall figure in a uniform that until January had been unfamiliar. Caleb Fawcett was back, here on leave to see Beatrice.

Amy had only met the sandy-haired, young officer a few times in January and had forgotten how strange his American accent seemed. He was staying at the inn, but Beatrice had invited him to dine with the family that evening.

As Cook served the consommé, Caleb looked relaxed, and there seemed to be a contented atmosphere between him and Beatrice, who was sitting beside him. She was wearing one of her less showy evening dresses, as though aware the officer was unaccustomed to smart society, but the deep green flattered her colouring.

Ma looked less impressed. 'How much leave will you have this time?' she asked stiffly.

'Only a week. I sure wish I had longer.'

Ma asked him to repeat what he had said.

Poor man, Amy thought, remembering how she had been scrutinised by Mrs Derwent when Edmond had first started courting her.

'We must make sure you visit the theatre in Wealdham while you're here,' Beatrice said. 'Sometimes they only stage music hall, but they're performing "The Importance of Being Earnest" this week.'

'They're anxious to tempt their old audiences back, now the war is over,' Edmond said. 'Next time we come to The Beeches we should go too, darling,' he told Amy.

'I'd love to!' They had seldom had the opportunity to visit the theatre together.

'We needed to go further afield, mostly to London, for good entertainment during the war years,' Beatrice said.

'Are you still stationed near the Marne?' Pa asked Caleb. As usual he was easy in his manner, welcoming to his guest.

An unspoken question hung over them all: would Caleb be sent back to America soon, maybe at short notice?

'Yes, we're still there. But we're expecting to remain in Europe for a while as part of the Army of Occupation, in the Rhineland.'

'What's that you said?' demanded Ma. 'I couldn't catch it.'

He repeated his words for her.

'Some of my friends who are still with their units are being sent to the Rhine,' Edmond said, happily exchanging news with the American soldier. 'They'll be stationed near the Cologne bridgehead.'

'We're being sent to a place called Koblenz.'

'That's further south, where the Mosel river joins the Rhine,' Edmond told him. 'It seems strange now, discussing troop movements, when we used to have to keep everything secret.'

After the meal they sat in the drawing room and Beatrice played some Chopin for them for a while. Then she offered to show Caleb around the conservatory.

Ma watched nervously while the pair left the room. 'Do we have to make this young fellow welcome?' she complained when Beatrice had closed the door.

'Really, Ma!' exclaimed Edmond. 'The Americans are our wartime allies. Peter will tell you how relieved they were at High Command when US soldiers arrived in France. Besides, Bea is twenty-six now. She's old enough to decide for herself who she spends time with.'

'I don't believe she'll do anything foolish,' Pa said.

Amy had hardly expected Beatrice to be attracted to Caleb for long. Her sister-in-law had been admired by several well-off young men, some of whom had not survived the war. She had been engaged to Charles Shenwood for several months, but he had been badly injured in 1918, and she had made the questionable decision to accept his offer to release her from the engagement. Later Amy had been delighted when Lavinia had become engaged to Charles.

Now Beatrice seemed to value the American's company.

'Won't you play the piano for us, darling?' Edmond asked Amy.

'Oh – you know how feeble my attempts seem after Beatrice has played!' She had been trying to improve since she had returned from France, but lacked a piano at home. Beth and Edmond kept her busy, and she wondered if she would ever play well enough to feel competent in public. Now she ventured to the piano stool and performed Beethoven's *'Moonlight Sonata'*, very warily.

The others congratulated her on her progress, but she felt it was a travesty. She had at least provided a distraction to keep Ma from fretting about Beatrice.

She yawned. It was nearly time for her and Edmond to retire to their room.

The door opened and Beatrice returned with her admirer. 'Caleb has to leave now,' she said. 'We've arranged to go for a walk tomorrow if the weather's fine.'

Edmond was uneasy as they went upstairs. 'Caleb's not Bea's usual type.'

'No – but somehow she seems different, content with the way he is, not expecting too much from him.'

–

Next morning they piled their luggage back into the car, ready to return home. They were just saying their good-byes, and Beatrice was embracing Beth, when they saw Caleb making his way back up the drive.

'I've heard so much about the Sussex countryside,' he told them all as Beatrice hurried to his side. 'Yesterday it looked beautiful from the train.'

'The bluebells are out along the edge of the forest,' Amy told them.

'We'd better set off,' Edmond said. 'We've quite a long drive.' He kissed his mother and Beatrice, and shook Caleb's hand.

Soon he was motoring down the drive. 'Those two seem very close,' Edmond said. 'But what will happen in the future? He'll want to go back to America – can you imagine Bea leaving for the United States? His family sound quite everyday folks.'

'Yes, I thought that, too.'

'I'm afraid Bea's going to get badly hurt in the future.'

–

'That young trollop Elsie has had her baby,' Beatrice told her parents one day in June. Mrs Johnson had told her that she had a new grandchild. 'A boy.'

Pa looked at her critically.

'Well, that's what she is!' Beatrice insisted. 'Either she was walking out with a soldier while encouraging the affections of an airman, or else she's telling a pack of lies to try to get the support of a well-off family.'

'Amy doesn't think Elsie is that devious,' Pa said. 'She's more likely to be enjoying some kind of fantasy.'

Beatrice wondered whether the baby looked at all like Philip Brownlee, but supposed it was much too soon to tell.

–

Soon afterwards, George Smith, the former gardener, called at the back door of The Beeches to formally tell Mr Derwent he was home.

'How wonderful to see you back,' the master said, stepping outside to join him, near the kitchen garden and greenhouse. 'Finally you've seen the last of the battlefields. How pleased your family must be to have you home!'

'Yes, Sir, they are.' Henry, the brother next in age to him, was still missing, presumed dead.

'You've been greatly needed here. You can have your job back as gardener – begin as soon as you like.'

He was grateful for the offer, but hesitated.

'I'll go on employing Joe too,' his master assured him to his relief, 'though I'll probably send him to work in the forest.'

Joe, the youngest of the three of them, too young to be called up, had been gardener for the past two years.

George was happy to shake Mr Derwent's hand and agree to begin work on Monday. They walked around the house to the front, with its lawns and flowerbeds.

'There's only a few weeks to get the garden in good order before the Peace Celebrations on the nineteenth of July,' the master told him.

The exact date was news to George. In letters his mother had mentioned plans for a celebration, and it had turned out popular to postpone it to the summer. In London the great Victory Parade would take place, and lesser ceremonies would be held around the country.

'The vicar proposed holding a fête in the church grounds,' Mr Derwent told George, 'but some of his congregation preferred it to be elsewhere.'

George had heard that the vicar had lost popularity by wanting to forgive the Germans for the war.

'In the end I offered the grounds of The Beeches – it just amounts to bringing forward our usual fête to July.'

'I'll do my best to help you be ready,' George said.

'Joe has been working hard but there are several areas where the weeds have taken hold.' He pointed out some overgrown flowerbeds.

'I don't mind working late, these light evenings.'

'Thank you, George.'

As he was about to leave, George noticed Mrs Johnson coming out of the house. He waited for her to catch up with him.

'It's good to see you back,' she said in her usual friendly fashion.

'How's Elsie's baby?' George asked.

'Little Philip is doing well,' she said uneasily.

'Philip? Is that what she's calling him?'

'I'm afraid so. We couldn't persuade her otherwise. The Brownlees very much disapprove.' She walked along with George, an unfamiliar frown on her face. 'There's not a scrap of evidence the young airman had anything to do with the baby, so far as I can tell. Of course, it's much too soon to see who he looks like. Elsie seems to be living in some kind of fantasy world.'

'If he's Henry's child, as people suppose, Mum and I want to do the decent thing by Elsie and the boy, and contribute to his support. We could find room for them in the cottage.'

'That's very honourable of you, in the circumstances.' Her expression still looked wary, as though she expected them to change their mind if Elsie persisted with her version of events.

—

If only it'll stay fine today, Vicky thought. The weather had been poor for most of the year so far. As her train steamed towards Larchbury there were light clouds moving fast across the sky. She was wearing her best hat, decorated with silk flowers, and a lemon lawn dress with a pattern of white daisies. A thin white jacket would provide some protection if it rained, but how could she bear to dress for poor weather on this day of celebration? She had gratefully accepted her aunt and uncle's invitation to join them at The Beeches.

She yawned. Matron had reluctantly allowed her the day off, but the hospital was quite full, as there were still a few war wounded making a slow recovery, and the occasional case of Spanish flu. She had been obliged to stay late the previous evening before heading to her iron bedstead in the nurses' hostel.

I knew nursing wouldn't be a glamorous profession, she told herself sternly. *Amy warned me the work is liable to be gruelling, even now the war is over.* She was wearing lacy gloves this afternoon, but beneath them her hands were becoming red from hard work. When she managed to go home to her parents on the occasional weekend, they sometimes looked at her and asked what she was thinking of, beginning such a demanding vocation.

At Larchbury she alighted and left the station, walking along the street in the pale sunshine. Before long she could hear a commotion from *The Farmers*. Union Jacks were festooned across its porch. There was a neat garden at the front and today it was crowded. There were many people enjoying the peace celebrations and the patrons of the inn were spilling out of the interior. There were tables full of men who would have been too old to fight, and rowdy groups of younger men, some showing signs of injury, who had been recently discharged from their units.

I hope they're not all going to the fête at The Beeches, she thought. She seemed to remember that her aunt had told her they had reluctantly decided to restrict the welcome to friends and prominent villagers, issuing invitations. The mayor had arranged for tables and chairs to be set out on the village green for others who were eager to celebrate together.

As she passed the inn, two soldiers in scruffy uniforms were involved in an altercation. It was only early afternoon but already they seemed drunk. A dark-haired, young waiter was urging them in slightly accented English to behave decently.

'For years we've been ordered around!' one complained, rising to his feet. 'Sent to fight by young officers straight from school who had no idea what orders to give – sent to fight against impossible odds!'

His friend nodded in agreement. The first man limped as they rushed towards the street. As he passed a table laden with glasses he knocked some to the floor. This table was crowded with middle-aged and older men, who shook their fists as their unfinished drinks landed on the ground, the glasses smashing.

Vicky hovered, keeping her distance as the soldiers ran past, and on down the High Street. Shocked glances followed them.

'Hooligans!' an older man cried after the young louts.

The young waiter put down his tray on the nearest table that had room for it. Vicky felt sorry for him as he bent to clear the wreckage from the floor.

'Don't touch the broken glass!' she cried. 'Fetch a broom and sweep it up.'

The young man looked at her, his eyes deep blue, and shrugged. She understood his impatience, for the area was crowded. He called to an older waiter to bring a broom, but continued to remove the larger pieces of glass, seeming determined to clear the area.

'Ach!' he cried suddenly. It was as she had feared: he had cut his arm and blood was beginning to pour from the wound.

'Now then, everyone,' cried an older man, taking charge of the situation. 'Keep away until the debris is cleared up.' A woman, probably his wife, stood up from their table. Gently, she helped the young waiter into a chair. 'Sit still, you can't go on working while you're bleeding like that.'

'Let me take a look at it,' Vicky said, taking off her gloves. 'I'm training to be a nurse. They should have some bandages here.'

The injured man relented. Blood was still pouring from near his wrist, though the glass had missed the main blood vessels, thank goodness. He let her push up the cuff of his shirt.

The older waiter came with a brush and dustpan, and began clearing the rest of the glass, working efficiently as though accustomed to this kind of accident. The helpful older man kept other customers from crowding around.

'I'll go and fetch some bandages,' the woman said.

Vicky held up the waiter's hand, to make it less likely to bleed heavily. 'I don't think it's very bad,' she said, as calmly as possible.

Now the woman was back with some first aid items in a wooden box. Another woman had come with her, and enquired after the young man.

Vicky seemed to remember she was the innkeeper's wife. *Didn't I meet her at one of the fêtes at The Beeches? Mrs Spencer, isn't it? I think their son was lost early in the war.*

A few of the customers decided that now was a good time to leave, and order was gradually being restored.

Mrs Spencer had brought some water in a bowl. Vicky dipped some cotton wool in the water and wiped the casualty's arm. She found a bottle of antiseptic and wiped it some more. She examined it carefully.

'I can't see any fragments of glass in it,' she said. 'Does it feel as though there might be some?'

'No — it's just scratched, that's all.'

She searched for a bandage. *Heavens, I've only dealt with injuries a few times, and then it was under supervision.*

Mrs Spencer set about clearing glasses from the tables. Vicky bandaged the young man's arm as neatly as she could.

He was smiling at her; what fine blue eyes he had. His skin was light brown in tone. 'Are you from somewhere abroad?' she asked him.

'From France. I'm Maxim. I'm working as a chef part of the time, besides being a waiter. What's your name?'

'Vicky. I don't know if you've met the Derwents, but I'm their niece.'

He smiled again. 'I know Peter Derwent very well. I knew him in France.'

As she secured the bandage she noticed a scar further up, with signs that it had once been stitched. It extended up beneath his shirt sleeve.

'How did you get that other injury?'

He smiled ruefully. 'We were at war in France for over four years, you know.'

'Of course. Forgive my stupid question.'

She could easily become distracted, talking to this young man, but she supposed she should really be getting to The Beeches. If she arrived very late her aunt would be put out. She looked again at the bandage. Just a tiny streak of blood was visible, but it did not look as though it was going to seep.

'Where do you work?' Maxim asked her.

'At Wealdham Hospital.'

'I'd like to see you again... Do you think that would be possible?'

She was taken aback a little, but welcomed the prospect.

'Yes, that would be lovely.' *She wondered if there would be an opportunity.*

Mrs Spencer came across to check her handiwork. 'How is the wound?' she asked.

'It's fine,' Maxim told her.

'If it starts bleeding badly you'll need to call a doctor,' Vicky warned them.

'You're Vicky Derwent, aren't you?' asked Mrs Spencer. 'Why, you're quite grown up now. What a lovely dress you're wearing.'

'I'm Vicky Harper, remember – my father is brother to Mrs Derwent. I'm on my way to The Beeches,' she said.

Mrs Spencer looked her up and down. 'I'm afraid there's a small bloodstain on your skirt. Come with me to the kitchen and I'll rinse it off for you. Maxim, you'd better go to the storeroom; you should sit quietly for a while before you go back to work.'

'Thank you for helping me, Vicky,' Maxim said.

Mrs Spencer rinsed Vicky's skirt until the blood hardly showed, and patted her dress dry with a towel. 'Now then, are you walking to The Beeches?'

'Yes – I'd better be on my way.' She pulled on her gloves and picked up her bag.

'Thank you for dealing with Maxim's injury.' Mrs Spencer accompanied Vicky out to the front again. 'I'm afraid the village is growing wild today.' The inn was quite smart, sometimes referred to as a hotel, and she must be concerned to see some of the rougher elements it had attracted on this occasion. 'I wonder if there's anyone who could accompany you?'

Just then they noticed the Brownlees and their daughter Caroline going past on the other side of the street. Vicky had met them once or twice at parties. Mrs

Spencer called out to them. She checked that they were heading to The Beeches and asked them to escort Vicky there. Vicky joined the family, remembering that it was not many months since they had suffered the tragic loss of their son Philip.

When she finally reached the fête, Vicky found it crowded with exuberant guests. Some of the stalls were decorated with flags or bunting. Her relatives greeted her warmly.

'How pretty you look in that dress,' Beatrice said, apparently not noticing the faint remains of the blood stain.

Was she implying that her usual range of clothes lacked style, Vicky wondered. But occasionally she fancied Bea was becoming less critical.

'Are Edmond and Amy here?' she asked.

'No, they're in Cambridge,' her Aunt Mabel said. 'And Peter is in France.'

Her Uncle Hugh found some refreshments for Vicky and the Brownlees.

'If you can visit some of the stalls I'd be grateful,' Uncle Hugh said. 'They're raising money for the Save the Children fund.'

She gathered that there would be a speech at around five. 'The mayor is coming,' Beatrice said. 'Ma is hoping the vicar won't be here, as he's upset some of his congregation recently with his views about making peace with the Germans.'

Vicky could hear military music from the bandstand. *When did they last have a band at the summer fête?* she wondered. *Probably not since early in the war.*

She had consumed her slice of cake with unseemly haste, as she had set out from the hospital just before lunch.

'Are you hungry?' Beatrice asked her. 'Come to the upper garden and I'll ask Daisy to fetch you some more.'

Her cousin led her up the steps to the upper lawn, near the hydrangeas, which was reserved for family and close friends.

They sat in wicker chairs and Beatrice asked Daisy to bring tea and cakes. Ahead, the garden sloped downward towards Larchbury village. In the distance she could see the church and catch a glimpse of the brook. The band was playing '*Land of Hope and Glory*'.

'I suppose Caleb is back in France now?' she asked Beatrice.

'Yes – he's being sent to the German border area, near the Rhine,' Beatrice said wistfully. 'He's hoping to get some more leave later in the summer.'

'How did you come to meet him?' Vicky asked curiously.

'It was Florence who first met Caleb,' her cousin explained. 'Last summer she insisted on visiting France to see James at his convalescent hospital. When she was obliged to get a lift back to the coast with some American soldiers, Caleb was the driver. By the time he had obtained leave, intending to pursue his acquaintance with her, Florence was engaged to James. Then he and I met...' Her pretty features formed a dreamy expression.

Presently they went round the stalls and Vicky bought some fresh cherries to take back with her to augment her diet of hospital food.

The sky was clouding over and the mayor arrived at The Beeches although it was little after four, having left the other group of merrymakers on the village green. It seemed he had decided to bring his speech forward in case it rained.

The broad-shouldered, middle-aged man took a prominent position on the steps nearby. The band brought '*The British Grenadiers*' to a rapid conclusion, then clashed the cymbals.

'I'm delighted to see such a wonderful response to the fête,' the mayor announced in his loud, clear voice. 'I'm happy to see all the stalls offering produce and handmade goods. What a magnificent effort you have made to raise funds for Eglantyne Jebb's Save the Children fund to help the starving children in Germany and Austria. They at least are innocent victims of the Great War.'

Vicky noticed Mrs Fletcher, Amy's mother, nodding at this, and a few others, mainly women, followed her example.

'At last the Treaty of Versailles has been signed,' His Worship continued. The Peace Treaty had been under discussion in Paris since the beginning of the year. It had been signed on the fifth anniversary of the assassination of Archduke Franz Ferdinand at Sarajevo, which had precipitated the war. 'Finally we can be certain of a lasting peace.'

Is it really over? Vicky wondered. All the while she had been growing up they had been at war.

Mr Brownlee was standing nearby. 'If only it was that easy,' he grumbled. 'They say the reparations are too severe on the Germans. And the Americans haven't signed the treaty.'

Looking around, Vicky could see the Smith brothers, the gardeners, standing respectfully by the path, where they had been listening to the speech. The other brother was missing, presumed dead, she knew.

She was aware that all around the village there were fractured families. The Brownlees had lost their son and Caroline's fiancé had been killed.

Beatrice seemed to guess her thoughts. 'You're lucky being younger,' she told Vicky. 'Men of your age weren't called up.'

Already Vicky had received admiring glances from young men, but up till now she had not felt especially drawn to any of them.

'Did you never think of finding a wartime job, Beatrice?' she could not resist asking, for she had often wondered.

'Like Amy, you mean?' Her cousin's eyebrows shot up at the idea. 'I can see now how valuable her nursing was, but I don't believe I could have tackled anything so demanding. I suppose I might have taken some clerical job in an office, a position normally held by a man, but at the time the idea didn't appeal.' She seemed a little regretful now, trying to explain herself. 'You see, I've been brought up to behave in a ladylike manner, and Ma always told me that for a woman in my position to take paid work was unfeminine.'

'Oh, I see.' Her cousin struck her as having very Edwardian attitudes – more like her parents' outlook than Vicky's own.

'Perhaps I should have considered participating in some way,' Beatrice owned.

A few raindrops started falling and the visitors started to disperse. Vicky's relatives began to say goodbye to their most important guests.

Vicky's mind drifted away from the ceremony. She found herself remembering the handsome face of the young Frenchman. *Working at the inn, I don't suppose he gets much free time,* she thought. *He's a friend of Peter, though. Will I get the chance to meet him again?*

Chapter 5

Vicky was weary when she left the ward one Thursday evening, as one of the other nurses was on leave and she had been made to stay late again. At this time of year it was at least still light when she left the hospital. As she stepped out on to the road and turned towards the hostel she was vaguely aware of a young man lounging against the railings.

'Vicky!' he called, to her surprise.

Gracious! It was that young Frenchman. 'Maxim? What are you doing here in Wealdham?'

'I wanted to see you again! It's my night off.'

Suddenly she felt less tired; she had wondered if they might meet again. In the reddish evening light he was every bit as good-looking as she remembered.

'Shall we go for a walk somewhere? We could go downhill to the town centre.' She pulled off her nurse's cap and crammed it into her bag. An indifferent meal would be awaiting her at the hostel, probably dried up as she was late, and it would be so much more fun to spend time with this young man.

'Is there anywhere we could get a meal?' he asked.

'There are two or three restaurants.' Her friend was just a waiter and trainee chef at the inn in Larchbury; she had better not suggest anywhere expensive.

68

'Let's find a good-quality one,' he urged her. 'The Spencers are teaching me to make English roast dinners, but I'm sure there's much else I need to try.' He took hold of her hand.

'But I'm still wearing my uniform! Shall I go back to the hostel and change?'

'You look fine. Your hair is such a lovely colour!'

She was thankful that her discarded apron had shielded her dress from blood and splashes of medicine.

'It's not very warm, though,' he realised. 'Will you be all right if we stay out for... perhaps two hours?'

'I've got my cape.'

They wandered downhill. To the right, beyond the railway, there were the ugly factories down by the river.

'It was quite a surprise to see you,' she admitted. *Goodness, I hardly know him*, she realised, *yet I feel comfortable being with him.*

'I was — what's the word — grateful for the way you treated my cut that day,' he told her. Over a week had passed since then. 'It healed very well.' He pulled up his sleeve to show her. 'Look — you cannot see it well now.' There was just a faint scar to show where the glass had cut him.

'I'm not used to my patients coming back to thank me!' she said.

In the main street there were two restaurants recommended for their good food. *The Crown* was expensive, she had heard.

'I'm afraid I normally eat at my hostel,' she told him, 'but I understand *The Pigeons* serves good food.' It was just beyond the theatre.

'Then let's go there.' They walked the short distance and he ushered her inside and found a table.

The waiter was an older man. The younger ones had generally left to join the war effort. Some would be returning, but many had still to be discharged. He passed her the printed menu.

'There is also a speciality of the day,' the man told them. 'It's game pie.'

'That will be tasty – I think you'd like it,' Vicky suggested. Maxim ordered it for both of them.

'There's a large cookery book at the inn,' Maxim said. 'If I want to try a new dish I need to ask permission and list the – how you say, food things…'

'Ingredients.'

'Yes, that's it.'

Being midweek the dining room was half empty. The waiter lit a candle on their table. She smiled across at him in the mellow light.

'So, where do your family live?' he asked.

'In Melbridge, in Surrey, north of here, towards London,' she told him. 'My father is Mrs Derwent's brother. He works as a banker. Mother was very ill with tuberculosis when she was a young woman and she's been frail ever since. Aunt has been very kind in inviting me to parties at The Beeches, for my parents live very quietly. I'm used to running errands for Mother, and I suppose that was partly what gave me the idea of becoming a nurse.'

The waiter returned with some wine that Maxim had ordered, allowed him to sample it, and poured it for them.

'I was worried about leaving her, when I considered training,' she said, 'but she wanted me to have the opportunity. I'm relieved that they have a new servant now who once trained as a nurse.'

The meal arrived, and Vicky was thankful that it met her expectations.

'What exactly do they put in it?' he asked. 'Is that rabbit that I can taste?'

'Yes. And there'll be other assorted meat, maybe duck, partridge and venison. I watched Aunt Mabel's cook make game pie once, and it's one of her most complicated recipes, so you might not want to attempt one.' She mentioned the various stages, from marinating the meat and spices to boiling the bones, baking the meat, preparing pastry and making jelly from the stock.

'What a hard task! I perhaps shall not make one!'

'Where do you come from in France?' she asked him.

'Bar-le-Duc – it's in the east.'

By the time they had enjoyed trifle for dessert, it was growing late. Maxim paid the bill without looking too shocked at the amount. Outside it was dark and the pavement was crowded, for the audience were leaving the theatre, mostly in a merry mood.

'They sometimes put on plays here,' she told her escort, 'but they're showing music hall this week.'

'Vicky – is that you?'

She looked around and saw Edmond and Amy, who had returned to The Beeches for the summer vacation.

'Hello – have you been to the music hall? Do you know Peter's friend, Maxim?'

'Yes, we've met him at The Beeches,' Amy said. 'It was great fun at the theatre tonight.'

'We spent so long apart when we were first married that we've hardly had the chance to go out together,' Edmond said.

'I've never even been to a music hall performance before,' Amy said, 'but they actually had Vesta Tilley tonight, on her farewell tour. She's great fun!'

'I'm afraid I've never been to music hall,' Vicky said. How her parents would disapprove of her going to such a show, known for sometimes being risqué! She thought Vesta Tilley was one of the stars who often performed dressed as a man.

'We'd better be getting back, in case Beth has missed us,' Amy said.

'We've got the car,' Edmond said. 'Shall we take Vicky back to her hostel and then bring you back to Larchbury, Maxim?'

'I can see Vicky back,' he said firmly. 'I'll have time to catch the last train.'

Vicky waved goodbye to her cousin, thankful that Maxim was able to accompany her back. They began the walk uphill, her hand in his once more.

'Will you come out with me again?'

'Yes, Maxim, I'd like to.'

'Call me Max. Perhaps we could go for a walk somewhere in the country around here.'

'It's not very pleasant near here,' Vicky said, explaining about the factories. 'Edmond came here soon after his lung was wounded in the war. He visited a soldier who lived in the factory area, and the smoky atmosphere set back his recovery. Amy won't let him come here when it's winter and the smoke from the fires mixes with the factory emissions.'

'I didn't know it was so bad,' Max said. 'We must meet in Larchbury instead and go for a walk there.'

When they reached her hostel, near the hospital, he seemed reluctant to leave.

'Thank you for a lovely evening. Make sure you don't miss your train!'

He reached for her hand and kissed it tenderly. Then he set off, hurrying back down the hill.

She let herself in. She had had the feeling someone had been staring out of the window at them.

'Who's that young man?' Nora came out of her room, anxious to ask her about him. 'I didn't know you had a follower.'

'Neither did I!' The evening had been unexpected but blissful.

Peter soon arrived at The Beeches on a week's leave. He and Edmond had plenty to discuss about current events. They would linger with Pa in his study after the evening meal, and Amy gathered they were discussing the arrangements for the Army of Occupation in Germany. Sometimes they went out for a ride together, Edmond on his faithful Wanderer and Peter on one of the younger horses which were chiefly used in the forest but could be spared occasionally.

One morning Amy was taking Beth for a walk in the garden. She toddled about on her little legs and stopped to pick daisies, where a few were appearing on the lawn. George was working on one of the flowerbeds which still showed signs of neglect.

'We went around the south garden yesterday,' Amy told him. 'The roses on the pergola are looking fine now.'

'I'm glad you can see the difference, Mrs Derwent. There's still a great deal to do. The weather has been so poor this year. When it's been fine Joe and I have worked late. We've been concentrating on the kitchen garden, to make sure there are plenty of vegetables.'

'There's been a great improvement, since you've been back from France.' The sky was clouding over again and she took hold of Beth's hand and headed for the house.

Soon there was the sound of voices and horses' hooves, and Edmond and his brother rode into view. The first drops of rain were beginning to fall, but Beth was jumping up and down in excitement at seeing the horses, and they followed the men to the stables.

When he had dismounted, Edmond picked up the little girl to allow her to pat Wanderer. He produced a sugar lump from his pocket and showed Beth how to hold it out to the old horse and let him take it from her gently.

They all walked together towards the house. 'I might be discharged early next year,' Peter told her. 'Then I'm determined to go back to India.'

'Are you still writing to Patricia?'

'Yes – she's longing to see me again. She's been very patient, though I suppose many women have missed seeing their men friends for months or years. I need to get back there as soon as I can. It won't be easy telling Pa, though. He's always hoped I'd take over the forestry business, though I've never encouraged him in that expectation.'

'You must do whatever is right for you,' Amy told him. 'Pa is a reasonable man – he'll accept it.' Ma would be less understanding, she thought, and Beatrice too would miss him.

'I must go up to the plantation and help as best I can while I'm here,' Peter said.

'I'm helping Pa with the accounts,' Edmond said.

They went into the house and plans for the future were set aside while they joined the others for lunch.

'Have you seen Maxim at all lately?' Peter asked. 'Is he doing well at the inn?'

'I've heard from the Spencers that he's making good progress,' Pa said. 'He's skilled as a chef.'

'And he's made quite an impression on Vicky,' Amy said happily. Edmond's cousin had looked captivated by her companion, the night they had seen them together. She had since discovered how they had met on the day of the peace celebrations. The closeness of the young couple had reminded her of her own encounters with Edmond, early in their courtship.

'Well, that's a development I hadn't bargained for!' For a moment Peter seemed almost shocked by the sudden attraction between his friend and Vicky. 'He's a few years older than her.'

'I've always thought Vicky was mature for her age,' Amy said.

Ma looked uncertain about the friendship, probably because Maxim did not have a well-paid occupation.

Later that afternoon, while Amy was showing Beth the little orange trees in the conservatory, Peter joined them.

'You'll be wanting to hear about Wilfrid Fairlawn…'

'Yes…' She had been wondering when he would find the opportunity to speak to her alone.

'Robert Lambert made great efforts collating all the evidence. Fairlawn was charged with assaulting two young women. He denied it, but the evidence was convincing.'

A feeling of relief coursed through her. 'At last!' she said. *Thank goodness Beth is too young to understand what we're talking about.*

'They haven't punished him as severely as I'd hoped. He's a major, and his wartime record is impressive, but the army have recognised that such behaviour is completely unacceptable. He's been suspended for three months and his disreputable conduct noted. I don't expect him to be granted any further promotion.'

'I'm so glad. You know, once I was a confident young woman, even walking back to the nurses' hostel in London on my own after dark. Now, if I'm occasionally out alone as it's getting dark, the memory of his behaviour in Ypres makes me anxious.'

'I'm dreadfully sorry it's had such a long-term effect. At least you helped bring him to justice.'

'Yes.' Her spirits rose. 'I'm so grateful to you and Robert for persisting with this. Thank him for me when you see him.'

'I'm relieved that justice has been done at last. And the case provides a warning to any other officer who might behave inappropriately.'

A glow of satisfaction filled her.

'Robert's getting married soon,' Peter told her.

'Really?' When he had attended the party at The Beeches at Christmas, he had given the appearance of being unattached.

'Apparently he was very keen on a young woman two years ago, but she didn't return his affections. But in the last year of the war her fiancé was killed, and now she's warmed towards him.'

'Give them my best wishes.'

'Bea was friendly towards him last Christmas,' he said. 'I told her he's engaged now and she didn't seem too upset.'

Amy knew there was a shortage of single men now, owing to the appalling losses during the war. At one time she had expected Florence and Lavinia to remain single, but they had been fortunate after all. 'I'm glad Beatrice isn't too disappointed.'

No one in the family but Amy knew that Wilfrid had also tried to force himself on Beatrice in a taxi. Later she would seek out her sister-in-law in the privacy of her room, and tell her that Wilfrid had finally been punished for molesting nurses while serving abroad.

-

On a Saturday in early August, Charles and Lavinia were married. Edmond and Amy attended the church at Alderbank, and the reception afterwards at her parents' large house nearby.

'Charles has improved greatly in the last year,' Edmond said as they made their way the short distance from the church to the reception. Below his morning dress the groom wore a substantial appliance on his right leg, and a much lesser one on his left foot, so Edmond understood. He had still needed a crutch to improve his smooth passage down the aisle with Lavinia, who had given him only limited support. 'I always knew he'd have the resolution to make a good recovery.'

'Lavinia looks unusually elegant,' Amy said. The bride had chosen a dress in a classical style and was attended by Charles's sisters. Alice, the younger one, was the girl who had been writing to Philip Brownlee before he had died of his injuries. On this special day she looked serene and glad to welcome Lavinia into her family.

Florence accompanied them into the Westholmes' house. It was disappointing for her that James was in France and had been unable to obtain leave. Together the three of them greeted the Westholme and Shenwood families.

'Are you keeping healthy, Lieutenant Derwent?' Mr Westholme asked him.

'Yes, thank you. I'll always be grateful to you for my recovery.' The surgeon had operated on him in Ypres.

'I believe your ankle has knit together well this time,' Mr Westholme said to Amy.

'Oh, yes – it's so much better now!'

Edmond knew she had been injured in Ypres, while Mr Westholme and other doctors were fighting to save his life. He had hazy memories of those days. In the frantic wartime hospital the staff were exhausted, and the first hasty operation on her ankle had left her handicapped. At the second attempt, soon after the Armistice, Mr Westholme had restored it almost to its original healthy state.

'Are you working in London?' Amy asked the surgeon.

He mentioned the name of a well-known hospital in south London. 'I can get there easily by train,' he said. 'And I sometimes help with emergencies at Wealdham, if I'm at home.'

Edmond took Amy and Florence to find places in a large, airy room where a massive buffet was laid out.

'I owe Mr Westholme so much,' Amy told Florence. 'It was he who brought me the news that Edmond was badly injured and drove me to the hospital in Ypres to be with him.'

'Seeing Amy come through the door and hearing her news that she was expecting our child, made me determined I had to survive somehow,' Edmond said, moved at the memory of that day nearly two years earlier.

Soon they were invited to the large table with its dazzling linen and fragrant roses, to be served with the delicacies that had been prepared. The Westholmes had contrived to provide a meal that was almost as lavish as one they might have enjoyed before the war.

'Are you settling now at the vicarage?' Amy asked Florence. She had managed to visit her there once since they had arrived in Larchbury for the summer.

'Yes – the controversy about the vicar's plans for reconciliation seems to be subsiding.'

'Soon everyone will see the sense in his views,' Amy said.

After the meal and the speeches they went out into the garden, where a variety of chairs had been provided. The afternoon was warm and sunny.

Charles was sitting at a nearby table with some old comrades. 'Come and meet my officer friends,' he invited Edmond. He joined them, while Amy and Florence sat down with some of the women guests.

Charles introduced a lanky man in uniform. 'This is Captain Leonard Turnbull – we were at the same hospital last year.'

'Pleased to meet you.'

'And this is Hector Anderson – he's an old school friend who lives locally.'

'Yes, of course,' Edmond said, sitting down with them. He remembered meeting the broad-shouldered man at a party.

'Do you think you'll stay on in the army?' Charles asked Hector.

'I only joined up when I was conscripted,' he admitted. 'I'm longing to be discharged.'

'I shall stay,' asserted Turnbull. 'I'm a regular soldier – I joined up before the war, remember.'

'Of course. You had that hair-raising escape from Belgium, didn't you?'

Edmond listened to Leonard Turnbull's account of being injured near Mons soon after the start of the war and being left behind in a hospital near Brussels. He had somehow contrived to escape to neutral Holland. Edmond and Hector were hugely impressed. For a while they went on reminiscing about life in the trenches. Nowadays Edmond's bad dreams were fewer, but the memories remained. Some of them, those of camaraderie, were ones he valued.

Turnbull went on to describe his part in the recent victory parade in London. The others listened respectfully, though Charles and Edmond exchanged glances. They were among those who had been invalided out before the end.

They sat around in their group, reliving their experiences.

—

Amy sat with Lavinia and other friends in the half shade provided by a cherry tree.

'You and Charles are fortunate to have your own house.' Florence could not avoid a tinge of envy, having heard about their new home nearby. They knew he had a legacy from his grandfather, and his parents had been very supportive.

'We drove past your house one day soon after Easter,' Amy told Lavinia, 'only we couldn't call in, because you hadn't completed the purchase then.'

'It's called Appletrees,' Lavinia said, 'and it's modest, compared with this house, but it's in a lovely area, in an old orchard.'

She rose to her feet to join Charles. She helped him up and the newlyweds began to circulate slowly among their guests. As they came to Amy's table, Edmond was following them.

'I'm impressed with how well you're managing to get around,' Edmond told Charles.

'I believe the excitement has given me a new lease of life!' He grinned, his face as handsome as ever.

'Are you still planning to study to be a solicitor?' Amy asked.

'I've changed my mind,' he told them. 'I didn't want to study in London. We'd probably have needed to live there, and I much prefer settling here, with a fine view and horses in the paddock. I'm going to study accountancy instead, at the business school in Wealdham. I'm starting next month.'

'That's where Bertie went,' Amy said, though he had only studied there part-time. *He had found it tedious but Charles seemed anxious to settle in a profession.*

Lavinia clung to her new husband, apparently overcome with the excitement of the occasion. She and Charles sat down with them.

'Will you go on nursing?' Amy asked her.

'Yes, I believe I should continue, at least for a while, as I have an aptitude,' she said. She looked serious for a moment. 'Do you remember, soon after you and Florence joined the Suffragettes, when we discussed the role of married women?'

'Goodness, I can't remember what we talked of so long ago!' cried Florence. 'It must have been before the war.'

'Yes, it was,' Amy said, 'and I can recall saying that women should not only have meaningful occupations but be able to continue them after marriage if they chose.'

'Yes, we did believe that,' Lavinia said. 'We've made such progress during the war, taking responsible jobs that demanded respect.'

'Now we've got the vote, and they're talking of women even becoming MPs,' Florence said.

'They are,' Lavinia said, 'but there's an unfortunate attitude that we should return to our domestic duties now, particularly those of us that marry. I'm in no hurry to do that.' She reached for a glass of wine as a servant passed by with a tray, and her companions did the same.

Amy was a little uneasy, wondering how Charles would feel.

'I know what you're thinking,' Lavinia said. 'Charles is handicapped and I must be mindful of his needs. So I've decided I shall apply for a position at Wealdham Hospital as soon as one becomes available, and I'll work for fewer hours, if they let me.'

'That should suit you,' Florence said.

'It'll suit both of us,' Charles agreed.

'My cousin Vicky works there now,' Edmond said. 'I'll make sure she lets me know if she hears of a vacancy.'

Amy considered. 'It's different for me as I have Beth to care for, but I do mean to go back to nursing one day.' *But I want to have another child or two,* she thought. *When will I ever have time to do more nursing?*

Before long Lavinia stood up, statuesque in her white gown. 'I must spirit Charles away to the seaside hotel where we're spending a week,' she said. 'Otherwise I'm afraid he'll wear himself out.' She helped him to his feet.

'I'm glad Lavinia's continuing with her vocation,' Amy said.

'She's always been tremendously confident,' Florence said, when she was a short distance away. 'She's so fortunate, having parents who understand her views.' Lavinia's surgeon father was sympathetic to her feminist ideals. Her mother, an artist, dramatically dressed in a multi-coloured gown, was regarded as unconventional, and was equally supportive.

'When I feel I should make a stand, I try to be assertive,' Florence went on, 'but I feel awkward about questioning my parents' views, however old-fashioned. It somehow seems disrespectful.'

'I understand how you feel,' Amy said. She looked across the garden at the bride. 'Lavinia looks wonderful today but I like to remember her with her hair messy, riding her motorbike through the mud in Flanders.'

Florence burst out laughing at the memory.

Chapter 6

One day in September Vicky telephoned Max at the inn from a public phone box and told him when she would have a day off. It was a weekday, and he could get time off till late afternoon as the inn had few bookings. He suggested she met him in Larchbury to go for a walk.

She set out very early, as he had to work later. When she got off the train he was waiting for her. 'How lovely to see you again,' he said. He was wearing casual clothes, a little foreign-looking and less well tailored than the ones Edmond might have worn. She was wearing a pale green, cotton dress, a straw hat and stout shoes. It was the beginning of September and the weather was fine.

By mid-morning they had walked up to the top of the hill, just outside the land belonging to her family, and near the forest, with its resinous, towering pine trees. There was a seat where they could look down over the Derwents' fine house and towards Larchbury village.

'This is a lovely part of your country,' he said. His dark lashes emphasised the deep blue of his eyes.

She asked what his area of France was like and he briefly described the vineyards on the hills near Bar-le-Duc. It sounded an attractive area.

'Shall we follow the path further on?' he asked. It ran along the edge of the forest and over the summit of the hill.

'Yes, let's. I've never walked in that direction.' He took her pale, freckled hand in his tanned one.

The path continued beyond the boundary of the Derwents' forest. Now they were looking towards fields with cattle, orchards and another village. 'That must be Alderbank,' she said. She had come through it on the train.

He indicated another bench to sit admiring the view, although now they were facing north, away from the sun.

'Let me pour you some lemonade.' He took a bottle and two enamel cups from his knapsack and poured her a drink.

Two tortoiseshell butterflies fluttered past.

Her attention was caught suddenly by movement through the fields below them. A group of horsemen in red jackets were galloping across the fields, accompanied by a pack of yelping dogs.

'A hunt!' she cried. 'I didn't know there were any huntsmen near here. They must be finishing for the day – it's late for them still to be out.' Besides the huntsmen in red, the oldest of the men was wearing army uniform with a lot of braid. A younger man was particularly large, riding furiously and urging on his horse.

'They make a fine sight,' Max said.

For a moment Vicky had been beguiled by the spectacle, but on the whole she found hunting distasteful. They watched as the huntsmen continued towards Alderbank.

'I've brought some food in my knapsack,' he said.

It was not yet noon, but she had set out early. She had not liked to mention that she was growing hungry, and was beginning to wonder where they would eat. He brought out some slices of pork pie. 'It's from what we made yesterday,' he said. 'I hope you don't mind. It's been kept in the cool pantry until I left this morning.'

She bit into the crisp crust and munched the tasty meat. 'It's delicious. Did you make it?'

'Yes.'

She looked at him curiously. 'You're obviously talented at cooking. I'm surprised you didn't stay in France though, as the country's famed for its cuisine.'

His face clouded. 'You don't understand what it's like there now. We won't attract many tourists for a while. The country has suffered a lot of damage and people are gloomy.'

'I'm sorry. I should have realised.'

'When the farmers till the ground they often find it is full of shell debris, and even live, unexploded shells sometimes. It will take years to restore some areas to normality. At the moment we are short of food, compared with before the war.'

'I didn't think it was so bad. Forgive me for being ignorant.'

'You weren't to know. You were still at school when the war started.'

'So, you fought in the war? Which battles were you in?'

'Verdun.'

'I don't remember much about that one.'

'It was the main confrontation between the French and the Germans.'

She wanted to ask him if he had fought throughout the war, but shrank from the horrific subject.

Presently they got up and retraced their steps uphill. Max reached for her hand. 'Should we call on your relatives, do you think?'

'They don't know I'm here today – I daresay they're busy.'

'Peter's gone back to France now.'

Vicky felt she needed time to decide her feelings for Max. He was a few years older than her, but there was a growing closeness between them. She could not help being conscious that she was just starting her nursing training. It was not the best time to consider finding a husband.

As it happened, a relative appeared as they reached the forest again. Her uncle was supervising the loading of timber on to a wagon.

'Hello, Vicky – and Maxim.' He came through a gate on to the path, looking a little surprised to see them together.

'We have been walking,' Max said. 'It is such a fine day.'

'We saw huntsmen, over towards Alderbank.'

'Oh, yes, they're becoming more active, now the war is over. They're a bit of a rabble, the Alderbank Hunt. Colonel Fairlawn and his son ride with them, I understand.' He looked disapproving as he mentioned them. Vicky remembered that the colonel was the one who had urged the court to prosecute Amy for her Suffragette activity.

'Will you call at the house to see Edmond and Amy? They're spending most of the university holidays here.' How kind and jovial he always was.

'Not this time, I think. I should get back to Wealdham in good time. I have to begin work very early tomorrow.'

She said goodbye to her uncle and continued downhill. *I hope he doesn't tell my parents that a man is courting me*, she thought. *It's too soon to introduce him to them.*

They dawdled through Larchbury, past the inn and on to the station. As her train steamed into the platform Max stooped and kissed her gently on the cheek.

'Thank you for a lovely day,' she said as he helped her into her carriage. *Maybe I'm becoming involved, whether I intended to or not*, she thought.

–

Amy set out with Beth early one morning to visit her parents in Sebastopol Terrace. As she walked along the familiar street of modest brick houses she saw Mrs Johnson arriving, for it was her day to help Mother with the cleaning.

Elsie was there too, with her baby in a pram. 'See you later, Mum,' she said, as her mother rang the doorbell.

'Hello, Elsie,' Amy said. She peered into the pram; she had not seen the baby before. He was sleeping peacefully. 'How are you?' she asked Elsie.

'All right,' said the young, fair-haired girl, with her usual vague expression. 'Mum helps me with Philip, and the Smith family do too, though I don't want their help.'

Mother came to let Mrs Johnson in, and left the front door open for Amy.

As Elsie went off down the street Miss Miller came out of the house next door. Amy greeted her and she commented on how Beth was growing.

'Will you be having another kiddie soon?' she asked.

'We'd love to have one before long.'

The grey-haired busybody watched as Elsie wheeled the pram across the road. 'Who do you think her baby looks like?' she asked, when Elsie was barely out of earshot.

'I fancied he looked a little like Henry Smith,' Amy said.

'Strange the girl doesn't acknowledge him as the father. Do you think she really went with that young airman?'

'Probably she just admired his good looks – I don't think Elsie is very bright.' *I really shouldn't encourage Miss Miller*, she thought. 'I hope no one will hold it against the child when he's growing up.'

Miss Miller stared after Elsie, her mouth opening as though she had more to say on the matter.

'I gather Maxim is lodging with you,' Amy said quickly. 'He's doing well at the inn, I understand.'

'Yes…' She was thoughtful. 'I wasn't sure about taking in a foreigner, but he's polite enough. I daresay I'll get used to his strange accent. He plays the violin very well, did you know? I enjoy hearing him practise.' Miss Miller was a fine singer and played the piano well enough to perform in public. She had briefly given Beatrice singing lessons when she was young.

'Yes, so I heard. I believe Edmond's family are inviting him to play for them one evening.'

'He's keen on Mr Edmond's young cousin Vicky, so I understand.' Her pale blue eyes probed Amy's face.

'She helped him once when he hurt his arm,' Amy said, anxious to spare Vicky the woman's curiosity. 'Will you excuse me, Miss Miller? Mother is expecting me.'

She hurried into her parents' house. Her father was back at school for the autumn term now. Mother picked up Beth for a cuddle, then set her down in a chair and brought them both glasses of homemade lemonade.

Beth smiled at her grandmother. She had a slight suntan from the summer and her pale blonde hair was curling; she was developing into a pretty little girl.

'Did you enjoy your week at Hove?' Mother asked.

'It was lovely. We revisited that beach where Edmond and I first met as adults. There aren't minesweepers offshore now. The bathing machines are back there, now the war's over. Beth loved paddling.'

'How much longer is it till you go back to Cambridge?' Mother asked.

'Another two weeks.' Amy wondered whether to tell Mother that she was eager to return to their own little house. She was glad to visit her parents, and was feeling more comfortable with her in-laws than when she was first married, but their own little house beckoned.

--

Beatrice reminded her parents they had proposed a musical evening. 'Let's hold it before Edmond and Amy have to leave, and while Caleb is here.' The American was on leave again.

They invited Maxim and Miss Miller, and then found that Vicky could not come, because she had promised to spend that whole week with her parents, not having gone back to Surrey for some weeks. The recital would need to go ahead without her.

Beatrice watched as they moved the piano into the reception room where they sometimes held a buffet for a party, and positioned two lines of chairs in front. Chambers served drinks as the guests arrived. Edmond led Amy to join the others gathering there. She was smiling in anticipation.

'Where are you stationed now?' Edmond asked Caleb.

'We're near the Rhine, at a place called Boppard, just south of Koblenz. I'm sure seeing Europe while I'm here!'

Beatrice was impressed by his increasing confidence. 'Caleb's been promoted,' she said, without mentioning any rank.

He had told them he was responsible for the upkeep of some army vehicles now. 'I took to vehicle maintenance quickly,' he had told her. 'Before I was drafted, I was used to keeping tractors in good working order.' Though apparently from an undistinguished background, he was clearly resourceful.

He turned towards Maxim. 'So, you're from France? Where did you serve in the war?'

'Verdun.' When Caleb mentioned the manoeuvres of his unit in the Marne area Maxim did not reciprocate with his own experiences. *Some men prefer to forget*, Beatrice thought. When Maxim told Caleb he came from Bar-le-Duc, the American tried to work out how near that area his unit had stayed.

'Our town lies south-east of your campaign,' Maxim said. He seemed to hesitate before continuing, as though reluctant to relive the war. 'Bar-le-Duc was a major assembly point for supplies for Verdun when it was besieged in 1916,' he said.

Now Caleb found little to say, perhaps because his nation had not joined the conflict until 1917.

'It's time we started,' Beatrice announced. 'Miss Miller, would you like to begin with *"Für Elise"?*'

Her former teacher had arranged her grey hair smartly and wore a dark red evening gown, attractive if old-fashioned. She sat at the piano and played the Beethoven tune, showing considerable talent.

After congratulating her, Beatrice sang the new song from Puccini, 'O my Beloved Father'. She stood beside the piano, wearing a favourite evening dress in pale yellow. She had managed to buy a copy of the song with the words in English. A young girl was asking her father to give his blessing on her marriage to a youth from a humble background. As she sang the sweet romantic words she felt wistful. The song was over all too quickly.

'What a lovely song!' Amy said. 'I haven't heard it before.'

Caleb and Pa clapped vigorously.

'What a beautiful voice you have,' Caleb said, leaning back in his chair, with his eyes fixed on her. She felt herself blushing.

'Bea has always sung for us,' Edmond said.

'She sings lullabies too,' said Amy. 'Beth loves them.'

The little girl always wanted to hear 'Ride a Cock-horse to Banbury Cross'. It was a family favourite, for Beatrice could remember singing it to Edmond, when she had been a very young girl and he little more than a baby.

'Are you musical at all, Caleb?' Amy went on.

'Unfortunately not, though I love hearing music. I have an aunt who can play the piano and sing, but I've never studied music myself. I seize what chances I get to hear good music. When we had the opportunity to visit Paris a few months back, I was determined to make the most of it. I managed to visit the Opera with some comrades.' Once more, Beatrice was impressed with his determination to seek out the best in life.

Miss Miller followed, with a simple folk song, well performed.

It was turning out to be an enjoyable evening, almost like ones they had held before the war. 'Maxim, it's time you gave us some music!' Beatrice said.

Miss Miller offered to accompany him on the piano while he played part of the sonata by César Franck for violin and piano. Maxim's violin had a fine tone, and compared with many amateur musicians Beatrice had heard, his playing seemed almost faultless.

'Miss Miller is right, you have a great talent, Maxim,' she told him.

'Please call me Max,' he said.

There was a short interval while Daisy circulated with some refreshments.

'Now, let's see,' Beatrice said afterwards, 'how about you, Amy? You've been practising on the piano, I know.' She felt she should at least invite her sister-in-law to play, though she might sound amateurish.

'Goodness, no! I couldn't possibly!' Amy cried. 'I've not reached a standard where I'm ready to perform in public.'

'I believe we should hear Amy play in a year or two,' Ma said quickly. 'Let's hear you play, Beatrice dear.'

Beatrice smiled, took her place on the piano stool and waited a little impatiently while Edmond finished telling Max about Amy's unfortunate lack of a piano at their home.

Soon she was launching into one of her impressive Chopin études. As her slender fingers flew over the keys she was thankful that after all her practice she had reached a good standard.

Max was quick to congratulate her on her playing.

'I'm proud that you find me talented,' she told him. 'I'm very impressed with your playing. Did you take lessons somewhere prominent in France?'

'I was very fortunate to be accepted by the conservatoire at Cologne.'

Edmond's jaw fell open. 'But that's in Germany!'

Now Amy, Pa and Miss Miller were all looking at Max curiously.

There was a confused expression on the young musician's face. 'It was before the war that I went there, naturally. And it was only intended to be a brief summer course. When I began to show talent for the instrument a maestro there tried to persuade me to continue, but my parents could not afford the cost of the lessons. We were wondering whether or not I should apply for a scholarship, when there was the crisis that led to the outbreak of war, and then of course it became out of the question.'

'All the same,' Miss Miller pursued, 'there must be fine musical colleges in France.'

'I thought of applying to Rheims,' he told them, 'but they were slow founding the college there. It was only opened in 1913 and had not gained much of a reputation. The one in Cologne was outstanding.'

Soon afterwards their soirée drew to an end. Caleb took Beatrice's hand as he said goodnight.

'Thank you for a wonderful evening,' he said, his light blue eyes fixed on hers. *How shall I bear it if he eventually returns to the United States*, she thought, as he set off to the inn.

–

'Do you think Max is all he seems?' Amy asked Edmond later, as they prepared for bed. She was disturbed by the evasive look she had seen on his face.

'What are you suggesting?'

'Could he actually be German?' she asked. 'Madame Rousseau said he had a strange accent for a Frenchman.' She was chiefly concerned because she knew Vicky was growing close to him.

In the dim light of the lamp Edmond looked thoughtful. 'It was Peter who encouraged him to come here,' he said. 'I don't believe he would introduce us to anyone who could not be relied upon to behave decently.' He paused, looking as though he was wondering whether to confide in her.

'Listen, in the war, besides his official duties at headquarters, Peter carried out one or two clandestine missions…'

'What do you mean? Spying or something?'

'Yes. He had various contacts, including people who were able to bring him messages from Germany, or translate enemy messages they had intercepted.'

She was intrigued. 'You never told me about that before!'

'No – Peter confided in me and I promised I wouldn't let it go any further. Remember that time, around the end of 1917, when he went missing?'

'Yes, of course – we were all alarmed because there was no news at all of his whereabouts.'

'He told me a little of his secret mission. I shouldn't be telling you about it, but at least the war's over now.'

She was a little hurt that he had kept Peter's exploits to himself.

'You can imagine how dangerous it is to carry out that kind of subterfuge. There are people whose loyalties are conflicted. Can you see how they can become suspect to both sides, and the perils they face? Perhaps Maxim is someone like that, under suspicion because of some undercover work he has done.' There was a faraway look in his eyes, as though he was visualising hazardous manoeuvres in wartime.

'I can barely imagine what it might be like,' she said.

'I believe we must give Max the benefit of the doubt.'

He was an attractive and gifted young man, and always seemed pleasant. She was eager to think well of him, and decided to trust the judgement of Edmond and his brother.

His arms came around her as they settled into bed.

Chapter 7

Cambridge, autumn 1919

'How could I have reached twenty-five already?' Edmond complained. 'I always imagined by this age I'd be launched on a career.'

Amy looked at him, serious for once, as they settled at a table in the Cambridge restaurant. 'You know why you haven't got further. The war interrupted your plans. Yours and those of most other young men.' *Some of them never had the chance to return to their planned occupations afterwards*, she thought miserably, remembering Bertie.

'You're right.'

'And you enjoy being at College, don't you?'

'Yes – it's stimulating. Sometimes other undergraduates seem young and foolish – they haven't been to war like me.'

'But they respect you when you talk about your experiences.'

'Yes, Horace certainly does. But I seldom want to relive those days.'

Usually he sees his challenges in perspective, she thought.

'I'm one of the fortunate ones,' he said, becoming his usual cheerful self. 'The doctors managed to make me fit again.'

A waiter brought them menus.

'I'm so glad you brought me here,' she said. Grace was spending the evening in their house with Beth, and he had driven them into the town centre through the wet evening. She was wearing her best blue satin gown.

The little restaurant was half-full and some of the other customers looked like undergraduates, for the food was well known for being delicious, while the prices were not too high. Outside they could see the rain still pouring down, puddles enlarging in the street.

Edmond scanned the choices. 'Horace was right when he told me they've got a more extensive menu now. I'm going to order the pheasant – would you like some too?'

'The duck à l'orange sounds tempting. I'll have that.' Their table, like the others, had a single chrysanthemum in a small china vase, in the centre of its spotless white cloth. 'I didn't imagine we'd come here again till our anniversary next month.' Edmond's birthday fell in October, for he was just over six months older than she was.

He ordered a bottle of wine. 'You deserve to be taken out far more often,' he said.

There was a draught behind them as the door opened and three new customers arrived, carrying umbrellas. They walked across the restaurant, their backs to Amy. There were two men, one of them very tall, and a young lady.

'Is this place all right, Zadie?' asked the shorter man.

'Let's stay here – I don't want to go out again into the rain.' A waiter took their wet coats and hung them up. They were all wearing formal evening dress.

As they settled at a table on the opposite side of the room Amy caught her breath. Now she saw his face she recognised the tall man as the last person she wished to see again.

'Are you all right, darling?'

'Yes,' she said quickly. 'Wilfrid Fairlawn has just come in – what's he doing here?' She did not recognise the others.

The newcomers were talking noisily and paying no attention to other customers.

'That's annoying,' Edmond said. 'It was his father, the colonel, who insisted on you being punished for that damage you did as a Suffragette, wasn't it? It was a few years ago now but I can't forgive him for that, especially as our marriage was delayed. At least the colonel isn't here, only his son.'

The man was sitting sideways on to her, and she hoped he would not notice her. If only he and his companions had sought out one of the smarter restaurants instead of rushing in here to escape the downpour. The waiter was presenting them with menus.

'When Peter was on leave he told me Wilfrid Fairlawn is in disgrace,' Edmond whispered, as the waiter brought their own wine. He took a sip and approved it. 'The major was in trouble for pestering nurses, remember?'

She shivered.

'Horace's brother Dennis heard some gossip about it,' he went on. 'There's talk that they'll send Wilfrid to some especially tedious posting a few miles north of Cologne, some backwater where he'll only hold a dreary position.'

She sat miserably, wishing she had at some time managed to tell Edmond how the man had molested her that hideous night in Ypres. She felt giddy at the memory of his large hands groping her body. Even now she shrank from recounting her misadventure.

Soon the waiter set down their meals. She began cutting up the meat and eating small morsels, but the evening was spoilt. She tried to focus her attention on the undergraduate and his young lady friend at the nearest table. She reached for the wine and took a gulp.

Edmond was relishing his meal. *I mustn't spoil his birthday*, she thought.

'I'm so pleased that term has started and we're back in our little house,' he said. 'I needed to visit the family, of course, but I love having our own place, just the three of us. It was what I longed for when I was away fighting.'

She looked up gratefully at his smiling face. *It came right*, she thought, *in spite of everything, we're together as a family, and Edmond's health is better.*

Wilfrid's table was noisy and it was hard to ignore him. He stood up suddenly, looking around for the waiter. Amy looked down at her plate, hoping he would not notice her.

'Waiter!' Wilfrid called loudly. The young man went and took his order for more wine. Nervously she looked up just a little. Then suddenly the officer was staring in her direction.

Now he was crossing the room, heading for their table. Amy felt she was frozen to the spot.

'Good evening, Derwent!' Wilfrid accosted Edmond loudly. 'Have you been discharged from your battalion now? Oh, no, you were invalided out, I'd forgotten.' He seemed to have drunk a good deal already.

'Yes, I was wounded at Wipers,' Edmond said. That was the name the soldiers often used for Ypres. He did not show any urge to discuss it further. Amy sat quietly, avoiding Wilfrid's gaze.

'I'm spending a few days here,' Wilfrid went on. 'My sister Zadie's just got married and settled nearby. My leave's over soon and I'm off to the Rhineland.' He looked across suddenly at Amy. 'And who's this little charmer? Have I met you before?'

Amy quailed, but hoped he would not remember her.

'My wife, Amy,' Edmond said coldly.

'Of course!' A foolish grin broke out on his red face. 'Amy Fletcher! How could I forget! I remember you from that night in Wipers! What a little tease your wife is, Derwent – she led me quite a dance!'

'How dare you!' Amy cried. 'You pestered me, you great bully, and now you're trying to insult me!' A tear ran down her face as she recalled her panic when he had hung on to her. Even when she had wriggled from his grasp, she had not been safe; as she ran she had lost her footing in the rubble of the street and fallen heavily on her ankle. Then she had seen him pursuing her as she lay there, at his mercy, unable to escape…

Edmond stood up, glowering at the tall major. 'I've heard all about you, Fairlawn. I know how you've plagued nurses.'

Fairlawn sneered. 'That's what they say, but only after they've led me on. Why, I remember now, Amy Fletcher, you actually accused me of molesting you!'

'Did he molest you, Amy? You've never mentioned it…' There was a questioning expression now on Edmond's face. 'I know about your record with women,' he said to Wilfrid.

'My war record is impeccable,' the major replied. 'I've been mentioned in despatches numerous times. Silly tittle-tattle by nurses who can't resist giving come-hither looks at officers hasn't damaged my prospects.'

Amy felt sick to hear him blaming young women in an attempt to justify his behaviour.

'...And there's a charming young lady shortly to become my bride. She's not taking any notice of the wild rumours.'

Was someone really about to marry Wilfrid? Amy felt sorry for the woman.

'Your brother Peter works for High Command, doesn't he?' Wilfrid asked Edmond. 'He was one of those trying to put together a case against me. I've heard talk about him, too. He was going on secret errands, meeting Germans – I've heard them say he was a spy.' His voice was rising.

'How dare you!' Now Edmond was furious. 'He's undertaken courageous missions. He's got an unimpeachable record, unlike you.' Customers at nearby tables were staring at them.

Wilfrid leered. 'Did I hear you've got a child, Derwent? How do you even know it's yours?'

Amy shuddered at his wild accusation.

Edmond was trembling with rage. He looked as though he was about to hit Wilfrid, who was so much taller and fitter.

In her terror Amy was a little relieved to see the waiter approaching, and an older, smartly dressed man coming from the kitchen area; she suspected he might be the manager.

Then suddenly the tall, dark-haired woman crossed to their table. She had arrived with Wilfrid, and Amy took her to be his sister. She was poised as she calmly caught hold of the major's arm. 'Wilfrid, darling, please don't get into an argument.' She looked appealingly at the others. 'I'm afraid he's had a little too much to drink. Come back to our table, Wilfrid – the waiter's just brought the fish course, and it looks first-rate.'

Edmond was not to be pacified. 'How dare you insult my wife like that! Apart from other considerations, you should know, Fairlawn, that Amy was already expecting a child when she was in Wipers, and Beth was born on New Year's Day...'

The waiter and the manager both took a few steps nearer.

The other man from Wilfrid's table, who Amy assumed to be Zadie's husband, was suddenly there beside his wife. He was barely as tall as Zadie, and a little plump. He seized Wilfrid's other arm. 'Your sole Véronique is getting cold, Wilfrid. Come back to our table.'

At last he allowed them to lead him back.

Amy put her hands over her face, unable to stop crying. Edmond got up and came to her side of the table. He took her in his arms. 'There, there, darling. I can't believe how he could talk to you like that. You know, I want to knock him down for the way he spoke to you...'

'You mustn't! He's strong and fit!' *And he comes from an influential family*, she wanted to add, remembering all their struggles to have him charged with offences against women.

She looked down at the remains of Edmond's meal, and her own plate which had barely been started.

'I'm sorry everything's spoilt, Edmond, but can we leave here?'

He looked at her and put his arm around her. 'Yes, we'd better go. Waiter, the bill, please.'

The waiter brought their coats. Edmond took out a pound note and gave it to him. 'Keep the change.'

He put his arm around her and hurried her out. It was still raining, if not quite so hard. He let her into the car and drove off. There was still a restless anger about his movements.

–

Edmond could scarcely believe the events of the evening. He said goodnight to Grace and closed the door behind her.

Amy sank onto the sofa. The fire she had lit earlier was dying down. 'Oh, Edmond, what an awful evening! It's completely spoilt your birthday.'

He had almost forgotten their reason for celebration, with the revelations of the evening. 'I know Fairlawn is a monster, but what happened between you and him in Wipers?' His wife was sweet and devoted, but she was also very pretty – had Fairlawn laid his hands on her?

'I was on my way to the nurses' hostel… and he appeared in the street and tried to make me go with him,' she faltered. 'He's the most hateful man. I don't want to talk about it, to remember that night. You surely don't believe I gave him any encouragement?' She was trembling.

He stared at her. 'Why ever didn't you tell me?'

'You'd just been wounded – you were lying in the hospital and I didn't even know if you'd recover. How could I tell you something like that when you were so ill?' She looked at him, her blue eyes wide and appealing.

His head ached as he remembered how they had struggled to repair his shattered chest, and how he had fought even to breathe. 'Oh, heavens, I suppose you couldn't.' He had failed her at the time she most needed him. He felt more helpless than he had done for months.

'But you managed to escape from him?' The officer was large and muscular. For a moment he had a ghastly image of the man pinning her down in some dismal Ypres street.

'He was drunk, and I ran away. Only I fell over some rubble, and that's how I broke my ankle.'

'You mean he was responsible for that?'

'Yes – I was desperate to get away.' She was beginning to cry again. She told him that a vehicle had passed, and Fairlawn had finally given up. As she lay unable to get to her feet, some nuns had come to her rescue.

He struggled for words. 'Why didn't you at least tell me when I was recovering?' he demanded. 'I could have helped you bring a charge against him. Goodness, he attacked you when you were actually expecting our child.'

'You were in poor shape for months afterwards. I was just so glad to have you recover that I couldn't bear to upset you.'

He got up and paced backwards and forwards. It was intolerable that she had kept the outrage from him. 'You had to bear all the misery on your own, and the damage to your ankle.'

'I did my best to get back at him. Peter will tell you. I made a complaint against Wilfrid. Peter and his friend Robert Lambert tried to bring a case against him, but while the war was on they didn't make any progress.'

'You told Peter about it? Who else knows what happened?

'Lavinia – she was very helpful. She encouraged me to make the complaint. It just happened to be Peter who had to deal with disciplinary matters like that. And in the end there were enough complaints against Captain Fairlawn – well, he's a major now – for him to be charged.'

He sat down beside her again. 'I'm a complete failure – you were attacked and I couldn't help you.'

She put her arm around him and stroked his face. 'No one could expect you to handle the situation at the time. You'd been critically injured, serving your country. Your priority was to get well, for me and for Beth. That was what mattered.'

He was thirsty and still a bit hungry, but could not collect his thoughts enough to fetch them food or drink. 'I could kill Wilfrid Fairlawn,' he said. 'I hate him even more than his father.'

'He got punished in the end.'

'Even tonight he was insulting you, making out it was your fault.' For a moment he imagined himself pointing a service revolver at the major and blowing out his brains.

'Darling, we have to put it behind us,' she implored.

What she had told him had completely shattered his composure. Could he ever forget what had happened to her? 'You kept it all secret from me.'

'There was a compelling reason. Listen, you didn't tell me about Peter's secret missions in the war, did you?'

'That was entirely different!' he snapped.

'I can just about understand why you didn't tell me.'

'Sweetheart, promise me we won't have any secrets from each other ever again.'

'Yes, darling, I promise. Put your arms around me to help me forget that dreadful evening.'

Chapter 8

Larchbury and London, autumn 1919

Florence alighted from the train at Alderbank. Outside the tiny station Lavinia was waiting for her in a modest Ford car.

'Lovely to see you!' she said, opening the door for her friend.

'I'm glad of an outing at half term,' she said, as Lavinia drove smoothly into the lane, past young birch trees which were shedding their leaves. For a moment Florence wondered if she herself would ever have the confidence to drive, but there was little prospect of James buying a car, and his father only had the pony trap. She could not imagine her own father allowing her to drive his car.

Soon they reached an area of apple orchards, with workers picking the last of the crop. Then they reached Appletrees, the house Charles had bought. They walked through the small garden with its Michaelmas daisies, now wilting, and windswept chrysanthemums. She followed Lavinia through the small hall into the drawing room, with its fire already flickering in the grate. Charles was sitting in an armchair and rose to his feet a little awkwardly.

They exchanged greetings, and he assured her that he was continuing to make progress with his artificial limbs. She gathered his accountancy studies were going well.

'Our maid isn't here today, but she cooked the ham joint for me yesterday,' Lavinia said. 'It's heating up and I just need to deal with the vegetables and make the sauce.' Florence followed her to the kitchen to help complete the preparations.

Before long they were seated at the dining room table. Florence poured mustard sauce on her slices of ham. 'You've a lovely outlook here,' she said, for there was a pleasant view of the orchards.

'The nearest field is ours,' Charles said. 'We use it as a paddock for our horses.'

'How's life at the vicarage?' Lavinia asked her.

'They're very kind to me.' All the same, she envied her friend being established in such a charming house. 'James's father has toned down his pleas to make peace with the Germans, though I feel sure he'll return to those sentiments in a year or two, when the congregation might be more ready to accept his views. ...How's your nursing going? Are you fitting in well at Wealdham Hospital?'

'Yes... but there's a complication now. I shall have to give up my work in a few months.'

'Why's that?'

'I'm fairly sure I'm expecting a child!' Lavinia was smiling broadly. 'To be honest, I hadn't expected it to happen so quickly. But it will be wonderful to bring Charles's child into the world.'

'Oh, yes! I'm delighted for you. I remember how thrilled Amy was when Beth was born, that a new life had come after all the losses.' Now she felt envious all over again. 'You two were married after us!'

'I believe I'll be a mother by the time of our first anniversary!'

'It's all happened quite fast for Lavinia,' Charles said. 'There are so many projects that interest her – I think she expected motherhood to wait a while longer.'

'It is somewhat bad timing, just when there are so many opportunities for women,' Lavinia said, leaning back in her seat with an intense expression in her dark eyes, rather the way she had looked in the days when they had been Suffragettes. 'There's the prospect of getting seats in parliament, becoming jurors, being awarded degrees – it's all suddenly coming about, but I shan't have much opportunity to take part while I have a young baby.'

'You're bound to find some important tasks to occupy you,' Charles said.

'I do hope so.'

After the meal they went back to their seats around the fire. 'As for you, Florence, I'm sure you'll become a mother before too long,' Lavinia said. 'Is there any prospect of James being discharged?'

'By the end of the year, I hope. He's talked of studying at university, but if he does he'll need to wait till next autumn.' How she longed to have him home with her. 'We've only spent two weeks together since we've been married.'

'Amy and Edmond didn't see each other for nearly a year after they were wed,' Lavinia reminded her. 'And at least the fighting is over.'

They had thought of taking a walk, but it was a dull day, and the light was fading fast. 'It's becoming dreary in the afternoons,' Florence complained. 'Soon it'll be getting dark when we come out of school. When the weather was better in the spring and summer it seemed we were moving on and putting the war behind us, but now it's dark and the plants are dying back – James's mother was saying the other day, people are becoming sad again.'

'There's a ceremony planned for the anniversary of the Armistice,' Charles said.

'And war memorials will be erected before long,' Lavinia said.

Soon afterwards, Florence got into the car and Lavinia drove her back to the station. The short day was beginning to draw to its close.

—

It was about a year since Beatrice had visited London, and she and Pa were staying at the same hotel in the street of multi-storeyed terraced houses where they had stayed when Charles was in hospital. There were fewer passers-by in uniform, and more men with crutches and a trouser leg folded up while the man waited to be fitted with an appliance. Such sights were common now. It was late afternoon and the street was growing dark, but the sombre memories haunted her. She closed the curtains and changed quickly into her evening dress. She had chosen it that morning in Harrods, but it was less showy than the ones she used to choose. She had less interest now in buying classy dresses, and in any case the styles had changed from the heavily embellished gowns they had used to wear. Most of the year had passed without her spending all her allowance before the end of the month and having to appeal to Pa. *Times have changed,* she told herself. *I must accept we'll never return to those days when I had a choice of eager escorts.*

She joined Pa in the restaurant, wishing they were staying at a different hotel, but he was still very preoccupied with the forest, and it had been a struggle to persuade him she needed a change of scene.

'Does your friend Harriet Patterson's family still have a house near here?' he asked her now. 'You used to enjoy visiting her.'

'I don't believe they stay there so often now,' she said. She was unwilling to tell him the real reason she no longer visited them. That time she had stayed with the Pattersons while Ma was ill, she had spent the evening at a restaurant with friends, and Major Wilfrid Fairlawn had accompanied her in a taxi and made unwelcome advances to her. When she had told them what had happened, they had refused to believe the major would behave like that and implied she must have encouraged him. After her ordeal with Wilfrid she had been subjected to insults instead of sympathy.

She put down her soup spoon. She was a little heartened to know that the army had disciplined the major, but the memory still disturbed her. She could not imagine ever staying with Harriet's family again.

Pa was looking at her curiously. She had never told her family about what had taken place, except Amy, who believed her because she had heard rumours about Wilfrid Fairlawn. Apart from the Pattersons, she was the only person who knew what had happened, and she was kind and understanding.

'Have you finished, Bea? We should start the main course; we haven't got very long before we set off for the theatre.'

'Yes – I'm ready for the veal.'

She sat up and tried to look poised and serene. She must pretend Fairlawn's dreadful behaviour had never happened. *These days, one has to adjust, to make the best of a diminished world.*

Little more than half an hour later they were taking their seats to see the new musical by Ivor Novello. The theatre was almost completely full.

In the interval she accompanied Pa to the bar, where there was a long queue to be served. 'Perhaps you'd like to sit at a table while you're waiting,' he said.

They looked around for one, near other respectable-looking women so she might not attract any unwelcome attentions from men.

'Caroline!' cried Beatrice, noticing her old friend from Larchbury.

'Please join me,' Caroline Brownlee said. 'I'm waiting while Father fetches our drinks.'

'It's a brilliant show, isn't it?' Beatrice's spirits had risen at the diverting plot.

'Yes! Are you staying in a hotel? How long will you be in town?'

They compared notes. Caroline and her father were staying in a hotel not far from theirs.

'It's been a very hard year for us, with losing Philip,' Caroline said. She had fair hair and looked quite like her late brother. It was less than a year since he had died of his injuries, crashing his plane just after the war had ended. *And that business about Elsie and the baby can't have helped,* Beatrice thought, though she was too tactful to mention it. Elsie still maintained Philip was the father, though there was no evidence.

'I didn't think Father would want to bring me to London,' Caroline said, 'but he's heard about the special ceremony on Tuesday. Are you staying for that?'

'Special ceremony?'

'It's for the anniversary of the Armistice.'

Mr Brownlee arrived with a drink for her. 'Hello, Beatrice,' he said, 'how nice to see you.'

'I enticed Father to London with the promise that we'd stay for the ceremony,' Caroline said.

'Perhaps we should stay too. In fact, I believe Pa may have mentioned it.'

She waved to Pa as he approached. He passed her a glass of wine. Only a few minutes remained for her to drink it. He and Mr Brownlee exchanged notes about the planned ceremony. 'We can't actually witness it,' Pa said. 'It's to take place in the gardens of Buckingham Palace.'

'Perhaps we can take a look at the Cenotaph, that memorial they've erected.'

'Look, there's Harriet over there with Wilfrid Fairlawn,' Caroline said suddenly.

'What?' Beatrice stared in the direction she indicated, at the other end of the bar. The pair had their backs to her, which accounted for her not recognising them before.

A young man hurried past, ringing a bell, to indicate that the second act was about to begin. Beatrice was mightily relieved to see Wilfrid and Harriet rushing out without looking about them, so she would not have to face an embarrassing encounter.

'We'd better get back,' Pa said. They swallowed the remains of their drinks and joined the throng heading back to the auditorium.

'Do you know if Harriet spends much time with Wilfrid?' Beatrice could not resist asking Caroline.

'I should say so! They've just got married.'

Beatrice gasped. 'Are you sure?'

'Yes – it was all quite sudden and the engagement announcement wasn't very prominent in the *Wealdham*

Gazette. The wedding should be reported in this week's edition.'

Beatrice tried to conceal her shock at her former friend's choice of husband. They reached the auditorium and she said goodbye to Caroline and went down towards their row with Pa. She sat in her seat and as the lights went down she was thankful her dismay could not be witnessed. She would need to tell Amy about it when she saw her.

–

The show finished quite late and there was no opportunity to speak to the Brownlees again. Next morning Pa rang Caroline's father at their hotel and on the Tuesday they all dressed in their darkest clothes and went to Whitehall. The area was massively crowded with people and they could not see much of what was taking place, but some veterans of the war were marching down the street to the music of a military band.

It had been announced that the war would be commemorated each year on the eleventh hour of the eleventh day of the eleventh month, and as the time approached the crowd became subdued.

Beatrice was still curious about the news that Caroline had told her. 'I'm so surprised about Wilfrid Fairlawn and Harriet,' she whispered. 'I thought Harriet was interested in an officer called Gilbert Barnet. I met him once and he seemed a decent young man.'

'Then you haven't heard about the other whirlwind romance, which happened earlier,' Caroline whispered. 'Remember Zadie, Wilfrid's sister? She started flirting with Gilbert and enticed him away from Harriet. Zadie and Gilbert got married when he came on leave, and Harriet was very put out.'

Beatrice was stunned by this news, too. It seemed all kinds of events had been happening while she had remained quietly in Larchbury.

'Then Wilfrid came on leave,' Caroline went on. 'It seems he was allowed a whole three months away, for some reason.'

He was suspended from his duties, Beatrice wanted to tell her.

'It gave Harriet long enough to enjoy his company and persuade him it was time to settle down.'

Some people standing in front of them turned and stared at Caroline. 'Be quiet, for goodness' sake!' a man demanded. 'It's coming up to eleven o'clock!'

Beatrice was so shocked by what she had heard that she was not tempted to make any comment.

Big Ben began striking the hour. The crowd stood, united in their grief, as lost ones were called to mind. Pa put his hand on Beatrice's shoulder. As the notes stopped booming, silence fell. The trees were almost bare, but a few of the last leaves were blowing down the street.

At last some military music started up again. They followed the crowd further along Whitehall. 'See, that must be the Cenotaph!' Beatrice exclaimed. It was a tomb-like structure made of wood and plaster.

'They're planning to rebuild it in Portland stone by next year,' said Pa.

She wondered what kind of ceremony the King was holding in the gardens of Buckingham Palace.

Eventually the crowd dispersed and they set off back the way they had come. Now Beatrice's thoughts reverted to what Caroline had told her. *Harriet clearly didn't pay any attention to what I told her about Wilfrid*, she thought. For a moment she felt it served her right if she suffered as a result, but then she was shocked at her reaction. *I wish I could have warned her again and prevented her making such a mistake. Or will Wilfrid settle down as a married man and learn to behave?* Somehow she could not imagine him achieving such a change.

'So, Zadie and Harriet have both rushed into marriage,' she confined herself to saying to Caroline.

'Well, there's a shortage of young men now.'

'But even so, they sound very desperate.'

'I'm glad you've said that, Beatrice, for I thought the same.'

Chapter 9

Beatrice dawdled down Larchbury High Street. After a cold snap in early December it had turned milder, and she enjoyed looking at the displays in the shop windows, more brightly decorated this year. The toy shop was particularly festive, and she peered at the arrays of spinning tops and stuffed toys. She would love choosing something for her niece; besides enjoying Christmas, Beth would be two years old on New Year's Day.

A little further along the street was the smart milliner's shop. She was not short of hats, but she was eager to call inside. They stocked gloves too, and one of her old pairs was growing shabby, but she had another mission. She had heard that Caroline Brownlee was working there. It was a decent, feminine occupation, serving in a shop which sold quality fashionable goods, but she was still a little surprised.

The bell jangled as she stepped inside. Miss Parsons, an upright, grey-haired lady who was one of the owners, was serving a customer, but Caroline was there too and looked up from unpacking a hat which had just been delivered. 'Beatrice!' she exclaimed. 'Lovely to see you. Are you looking for a new hat?'

'Just gloves, this time. May I see what you have in brown leather?'

'Yes, of course. What size do you take?' She went and fetched a drawer full of suitable gloves. She was tall and neatly dressed, and gave a good impression of a smart, attentive shop girl. 'I expect you're surprised that I'm working here,' she said.

Beatrice had been wondering how to broach the topic tactfully.

'The older Miss Parsons is working fewer hours now,' she explained, 'and I heard there was a vacancy of sorts. It struck me as an interesting way to spend my days, besides giving me more financial independence from my family. When I discussed it with my parents they took a while to become used to the idea, but they had no objection.'

'Occasionally I wonder what it would be like to have an occupation,' Beatrice said. 'Amy became a nurse in the war, and Florence Clifford, I mean Fletcher, works as a schoolteacher.'

Miss Parsons was still attending to her customer.

Caroline lowered her voice. 'Since Herbert died I've given up the idea of ever marrying,' she admitted.

Her fiancé had died fighting near the Somme, Beatrice remembered. 'I'm in my mid-twenties now,' Caroline continued, 'and I don't suppose I shall have the opportunity. So I decided to find an agreeable way of spending my time.'

'You could do a lot worse.'

'Of course, it's different for you,' her friend said quickly. 'You're so pretty and elegant and accomplished. But I decided my chances of finding a husband were poor, as I could not imagine finding anyone I loved like Herbert.'

Beatrice was glad of the chance to speak what was on her mind. 'When I heard how Zadie and Harriet had rushed to marry I did wonder if they were panicking that they would remain spinsters,' she said, picking out a pair of gloves to try.

'One wonders if it's wise to marry so impulsively,' Caroline agreed. 'It's said they were quite forward, sometimes angling for invitations to events where young men would be present.'

Beatrice imagined Harriet coming to regret accepting Wilfrid's offer. She eased off the gloves. 'These will be fine, thank you.' She took out her purse to pay.

'That's a gorgeous hat you're wearing, Beatrice. May I ask where you bought it?'

'I chose it when we were in London. It was the nearest I could find to what I wanted, so I bought it and then changed the trimming so it looked more like one I'd seen in a magazine. I bought some fresh ribbon and arranged it like the photograph.'

Caroline's eyebrows rose. 'Did you fix it yourself? Those pleats are very stylish.'

'Yes – it was fun, getting it just so!'

'You're gifted, Beatrice. You could probably find employment with a milliner, trimming fine hats… if you ever wanted to, of course.'

'Thank you, Caroline – I'll bear in mind what you've said.'

Ma had been critical of Caroline's decision to take paid work, but as Beatrice said goodbye she resolved to stay good friends with her. For one thing she was short of close friends – she could hardly visit Zadie or Harriet anymore. She had never had much in common with Lavinia, and in any case, she too was unlikely to be well disposed towards her, since Beatrice had previously been engaged to Charles, before ending the commitment. She did not regret her decision, and was glad Charles had found a wife well-equipped to care for him, but for the time being at least there was an awkwardness between them.

How wise Caroline is, she thought, *not casting around for a husband who is second best*. Once she herself had felt desperate to avoid spinsterhood. But she knew now who she cared for, though she could not see any way ahead for her and Caleb. She wished her parents, Ma in particular, were less likely to reject him as a son-in-law. If only she could envisage some kind of future for them in America. *I haven't the slightest idea if I'd ever fit in there,* she thought. *His home sounds very basic and different from what I'm used to. He writes me loving letters, but what's to become of us?*

–

Soon after Edmond drove Amy and Beth to The Beeches for Christmas, Beatrice invited Amy into her bedroom and told her the latest news about Wilfrid.

'Married? His poor wife!' Amy remarked. Wilfrid's ugly confrontation with her and Edmond in the restaurant in Cambridge still preyed on her mind. Besides her shock at seeing him again, the man's distorted version of events had upset Edmond so greatly.

'Don't you just want to put it behind you?' she asked Beatrice. 'At least he's been punished now.'

'Yes, I intend to,' her sister-in-law said, a determined look in her greenish eyes. 'I just needed to tell someone about it, and you're the only one I can confide in.'

'I understand.'

Thank goodness Beatrice isn't likely to mention Wilfrid's behaviour in front of Edmond, Amy thought later. At last her husband seemed to be coming to terms with her own experience at the man's hands in Ypres.

'I've always hated that kind of behaviour,' Edmond had told her. 'If ever any young man in my command tried to take advantage of a woman left in a vulnerable situation, I would see he was disciplined. There's no excuse for it.'

Wilfrid had revealed himself as a man treating women as prey in contingencies of war. Edmond now admired her for having fought back and helped bring the officer to justice. The raw fury that had possessed him for the first few days after he heard of Wilfrid's assault had begun to abate.

She prepared Beth for bed, then changed for dinner. *The Fairlawns – what a family,* she thought. *Even the father is a bully, who was determined to send me to jail for a relatively minor offence. I'd rather meet a family of belligerent Huns.*

–

'What a simply lovely Christmas tree!' Vicky exclaimed. 'It almost reaches the ceiling.' It was two days after Christmas and guests were arriving for the Derwents' ball. Invitations were sought after for the annual event towards the end of the year.

Her aunt smiled. 'It's a fine specimen, isn't it? Do you remember when we used to have one, before they became unpopular in the war? Too German, people thought. We've sold quite a few this year. Your uncle selected this one for us, but we had to buy more baubles, to have enough to decorate it. We spent a whole morning fixing it, with Ross from the plantation, and George and Joe helping Chambers as he climbed up a ladder to reach the top of the tree.'

'You're looking very pretty tonight,' her aunt went on. 'I'm glad the hospital gave you the evening off.'

'I'm relieved I reached here in good time.' She had compared notes and discovered the same Matron was in charge as when Amy had done her preliminary training there. She was very strict, and liable to keep nurses working late. Sometimes Aunt Mabel invited Vicky for a meal and she would rush in at the last minute, to her aunt's obvious annoyance.

'Doesn't Vicky's hair suit her like that?' Beatrice asked.

Her auburn locks were drawn into the usual chignon, but her friend Nora had helped her style little curls at the front.

Beatrice was as attractive as ever but more retiring than she had once seemed. Even last Christmas she had seemed to spend her time looking around for young men. Vicky remembered her recently referring to a letter from Caleb. Her interest in the American seemed to be holding.

There was one thought prominent in Vicky's mind: *Will Max be here*? He had told her that he was invited, and would ask for the evening off, but she had wondered if he would change his mind at the last minute and go home to France to spend the festive season with his parents. She looked around her. Besides the magnificent Christmas tree there were pine garlands festooned around the walls.

'Vicky!' Amy hurried to join her. 'I love your dress.'

She had chosen a new one, loose around the waist in the modern style, in pale turquoise georgette crêpe. There was no sign of Max, but she greeted Amy and Edmond, and Florence, who was clinging to the arm of her husband James.

'He's home permanently now,' Florence said delight-edly.

'The hospitals in France are emptying, thank goodness,' he told them. 'Most of the battalions are settling in the Rhineland. They say that soon conscription might end, so we'll have a volunteer army.'

In one corner a quartet of musicians had arrived and were unpacking their instruments.

She sensed someone tall approaching from her left, and there suddenly was Max, handsome in evening dress. It was hard to take her eyes off him.

'Do I look all right?' he asked, an anxious expression in his blue eyes. 'Will I fit in at an English ball?'

'Of course!'

'Then you must be my partner, for you are looking beautiful.'

'I thought you might decide to go home to France. I suppose you could still go tomorrow and join your parents in time for New Year.'

'It's a long way to go, as I come from eastern France, quite a distance from the Channel.'

Chambers, the butler, approached with a tray. They both took glasses of wine. Vicky sipped it cautiously, for she was unused to drinking much alcohol. Max took a mouthful and swallowed it, looking dubious as though it was not what he was accustomed to.

'Have you heard from your parents recently?' she asked him.

'Yes – they are well, and making the best of the post-war situation.'

He scarcely ever mentioned them and she wondered if there was friction within the family. As for his country, she had heard a good deal from Amy and Edmond about the devastation in France.

'They are following the progress of the Peace Conference, at Versailles, of course,' he said.

'But the treaty was signed in June!'

'Yes, but the United States still have not signed it. In November they refused to ratify it. How about you, have you visited your parents recently?'

'Yes, I went there for Christmas Day.' She was glad to find time to see them again. She still had not mentioned that she was interested in a young man.

Soon they were following the other guests into the large reception room where her aunt's buffet was being served. As usual the long table, lit by candles and decorated with sprays of holly, was stacked with tempting food.

'What a fine selection!' Max said.

There were platters of cold meat, salmon and pies. Daisy and Mrs Johnson were cutting portions for the guests. The buffet seemed almost as lavish as at the beginning of the war.

She and Max compared notes on the feast. She gathered he had been involved in cooking and serving the Christmas meals at the inn.

Chambers brought some more wine, and Max took another glass.

'May I ask what you think of our wine, Sir?' the butler asked. 'It's a little easier to select good vintages, now the war is over. You French citizens are connoisseurs of wine.'

'I like Gewurztraminer,' Max told him.

Vicky had never heard of it, and Chambers looked surprised at Max's recommendation. Max's face clouded for a moment, as though he had made a faux pas.

They circulated, chatting to the Brownlees and other guests that she knew. The atmosphere was merrier than the previous year, when the fighting had only just ended, but there was still a shortage of young men and she felt especially fortunate to have Max at her side.

'Aunt and Uncle have been inviting me since I was first taking dancing lessons,' she told him, remembering how she had begged to be allowed to stay up to watch the first few dances, at least.

She was growing excited as they followed other guests back to the ballroom, where the quartet was tuning up. 'Is that Viennese music?' she asked Max.

'You're right, it is. It's "*Tales from the Vienna Woods*".'

'I seem to remember that kind of music was very popular when I was a child, then they stopped playing it so much in the war.'

'There's a peace treaty with Austria now, though their empire must be dissolved.'

'I know so little about the Continent. Beatrice travelled there before the war, and of course Edmond and Amy served there.' She wished she had known France in its heyday.

As the room filled, the musicians switched to a popular dance tune and her aunt and uncle took the floor to begin the dancing, rapidly followed by Amy and Edmond.

'Are you familiar with British dances?' she asked Max. For a moment she was worried that the French enjoyed exotic dances like the can-can.

'Yes, of course, we dance the waltz a good deal,' he said, to her relief. 'Come, let's join the others!'

She allowed him to take her into his arms and they stepped on to the dance floor. She looked up at his smiling face. Dancing with him was just as delightful as she had expected it to be. There had been the earlier years, when she had enjoyed her first tentative dances, and last year, when she had begun to gain confidence. Now she felt that she had the partner she had been waiting for.

She caught Amy smiling in her direction, seeming to sense her enchantment with her partner. But, thrilled though she was, she must be aware of the other guests. Aunt and Uncle were growing older, she had noticed when she began visiting regularly, and after the first dance they were content to sit and watch. When there was a pause she happily danced with Edmond, who was still apt to become a little out of breath after each number. She danced with James, too. Maxim partnered Amy and Beatrice, and she became a little impatient to see if he would return to her side.

Then, there he was again, and she melted into his arms for another waltz. He was holding her more closely now. She surely had not imagined his feelings for her were growing stronger.

As a dance finished, he made a slight bow and clicked his heels. She looked at him a little curiously and for a moment she thought she noticed a trace of embarrassment. *Isn't it Germans who click their heels? Very probably it's a common habit on the Continent,* she reasoned.

The quartet were beginning a new dance, with a merry modern air. Tunes like this were beginning to be played by dance bands; she thought it was a foxtrot. As they stood and watched, Alice Shenwood and her partner were the only pair to take to the floor and try the new steps, seeming to flow around the room. Vicky knew that Alice was Charles's younger sister. She and the young man accompanying her had been invited, but Charles and Lavinia could not be present: that would have been awkward as Beatrice had once been engaged to Charles.

Alice seemed to have quickly forgotten her young airman who had died. *But I believe she's even younger than I am*, she thought. 'What fun they do seem to be having!' she told Max. 'The other day Nora, my friend at the hospital, was showing me how to do the steps. Shall we try the dance too?'

He smiled and she showed him the basic steps. Next he drew her into his arms and they found a quiet corner and tried a short sequence together. Then they took to the floor and glided around in response to the music. She was not even certain they were getting the steps right, but at the end they burst out laughing at their efforts.

Edmond and Amy came to congratulate them, looking tempted to try it.

'At least we're dancing the waltzes more competently than we did when we were both injured,' Edmond said. Vicky remembered how much of a challenge it had been for them to take part in earlier years.

The musicians moved on to the final waltz. As Max led her to the floor her excitement soared – *what a handsome young admirer I've attracted,* she thought. *As a child I wondered what it would be like to meet a young man from abroad.* She stayed by his side until the ball was ending.

He fetched his coat and kissed her tenderly on her lips. They made a plan to meet one evening the following week, if they could both arrange time off. For a few moments more they clung together, unwilling to part. Then he set off, back towards his lodgings.

She was still a little dizzy at the memory of the dancing, and his kiss. *It's time I told my parents that I'm seeing a young man,* she decided, *especially as Aunt Mabel may write and tell them.*

It's nearly New Year. We'll grow even closer, I'm sure we will.

Chapter 10

Larchbury, spring 1920

'I should like you all to say Good Day to my guests,' Reverend Fletcher announced towards the end of his sermon. 'Herr Pastor Schulz is here from Germany, as my opposite number; he's concerned with reconciliation between our two countries. And Emil is his nephew, who joined up as a young officer at the end of the war.'

Many of the congregation drew their breath, those near the front straining to see the two men in the vicar's family pew. The pastor was plainly clad and the young man out of uniform.

'They'll be staying with us for a few days, and I hope you will take the opportunity to speak to them,' the vicar went on. 'They both learnt English at school.'

At the end of the service Florence's parents were among those who were quick to leave, but Amy's parents stayed to shake hands with the Germans. Amy and Edmond were back in Cambridge now. Mr Derwent stayed briefly to greet the guests, then hurried away to drive his womenfolk back to The Beeches. Maxim, the young man from France who was working at the inn, greeted the newcomers with enthusiasm, and was soon talking with them in their own language. The young chef was making a great impression with Vicky, Florence understood. Now he was gabbling away with his German counterpart as though he had never spoken anything else.

'Is German much like French?' she whispered to James curiously. She had the impression it was not.

'No, they're quite different, but Max knows German as well as English and his mother tongue.'

Soon they were back at the vicarage and she was helping James's mother prepare roast lamb for lunch. There were two extra places for the visitors. The pastor was polite and dignified, and Emil young, but able to speak well.

'We thought we'd go out for a walk by the brook this afternoon, as it's such a nice spring day,' James said. It was April, the week after Easter. 'Would you like to come with us?'

'Reverend Fletcher is going to show me some of his books,' the pastor said.

'Maxim from the inn said he'd take me for a walk,' Emil said.

'Make sure you speak some English while you are here,' the pastor told him sternly.

From the High Street a lane ran through to the brook. The day was cool but bright, and light green leaves were appearing on the trees.

'There must be some more universities you can try for a place,' Florence told her husband.

'There are a few more.' The results had been disappointing so far. Now the men were being discharged, many of them wanted to study, and his own qualifications were not as good as he wished.

'At least I'm making myself useful in the meantime,' he said. On most weekdays he went to the orphanage to help, handling the paperwork for them.

'There are a great many other worthwhile things I might do,' he went on. 'Look at all the new projects – Father's scheme for reconciliation, for one. Then there's the Save the Children Fund, and the Red Cross. There are all kind of organisations I might become involved with, and some might offer me paid work.'

She was relieved to hear it, for the orphanage only paid him a pittance for the work he did there. 'You were going to publish your memoirs, weren't you?' she whispered. She knew he had furtively written accounts of his life at the Front, but that as yet they were secret.

'The time hasn't come yet for those… one day, perhaps. Some of the top brass won't like what I said about them.'

In the distance they caught a glimpse of Emil and Max coming towards them.

'There'll be trips to France soon to visit the war graves,' James went on. 'Of course they'll take place around the battlefields in France, but I daresay people will need help with making arrangements here.'

'Are they still determined not to repatriate any of the bodies?'

'They won't change their resolve. Perhaps it's because there are just so many bodies out there?'

They both shivered. There would be a need for travelling to France, she realised. One day in a year or two she meant to go with Amy and Edmond to see where Bertie had fallen. How could you leave your loved ones abroad and not even visit their graves? But as for James making some kind of career from that work, she had no idea how it would come about. Would he need to travel, to know languages? And how well would it be paid? She could go on teaching for a while, but what if they had a family? She would prefer not to remain dependent on his parents.

Emil and Max were approaching, still talking in German. Emil pointed suddenly to the brook, and there were the first six tiny, fluffy ducklings, bobbing across the clear water, behind their mother.

–

'Thank goodness the Spanish flu is officially over now,' Lavinia said. She and Vicky were working on different wards, but they managed to stop for a cup of tea in the canteen at the same time. Lavinia was slumped wearily in her seat, her condition becoming very obvious. *Surely it must be time for her to give up work soon*, Vicky thought. Lavinia was married to Charles, Edmond's friend, and they often chatted.

'There's still no shortage of work here,' Vicky said. 'Not with that unhealthy area down by the factories.' The people who lived there were mainly poor, and often fell ill with bronchial infections. Some of them managed to put by a few pence each week to pay into a Friendly Society in case a family member needed to attend the hospital.

'There are a lot of waifs and strays now,' Lavinia said. That was what poor children were called, when the parents had difficulty supporting all of them, or one or both parents had died.

Vicky sighed. 'I used to think of nursing as a stimulating career,' she said. *It must partly have been the opportunities to travel that Amy enjoyed*, she thought. *There's little glamour in constant visits from snuffly children or old men with persistent coughs.*

'But you don't regret starting your training, do you?'

'No, I can see how vital it is that we do what we can for the folk here.' She was often tired out now, and relished her weekly breaks. There were delicious meetings with Max, when they could obtain time off on the same days. She also looked forward to trips home or to the Derwents, simply for the chance to relax.

'I hear Queen Alexandra unveiled a monument to Nurse Edith Cavell in London last month,' Vicky went on. She was the widow of the old king, Edward VII.

'Yes, I wished I'd managed to visit London to see the ceremony. It was very shocking in 1915 when Nurse Cavell was shot as a spy.'

'I can't imagine a nurse working as a spy.'

'There were some allied men still trapped in Belgium, and she was one of the team helping them to escape to Holland. She was a very strict woman, and deeply religious, and when she was captured she wouldn't deny what she had done.' Lavinia stood up and examined her watch. 'Time I was returning to the ward.'

'Will you miss working here?' Vicky could not resist asking her.

'I'd really like to take some political role, now women are more accepted in such positions. I'd like to raise questions about how the poor suffer in our society. But my husband still needs a lot of support, and I don't know how much time I can devote to my ideals once I have a child.'

Vicky watched her tall, striking figure heading back towards her ward.

—

Herr Pastor Schulz and Emil were spending their last weekend with Reverend Fletcher. They had originally crossed the Channel with another pastor, Herr Ritter. He was well known for his religious writing, and the vicar was delighted to welcome him too for three days. It was a wet weekend and the three ministers were happy to spend much of it indoors, discussing religious topics and the peace process. Many Germans hated the Occupation.

On Sunday morning Pastor Ritter joined them for the service. Afterwards James joined the visitors and soon Max came to talk to them. There was a light drizzle.

'So you have to go back soon?' James heard Max ask. The group were speaking English to each other.

'Yes, sadly. I do not know when we will be able to come again.' Emil turned to speak to Pastor Ritter. 'This is Max, the young Frenchman I have come to know here. He speaks German very well.'

The new pastor looked in his direction and James saw his mouth drop open. For a moment Max seemed to start too, but his reaction was so fleeting that James felt he might be mistaken.

There was anger now in the pastor's voice. 'He speaks German well! Indeed, I am not surprised. This man is as German as you or I. The last time I met him he was wearing a German lieutenant's uniform and answering to the name of Johann.'

'No, no, you are completely wrong,' Max cried. 'I am Maxim, and I assure you, I'm from Bar-le-Duc, in France. You must be mistaking me for someone else.'

'I think not,' the pastor maintained. 'It was some years ago I saw you in that uniform, early in the war, but I remember faces well.' His raised voice was attracting attention now from some of the dispersing congregation. It had stopped raining.

'But Max is my friend!' exclaimed Emil.

Florence looked from Emil to Pastor Ritter, clearly perplexed.

'Perhaps it is time we left,' Pastor Schulz said. 'We have to collect our luggage from the vicarage and make our way to the station for our train.'

James was thoroughly upset by the scene, and his father looked shocked.

'You are absolutely sure you do not wish to take lunch with us first?'

'No, it is best we take the next train.'

'Will you accompany all the guests back to the vicarage, please James, while I say goodbye to the last of the congregation.'

James did as his father asked and Florence went with him. It seemed best not to present an inharmonious appearance to the congregation, while trying to persuade them into ways of peace. His mother, who lacked any knowledge of foreign languages, went with them and helped their guests prepare to leave.

'How difficult this all is!' exclaimed Emil, as James helped him with his suitcase. 'French or German, it makes no difference, but I am convinced Max is a decent French fellow. Why would he say something untrue? If only we could have resolved this question!'

Up till now Pastor Ritter had seemed a reasonable man, but seeing his tight lips James could not see any point in trying to make him change his mind. When his father was back he hitched up his pony to his trap and took his guests to the station.

Until today, James had been regarding the Germans' visit as a great success. 'How disappointing it was to witness that confrontation,' he said as they eventually began lunch.

'I feel sure he's mistaken about Max,' his father said.

'He's such an agreeable chap!' Florence agreed.

'The very idea of him being a German officer!' James said. Then suddenly he remembered something strange about the young man's demeanour. At the Christmas party he had danced with Edmond's cousin Vicky, and there had been that moment when he had clicked his heels. He had seen German casualties doing the same when they had recovered enough in hospital to stand when addressed by senior officers. But his knowledge of France was by no means complete, and it was possible that there were some areas outside Germany where the practice was common.

–

Miss Enid Miller waited until her lodger left in late afternoon to work at the inn. The argument she had overheard outside St Stephen's had consolidated all her doubts. He was a polite, charming young man and he could play the violin admirably, but this was just the latest in a series of concerns about him. Someone had to resolve the question of his identity, and she was the best person to do so.

I'm glad to receive rent from a lodger, she thought, *but I should have known better than to take a foreigner. There had been the pastor's suspicions this morning, and at the Christmas party Chambers had told her Maxim had recommended a German wine. Before that Maxim admitted that he had studied music at Cologne, which was startling.*

She fetched the key and unlocked his room. She stepped inside. It was clean and orderly, with a fresh breeze blowing in as the window was open a little. *Now where exactly is he likely to keep his passport?*

There was a small writing desk with a drawer, so she began there. She found pens, a bottle of ink and blotting paper, along with some pencils and a small penknife.

There were an English dictionary and a diary. She flipped through the early pages of the diary and discovered a few appointments, including one with young Vicky, but there was nothing remotely incriminating. There was no sign of a passport. *Might he carry it on him when he goes out?*

There was a large suitcase and a smaller one, in different shades of brown leather. Neither was locked, which hardly suggested he was being furtive. Beginning with the smaller one she delved inside and found a small pocket containing – a passport. The cover said *République Française*, and inside there was a photograph of Maxim, with a fairly serious expression. The date inked in was presumably his date of birth, in 1895, and on another line she saw *Bar-le-Duc*, where he had told her he was born. She suspected that one of the other lines gave his profession, but her French was not good enough to tell. *Well, there's nothing suspicious about any of this.* She tried not to feel disappointed that her lodger was exactly who he claimed to be.

What if there's something else in his room that might be incriminating in some way? Another passport, even. She had to accept that this idea was a complete flight of fancy, but she turned to the larger suitcase, with the reinforced corners. Inside she discovered some magazines. From her limited knowledge of European languages she was confident that two were in French; they had the kinds of accents she expected. She caught her breath at the sight of the third one, which was printed in that bizarre gothic script that the Germans used, and had those double dots used on some of their vowels. When she looked at the pictures they were photographs of glamorous young men and women, and scenes she supposed were from moving pictures, like the ones you could see at the cinema in

Wealdham. None of the material seemed to relate to the war.

She closed everything up carefully. She did not think she had left any sign of rifling through Max's belongings.

Still she could not relax. There was a sound outside in Sebastopol Terrace, and she stood, a little behind the curtain, making sure Max was not returning, though he was not due back for hours yet. She waited quietly while a local family walked past her house. There had been showers in the early afternoon, then it had stopped raining.

With sudden resolution, she dragged the bedclothes from the bed. She changed the sheets weekly, of course, but he knew when to expect her to do so. Now she checked inside the pillowcase, without finding anything unexpected. She looked under the bottom sheet, above and below the mattress, and peered under the bed. There was nothing untoward to be seen. Wearily, she reassembled the bedding. *How stupid to waste the afternoon like this*, she thought.

As she walked towards the door, the loose floorboard creaked. *I might as well satisfy myself about that too*, she decided. She knelt down awkwardly and tried to prise it up. It was hard to move, and she had to resort to using the penknife from Max's drawer, an innocent looking tool, probably used for sharpening pencils. She slipped it into the crack and tried once more to shift the floorboard. This time it flipped up. By now she had given up any expectation of finding something incriminating, so it was a shock to see what looked like another passport lying there, with the words *Deutsches Reich* on its cover.

She stared at it, disbelieving, for a moment, before extending trembling fingers to seize it. A German passport! She gripped it and pulled it free – only to discover, underneath, yet another passport, also bearing the words *Deutsches Reich*.

Her heart seemed to be pounding in her chest. She carried both the documents over to the desk and sat down to examine them. Both contained photos of Max, though in one he looked younger, and in the last, and most shocking, he was wearing the uniform of a German officer.

In the one where Max looked younger, the pages themselves looked older and a little worn. The name and date of birth were the same, but the place of birth was written in gothic script, hard to read, and appeared to say *Straßburg*.

The third passport was a damning document, particularly as she had, that very morning, heard him deny that he was a German lieutenant. It was him again, the birth date was the same, and the place still *Straßburg*, but the young man was now identified as Leutnant Johann Bauer.

For a moment Enid Miller was proud of herself for her tenacity, and for unmasking her lodger. But what was she to do now?

She went and replaced the floorboard. *He can't go on staying here,* she thought, *that's certain.*

–

A movement outside in the fading light made Amy's father look out of his parlour window. Next door Miss Miller had stacked two suitcases in the street in front of her house. Other objects seemed to be crammed into cardboard boxes.

He went outside into the street. 'Is everything all right, Miss Miller?'

'No, indeed it isn't.' She looked indignant. 'I wish I'd never accepted that young man as my lodger.'

'What's wrong with him?' He suddenly remembered half-hearing an argument after church. 'You surely don't believe those allegations about him being German?'

Her eyebrows rose. 'Can you think of any innocent reason why he has three different passports, two of them from Germany? If you don't take my word for it I can show you!'

She went back into her house and returned, flourishing three documents. She followed him into his hallway and then into the parlour.

'Miss Miller has something important to show me,' he told his wife. He still imagined there must be some misunderstanding.

Their neighbour held the documents one by one under the light of their reading lamp, so he could not fail to see what was written there.

'It's as you say,' he agreed unwillingly, for he had liked the young man. His wife came and confirmed what he had witnessed.

'He can't live at my house any longer!' Miss Miller insisted.

'You're not going to throw him out this evening, are you?'

'I don't want him there a moment longer!'

'But what time does he get back from work? Not till ten or eleven?'

'It's what he deserves, deceiving everyone like that!'

He paced across the carpet: what was to be done? The young man and his luggage must have somewhere to go.

'Stay with my wife for now,' he told Miss Miller. 'I'm going to call on my brother and see if he has any idea what to do. He can come here with his pony and trap to collect Maxim's luggage… Can you make Miss Miller a cup of tea, dear?'

'Yes, right away.'

The vicar was equally horrified at Miss Miller's discovery. It was clear that she had been rummaging through the young man's belongings, but that was largely forgivable after the allegations made that morning.

'Who would have thought it!' exclaimed Reverend Fletcher. 'And where is Max to go? For tonight I had better invite him to one of our spare rooms here.' He hurried to make explanations to Sophie, who looked a little weary that there was already to be another guest to accommodate. Then he explained the situation to James, who was shocked at the new revelation, and Florence, who looked a little more willing to accept the situation.

It was fully dark as the brothers made their way back to Sebastopol Terrace in the trap. 'I don't see how the Spencers can go on employing him at the inn,' Arthur Fletcher told his brother. 'John Spencer was killed by the Germans in the first few months of the war.' He remembered how the news of his death had broken around Christmas time. 'They'll hardly want a German working there.'

His brother was still confused. Might there even now be some innocent explanation? But it all looked thoroughly incriminating.

They waited uneasily in his house with Miss Miller as the minutes passed slowly. Arthur sat by the window, with one of the curtains undrawn, and as ten o'clock approached, there was Maxim sauntering down the road, his pace only becoming less confident as he noticed the pile of luggage outside Miss Miller's house.

She hurried from the Fletcher home, with the two brothers following her.

'You've been found out!' she snarled, flinging his passports at him. He stood, staring in horror, as she went into her house. She emerged with his violin and bow and passed them to him. 'Take these, along with the rest of your belongings, Johann, Maxim, Maximilian or whoever you really are, and don't ever come back here!'

Chapter 11

Vicky had had a hectic Monday. Apart from her usual tasks on the ward, and some further training in splinting injured limbs, she had helped Sister Green run a clinic for mothers of young children.

The nurses were encouraging the women to feed the children well and tend them carefully through childhood illnesses. All too often their problems were not based in ignorance, she suspected. It was poverty that kept them from giving the children an adequate diet, and over-crowding that enabled diseases to spread through whole families.

She did up her cape as she left the hospital in early evening. She was excited to see Max waiting for her outside, as he had done a few times before. She rushed across to speak to him. 'What a lovely surprise!' she said.

But instead of kissing her he looked downcast. 'I need to speak to you urgently,' he said. 'Would you like to take a meal with me, while I explain some things?'

'I'd love to!' Recently she had told her parents she was seeing a young man. Father was dubious because he was French, and was not yet in a well-paid job. Soon she must arrange a meeting, and once they became accustomed to his slight accent they would soon grow to like him.

He led her to one of the modest cafés near the station, as though this meal was very far from being a celebration. Something about his demeanour made her anxious. They sat down and he ordered the hotpot she chose from the menu, and the same for himself.

For a moment afterwards he was silent. Then 'It's all gone wrong!' he blurted out. 'I've been thrown out by Miss Miller and lost my work at the inn.'

She looked at him in amazement. He was working hard and fitting in so well – how could he suddenly lose his lodgings and his job? But there was misery in his expression.

'What happened?'

'I was born a German,' he told her.

'What do you mean? You've told everyone you're French!'

'It is very complicated, and I fulfilled some secret roles for the French during the war. You have to understand there are some areas near the border where people have very conflicting loyalties.'

'No, I don't really understand.' Her eyes searched his face. Now she seemed to notice a tinge of deception in his expression. 'Wherever you come from, why couldn't you just tell me the truth?'

'Because people hate the Germans, and my role in helping the British and the French was very difficult to explain…'

Their regular meetings had seemed so happy and secure. 'But what will you do? Can you find another job around here and somewhere else to live?'

'It's dreadful in Larchbury now – people don't want me living in their house. Think how many families have lost relatives in the war. And the Spencers don't want me at the inn for the same reason. The vicar is letting me stay at the vicarage for the moment, and he says he'll provide a character reference when I move on. I think perhaps I must go to London for a better chance of finding work.'

Her heart seemed to lurch. 'To London? But that's so far away! Can't you find anything in this area?'

'Miss Miller has poisoned the atmosphere – no one in Larchbury trusts me anymore. The rumours will probably reach Wealdham soon…'

Rumours? A poisoned atmosphere? For a moment she hated Miss Miller. *How did she discover he was German*, she wondered. Then she considered the implications of what he had told her. 'So you don't really come from Bar-le-Duc…'

'No, from Strasbourg.'

People had commented on his fluency in German. She was suddenly angry that she had let him dupe her.

'Did you ever fight at Verdun, like you said?'

'No, but I was involved in other wartime activities, against the Germans…'

'You never told me much about your family or wanted to visit them – I should have known there was something very suspicious about you.' How long had she known him? Since last summer – maybe nine months.

There was a wholesome smell coming from the kitchen and a waiter was advancing with two steaming plates of food.

She rose to her feet. 'I've allowed myself to be taken in by you,' she said. 'I don't know how I could be so foolish and trusting…'

His face was pale and awkward. 'At least let me tell you the whole story now. It'll take a while.'

'I don't want to hear any more of what you've got to say. It's too late, Max.'

She picked up her cloak and ran from the café, tears pouring down her face.

–

One Wednesday Amy, Edmond and Beth came to stay at The Beeches. Edmond had an appointment on the Friday at Queen Mary's hospital in Roehampton in Surrey, for he was applying for work there when he had finished his course at Cambridge. He had completed the first year before the war, returning in 1918, and this summer he hoped to obtain his degree. Then he aimed to apply his engineering skills and knowledge of metallic alloys in the advances being made in the design of artificial limbs at Roehampton. He had heard of other graduates who had studied metallurgy going on to work there.

'I've been fortunate to study at Cambridge and meet some of the gifted academic young men here,' he said, 'but I always intended to make the most of my scientific course and learn something that could be put to practical use. Helping war victims must be one of the most important goals of our time.'

'I'll be proud if you can make that your occupation,' Amy assured him as they set out.

'It would mean moving again.'

She was sad, for they had become settled at their comfortable little home, and grown to like some of the young men he knew there. Still, if they had to move for him to find his mission in life, she must accept it. 'We can, if that's what you need to do,' she said. 'Wherever we go, we'll still be together as a family.' It was just that the timing was bad.

'I'll be sorry to inflict it on you.'

The Derwents were happy to welcome them to The Beeches again, soon after their Easter visit. 'I need to see Charles tomorrow,' Edmond explained, 'to hear of his experiences at Roehampton before I go there.'

As they took their places in the dining room for their evening meal, Amy told her in-laws their latest news. 'I'm expecting another baby!' she announced, merrily. By now their doctor in Cambridge had confirmed she was pregnant.

'That's capital!' Pa cried.

Ma and Beatrice added their congratulations.

'When's it due?' Ma asked.

'In the autumn. So there'll be less than three years between Beth and the baby.' She had been longing for another child, though it was a little unfortunate that their planned move to Roehampton would occur in the middle of her pregnancy. Maybe this time it would be a little boy, who they could call Albert, after her brother.

As they began their meal, the talk turned to the scandal about Maxim. 'He's left the vicar's house now and they say he's gone to London to find work,' Pa said.

'Shame he didn't go back to Germany,' Beatrice observed.

'Three separate passports, Miss Miller found,' said Ma. 'Goodness knows who he supported – she imagines he was some kind of mercenary.'

'It's all very confusing,' Pa said. 'I confess I always liked the young man, and Peter was impressed with his record. I'm impatient to discuss the matter with him, but he's in the Rhineland now and I'm unwilling to mention it in a letter.'

'Peter said that Max had supported the Allies in the war but came from a region where it made life dangerous for him now,' Edmond said.

'What about Vicky? She was getting very close to Max,' Amy said, anxious for the young girl.

'She's been hit hard by him leaving, and all the unpleasant talk,' Beatrice said. 'We tried to persuade her to come to see us on her day off last week, but she was too upset, and didn't want to face all the gossip. She went to see her own parents, though.'

'We've told her you two will be here this weekend,' Ma said to Edmond and Amy. 'That may persuade her to come.'

'It's very vexing,' Beatrice said. 'Think of all the families who've suffered losses during the war. For a year we've had a German among us all the time, posing as an innocent Frenchman. I should have taken notice when Miss Miller questioned his learning music in Cologne.'

Edmond said little more about Max, though Amy suspected he was still favourably disposed towards the young man. 'He was working for the Allies, bringing them information, as I understand it,' he told Amy when they were alone. 'Imagine how dangerous that is. If you come from an area where loyalties are divided, by helping one side you antagonise the other.'

–

The following day they went to see Charles and Lavinia, who had given up her work at the hospital with only a few weeks more to wait for the birth of her child. Her maid busied herself with their lunch.

Amy passed on the news of her own pregnancy, and Lavinia hugged her. 'How wonderful!'

'Before we came here I called in on Mother and told her,' Amy said. 'She was thrilled – they'd hardly stopped asking me when we'd have a brother or sister for Beth. If we move to Roehampton she's promised to help me, so I don't become overtired.' How kind and thoughtful Mother always was!

'I'm studying hard now,' Charles said. He explained that his father's chauffeur called at their house each day to drive him to the business college in Wealdham. 'When I'm more confident with my appliances I'm determined to drive our car myself.'

They spent time discussing his treatment at Roehampton, so that Edmond would be well-prepared for the following day. 'The house was requisitioned for soldiers during the war,' Charles told them. 'Queen Mary became a patron, and public funds were raised so amputees could be rehabilitated. At first the patients had to stay six weeks or more, like I did, but I hear that now some only need to be there for three weeks.'

Edmond looked eager to see the place for himself.

The question of Max surfaced presently. It was clear that the controversy about him was widespread, with most people indignant that he had courted popularity through his false identity.

Charles tended to Edmond's view. 'I've heard of young men from the disputed borderlands near the Rhine helping the Allies,' he told them.

Amy knew that Edmond instinctively trusted his brother's judgement. *Will we ever know the truth*, she wondered.

–

Next day Edmond went off to Roehampton. Amy set out with Beth in the late afternoon to visit Florence at the vicarage, after her teaching was over for the day. Florence took Beth on to her lap, and was next to learn Amy's happy news.

Aunt Sophie brought them cups of tea and slices of fruit cake and before long James joined them.

'Have you heard any more about getting a university place?' Amy asked him.

'No – it's not looking promising. I'm trying to think what else I might do. I've been writing a few little articles for the newspapers, about working as a medical orderly.'

'I know – I saw one of your pieces and it gives an excellent idea of what went on.' There were other young men who offered accounts of their wartime exploits, but James had a particular skill at conveying the impression of life in frontline hospitals. There was a reluctance to dwell on the horrors of the war, now it was over, but in James's accounts it was clear that the victims were generally courageous and at least some recovered well.

Max was soon mentioned again. 'Father was unwilling to believe he'd behaved in such an underhand way,' James said. 'He thinks there must be some explanation.'

'He always seemed a fine man to me,' Florence said. 'James's father is keeping in touch with him in London. And he persuaded Mr Spencer to provide a reference, even though he won't employ him anymore.'

'He won't tell us how Max is placed now, except that he's found work as a chef,' Aunt Sophie said. She poured Amy some more tea and left them to carry on talking.

'When are we going to France to see Bertie's grave?' Florence asked them. They had always planned to go together.

'We can't go this year,' Amy said, for she meant to take care of herself more in this pregnancy than she had been able to when she had first been expecting Beth, still nursing in France.

'Most of the cemeteries aren't ready yet,' James said.

'We haven't been notified of his final resting place,' Amy said.

'Perhaps you'll hear by next year,' Florence said.

But next year I'll have two children, Amy thought. *I can't expect Mother and Father to look after a baby and a three-year-old. We might have to wait a few years before I get the opportunity to travel to France.*

'It's admirable that they're treating all the fallen the same way,' James said. The Committee had maintained its insistence that there would be no special treatment for officers. Any man who had given his life for his country would have the same kind of headstone, giving his name, rank and regiment, as well as a cross.

Amy took Beth back from Florence, for she was wriggling impatiently. She reached for one of the fabric books she had brought to amuse her little girl.

'One day I'm determined Beth will know all about the uncle she never had the chance to meet,' she said, 'and how he gave his life for our country, when he was only twenty-two years old.'

—

Vicky agreed to join them at The Beeches on the Saturday, and arrived in good time for lunch. Amy found her looking pale and downcast.

'How did you get on at Roehampton?' she asked Edmond as she joined the others in the drawing room.

'It's an inspirational place,' he told her. 'The hospital is still expanding. The limb-makers manufacture prosthetic legs and arms, mainly in huts in the grounds.'

Amy had been impressed by his account of the hospital which was helping so many injured men.

'I definitely want to work there,' he continued. 'I won't know for a while whether or not they'll accept me, and if they offer me a job it'll be dependent on my getting a good degree.'

Amy hoped desperately he would prove fit enough to carry out practical work, which would require him to spend time on his feet.

Soon the family were sitting around the lunch table.

'How are your clinics going?' Amy asked Vicky, having heard about the new project at Wealdham.

'We try to help mothers become more aware of hygiene and a good diet, but we can't do as much for some families as we'd like,' Vicky said.

'If you help even one family it will be worthwhile.'

There was a subdued atmosphere, for everyone was avoiding the awkward topic of Max. Even Beatrice seemed to be learning tact.

After lunch Amy went to settle Beth in her cot in the nursery, for her afternoon nap, and Vicky followed them upstairs.

'So you're expecting again!' she said. 'I'm so glad for you and Edmond. Are you keeping well?'

'I feel tired sometimes – I didn't expect to, because last time I was pregnant I was working flat out in the hospital in France, and hardly found any time to rest. I wanted to stay there as long as possible, in case Edmond managed to get leave and we could meet.'

'Did no one guess your condition?'

'Emily, who shared my Alwyn hut, noticed I was being sick in the mornings. I had to swear her to secrecy. If they'd found out they might have sent me back to England straight away.'

Vicky's eyes opened wide. 'You were taking a risk,' she said.

'I'm determined that this time I'll look after myself properly while I'm expecting.'

'Make sure you do!

Then Vicky fell silent, in no hurry to join the others.

'I know how this business with Max has affected you,' Amy said, suspecting the girl was ready to talk to someone sympathetic. She remembered how close the young couple had appeared at the Christmas ball.

'I never expected it to turn out like this,' Vicky said miserably. 'It was as though he hoped I'd defend his behaviour. How could he expect that, after he'd been so deceitful?'

'I don't know.' Several of them still had difficulty believing the recent revelations, but how could they challenge the evidence?

'I miss Max so much,' Vicky said. 'I don't even know where he is now.'

Without encouraging the young girl to expect any improvement in the situation, Amy passed on the news from the vicarage, that Max had work in London. This seemed to offer her a faint degree of consolation.

'I don't think he knew anyone in London,' she said. 'He might be dreadfully lonely.'

Amy remembered her own distress during the war, when she had gone nearly a year without even seeing Edmond, and later there had been the horror of the wound to his lung. But all through that traumatic time she had at least had full confidence in his love for her, and his integrity.

'These days I throw myself into my work,' Vicky said. 'There's always plenty to do at the hospital and now I volunteer to stay behind when they need someone to work late.'

Amy put her arms around Vicky. She must go on writing to her, and stay close, to try to support her through her heartache.

Chapter 12

Cambridge and Larchbury, summer to autumn 1920

Amy allowed herself to linger a while after eating a bread and cheese lunch with Beth, and Grace, her part-time maid.

'I feel a little weary,' she said. *How did I largely avoid becoming overtired in my first pregnancy?* she wondered. *In the first few months in France I had to rush around the hospital all the time. Perhaps the tension of wondering when the next offensive would begin made me less aware of my health.*

'You must take things easy in your condition,' Grace said. 'You were very busy this morning, sorting out those blankets.'

'We won't use them in the summer. They needed putting away in a suitcase, ready for when we move. I've resolved to do a little sorting each week.' She got up from the table and felt slightly dizzy. 'Actually, I think I'll go and lie down for a while, while Beth has her afternoon nap.'

'Good idea, Mrs Derwent. You go and put your feet up.'

Once Beth was settled, Amy lay down on her bed, feeling weak and shivery.

Grace brought her a cup of tea. 'You look quite pale,' she said.

'I expect I'll be all right if I doze for a while.' She closed her eyes, but the day was bright and she could not fall asleep. She could hear the usual sounds outside: footsteps, the occasional car, bicycles and horses and carts. Someone was whistling cheerfully and neighbours were gossiping.

Presently she felt a stomach cramp, and then more alarming symptoms. 'Grace!' she called out, 'come and help me, please!'

She had to call her three times, before the maid heard her downstairs. Then she rushed in.

'I'm bleeding!' Amy said. 'Could you call the doctor for me, please?'

From the next room they heard Beth calling out.

'Yes – I'll get Beth up, then I'll go right away.'

Grace went off, taking Beth with her, to call the doctor from the nearest telephone box.

Amy waited anxiously for her return. Could she be about to suffer a miscarriage? But her last pregnancy had gone smoothly, in spite of everything.

Before long Doctor Richards arrived. She had only seen him once before. He was in his forties and his manner was reassuring. 'Let's just get your feet raised on a pillow, then lie calmly – with luck the bleeding might stop.'

After he had gone she lay as he said, uncertain whether or not the bleeding was starting to ease. *Will I need to take a lot of rest all through the pregnancy,* she worried. *Perhaps Mother can come to stay.*

After a while Grace brought her another cup of tea. 'How are you doing?' she asked.

'Not well. I had a pain, a kind of cramp, just now.'

Grace had children of her own, who were nearly grown up. She was normally calm, but now she could not disguise her anxiety, even though Beth chose this moment to follow her into the room. 'She's getting restless,' Grace said.

The little girl was curious about what was happening. 'I'm feeling a little unwell,' Amy managed.

'Is it cos of the baby?' Beth said. Amy wished they had not told her about the expected brother or sister, but in their excitement they had mentioned Amy's condition to friends and family, and soon it had been necessary to explain.

'Yes – I need to lie down for a while.'

'What time will Mr Derwent be home?' Grace asked.

'He finishes early today,' Amy said.

Grace looked relieved. Amy remembered she was due to leave at half past four.

'I'll stay till he gets home,' Grace said, 'then we'll see.'

She led Beth away, to water the plants in the garden with her own little watering can they had bought her. Amy winced as she experienced the pain again.

As the afternoon wore on, the band of sunlight moved further across the floral bedspread. At last she heard Edmond arrive. Grace and Beth were speaking to him and then he rushed up to see her.

'Darling!' he cried, embracing and kissing her.

'I keep getting pains,' she said. 'They're getting worse. I'm afraid I might be losing the baby.' She could hardly bear to pronounce the words.

'Just lie quietly, darling. Nothing is as important as your health.' He sat down in the chair by their bed and held her hand. For a moment she felt serene, then the treacherous pain came again.

There was a knock at the door and they heard Grace go to answer it. She came upstairs, followed by a woman of around thirty in a nurse's uniform.

'Doctor Richards sent me,' she said. 'Are you still having problems, Mrs Derwent?'

'Yes.'

'Just relax, dear.' The nurse examined her briefly. 'We'll hope for the best, shall we?'

'I'll go down to see Beth,' Edmond said. 'I believe Grace is getting a meal for us.'

The sunshine was less bright but Amy could not sleep, for the pains were becoming more frequent, remorselessly carrying her towards disaster. In the early evening, after Edmond had put Beth to bed, the unavoidable loss took place. It was clear that the baby was no more.

As she wept, Edmond took her into his arms. 'Dearest, I'm upset too, but I've still got you and Beth – I'm so thankful for what I already have.' His clear blue eyes focused on hers, full of concern.

'I shouldn't have done that sorting out this morning!' Amy cried. 'I didn't believe I could harm the baby…'

'Grace told me you only worked a little.'

'I should have rested more.'

'Don't blame yourself, darling. No one believes you harmed the baby.'

'We all know women who've lost babies,' the nurse said as she packed her bag. 'Even when they've taken the greatest care. Now let me get you some clean bedding and a nightie.'

As it grew dark, Amy stayed in bed, trying to accept what had happened. Soon Edmond joined her and she lay in his arms, comforted a little. *Haven't I always said I only need Edmond and Beth, and a home of our own?* she told herself. *I'm very fortunate.*

But tears still ran down her face at the loss of the new life that had started to grow within her.

'I got a glimpse of the little shape in its sac,' Amy said as her mother arrived at their house to care for her and Beth for a few days. 'I don't know if it was a boy or a girl.' She would never be certain now whether it would have been a future Albert. The nurse had whisked away the remains of her child, and now she wished she had looked more closely.

'You're bound to be expecting again before long.'

Amy wished she could be sure of that. She felt weary and could not sleep well, even in Edmond's arms.

When the postman arrived one day, there was a letter for Amy and one for her mother, in Father's handwriting.

'Mine's from Florence,' Amy said. Her friend had heard about her loss and was loving and sympathetic as always. 'What does Father say?'

'I don't know whether I should tell you this…'

'What? Tell me what it is!'

'Your friend Lavinia has had a little boy.'

'Oh!' Of course, she had known Lavinia's baby was due. 'How wonderful – I must write to her.'

I'm truly glad for her, she thought. *Only it's going to be hard going to her house to congratulate her.*

–

Lavinia lounged on a garden chair, while her baby boy lay quietly nearby in his perambulator. It was a sunny morning, though mostly the weather had been poor that August. She cast a bored glance at her newspaper. The Olympic Games were still in progress in Antwerp, she gathered.

She turned round at the sound of footsteps, and was delighted to see Ethel, her maid, bringing Amy through to the garden. 'How lovely to see you!' she cried, rushing to greet her.

'I'm sorry I haven't managed to get here before to see little Christopher,' Amy said. 'Goodness, he must be over two months old.'

She stooped to see the child, but did not touch him as he was fast asleep.

'Ethel, bring us some coffee and cake, would you, please?' Lavinia asked. 'I was desperately sorry to hear that you lost your little one,' she told her friend, embracing her. She had written to Amy at the time, expressing her sympathy. Amy was trying to smile, but she could see a shadow in her expression. It was brave of her to come. Florence had not yet fallen with child, so she too envied Lavinia.

Amy sat down in the chair next to hers. She did not look as blithe as usual. 'It's so strange,' she said. 'Remember what I was like when I was first expecting Beth? I was working at that hospital near Arras through midsummer 1917. I was on my feet for most of each day because I didn't want to tell anyone I was expecting.'

'Yes, life is peculiar, isn't it? You sailed through your first pregnancy.'

'I even had that bad fall in Ypres, but it didn't harm the baby. Beth was healthy and full-term.'

'There's no reason why you shouldn't have a perfectly normal pregnancy next time,' Lavinia said.

'I don't know much about the chances – I've nursed in France, but there was no call to study obstetrics, of course.'

'I had some training in it when I came back to London. It's always very sad when an expectant mother miscarries, but it's quite common. Often a young woman who loses her baby is back at the hospital the following year, expecting again.'

Amy looked a little more cheerful.

'How's Edmond? Did he drive you here?'

'Yes, he dropped me off. He has to go to Wealdham to see about getting a mortgage. He'll call for me on his way back. It's been so hectic this summer, with the move to Roehampton to fit in.'

Amy explained that they had travelled to the pleasant area not far south of the Thames and hunted for a small house they could afford to buy on the salary Edmond would be earning. Now they had chosen their future home and signed the paperwork.

'It's a little larger than our Cambridge house – I want to get a piano when we can afford it. And you must all come to visit when we're settled.'

It might be best for her that she has plenty to occupy her, Lavinia thought.

'Now we have to arrange for the furniture to be delivered there, engage a new maid...'

'What a heap of domestic duties we find ourselves charged with...' Lavinia sighed as Ethel poured their coffee. 'I have to spend half of each morning making sure everything is in order here that Charles and Christopher may need. It's boring after my nursing career.'

'I'm thankful I have time now to enjoy a normal life with Edmond. I'm thrilled I can see him improving. And as he takes on a demanding career it's important I still make certain he doesn't overexert himself. We couldn't want to go back to the war years.'

'No, but...' *Then there was that element of urgency,* she recalled, *that absence of choice which propelled us through the days.*

'I have household tasks that take nearly all my time.' It was Amy's turn to complain. 'Yet I seldom find time to entertain visitors. I can't imagine inviting the families, Edmond's and mine, for Christmas, not even in our new house: how would I fit them all around the dining table?'

'But that's to be expected – it's the same for me. It's our families who have the large homes, and more servants.'

'That's certainly true of the Derwents. But my parents have managed to entertain at Sebastopol Terrace. They've held birthday parties for Beth both years.' Beth's birthday was New Year's Day, so it came soon after the Derwents' annual ball, and Mother had persuaded them easily that she and Father should give the party for Beth. 'One day I must hold a proper party – somehow!'

'On quiet days I grow bored with nothing to divert me between domestic tasks,' Lavinia said. 'Make sure you come to see me when you can, Amy.'

'I promise I will. And we must keep writing to each other.'

Little cries came from the direction of the pram. 'Christopher is waking – it's time for his feed!' Lavinia hurried in his direction. She scooped him up. 'I'm here, sweetheart! Look, Amy, his hair is beginning to curl, like his father's.'

—

Beatrice asked for afternoon tea to be served on the veranda as there were intermittent showers. It had been another disappointing summer. Caleb joined her and she introduced him to Cook's ginger cake.

It seemed ages since he had last obtained leave. He had arrived just too late to see Amy and Edmond, who were now settling into their new home in Roehampton.

Caleb had told her in his letters some of his impressions of the Rhineland, of the scenic hills and fairy-tale castles there, and the lines of barges which progressed down the great river, but she was curious to hear how he and his comrades spent their days.

'In the evenings we enjoy the refreshing Riesling wine grown in the vineyards there.'

'And what are the Germans like? Are they ogres?'

'They heartily resent the occupation.' He leant back in the wicker chair, handsome in the uniform he still wore. 'They don't much care for Americans, but the ones they least like are the negroes. One of our black men fathered a child by a German woman, and the dark-skinned baby was a cause of scandal.'

'Sometimes I feel very inexperienced,' she said, 'and wish I'd done war work, like Amy. I've only travelled abroad as a tourist, to the south of France, the hot region along the Mediterranean, before the war.'

'I'd scarcely left Massachusetts before we got sent to France,' he said. 'I'd spent most of my life on a farm.' It was clear he had done outdoor work back home. In the army he had mostly been a driver. Anyone could see he was healthy and vigorous. 'Once we adjusted to the fighting, life seemed far more stimulating, and now some of us can't imagine going back to the States.'

She loved his enthusiasm for new experiences and for a moment she felt encouraged. But would he ever fit in to British society, where so much was made of what school you had attended, and the status of one's family? Perhaps that was partly what attracted her to him: he had an openness about him, and it never occurred to him to worry about his position within a class structure.

When he stayed at the inn for a few days, visiting her regularly, it was as though they had hardly been apart. And yet, a plan for any future together was still lacking. When he was staying in Britain it hardly seemed to matter.

'I love receiving your letters,' he told her. 'I sit in my quarters, wondering what you are doing at home here.'

She was unwilling to admit that there was less to occupy her now than in earlier years, when there had been plenty of other leisured friends to share shopping trips, or to join at parties or for playing card games. Since the war there had, of course, been the stampede of her female friends to get married, desperate to catch any remaining healthy bachelors. Recently she had heard that Harriet was expecting Wilfrid's child. He was now stationed somewhere north of Cologne, apparently. She realised the family must have largely hushed up Wilfrid's conviction for molesting women, but she could not help wondering sometimes whether Harriet was content with her husband when he came home on leave.

'Sometimes I make hats,' Beatrice ventured, hardly expecting Caleb to find it of interest. 'I like decorating them with ribbons and fabric flowers. My friend Caroline helps run the smart milliner's in Larchbury, and she encourages me to sell my creations.' There was less demand now for fancy styles, but she needed to keep aware of the evolving fashions.

'I didn't know you'd gone into business!' He smiled at her encouragingly.

Ma still had not quite forgiven her, as Beatrice had moved on from decorating completed hats to assembling them from basic materials upon a frame.

'It's a new pastime.' Her equipment was accumulating in one of their spare rooms.

She poured him a second cup of tea. *Our backgrounds are very different*, she thought, *yet he understands me well. Pa and Edmond and Amy recognise that he's a decent man. What would Caroline think of him, I wonder. I believe she'd like and respect him – and if she doesn't, I'll not worry too much about her opinion.*

She realised he was looking at her intensely. 'It's tantalising for me, seeing you so seldom,' he said. He caught hold of her hand. 'Do you think one day, if I can get my discharge, we can be together?'

A wave of happiness swept over her. 'Yes,' she said, 'I believe we belong together.'

His lips came down on hers eagerly, and she allowed him an extended kiss.

When eventually they moved apart, she felt herself glowing with happiness.

All the same, she looked around her. It seemed unlikely that anyone had seen them, and in any case her parents had not made any objection to her seeing Caleb. She felt sure Ma would have done so, if so many young men had not become casualties of the war.

'It's too soon to tell the others,' she said. 'You need to work out what you'll do after the war. We need to make some kind of plan.'

'Yes, my sweet.'

Would she end up needing to travel with him to America, she wondered nervously. She was certain now that no one else would overwhelm her emotions like Caleb.

–

Edmond looked weary, driving to The Beeches.

'Perhaps I should learn to drive,' Amy said, although the idea did not especially appeal.

In September they had moved to Roehampton. Mother had travelled there for a few days to help her arrange the house to their liking. Mostly their furniture consisted of familiar items, modest but precious to them, brought in their removal van from Cambridge.

Edmond was excited by his new work at the hospital there, but the week had tired him. Once a patient had had an artificial limb made, he needed teaching how to use it. He would practise walking in the gymnasium or using his new arm in the workshop. Edmond was elated at being able to help men recover, but the work was demanding.

Now they lived south of the Thames it was easy to visit The Beeches at the weekend. On this Saturday in late October they were keen to see Peter, newly arrived on leave from the Rhineland.

They drove through Larchbury, past the triangle of green in the fork in the road. Beside the horse trough there was now a stone pedestal, most of it concealed by a sheet of canvas.

'That must be the war memorial,' Amy said curiously. 'They'll unveil it sometime around Remembrance Day.' Father had written about it in one of his letters. Bertie's name would be there among those of all the other victims.

They continued sombrely, turning off for The Beeches. As they drove through the avenue of trees shedding their leaves, and along the drive to the house, Peter hurried out to greet them. The brothers exchanged news before Peter picked up Beth and hugged her. 'You've grown such a lot, little girl, since I last saw you,' he said.

'I believe I can obtain my discharge early next year,' he confided to the others. 'I mean to go back to India, but don't mention it to Ma and Pa as I haven't told them yet.' He helped them indoors with their bags.

The others were sitting in the drawing room. 'We've invited Vicky to lunch,' Ma said, 'but she's late again. She's as unreliable as you were, when you were nursing, Amy, but without the excuse that there's a war.'

'At a hospital you never know when an emergency case might arrive,' Amy tried to explain.

'I'll give her another quarter of an hour and then tell Cook to go ahead and serve lunch.'

Amy turned down Chambers' offer of a sherry, but the brothers accepted.

'They're sending the body of the Unknown Warrior to England very soon, ready to be buried on Remembrance Day,' said Peter. 'He'll be brought across the channel on HMS *Verdun*.'

'So, no one actually knows who he is?' Beatrice asked.

'No,' said Peter. 'I'm afraid that all over the cemeteries there are thousands of nameless graves, marked only "A Soldier known unto God." It seems fitting that one of them will be buried in Westminster Abbey.'

Amy exchanged a sober glance with Edmond, thinking of all the men who had been lost, some even lacking the dignity of being buried in a named grave. She recalled Henry Smith, the brother of their gardeners George and Joe, who had never been found.

'Last year, Remembrance Day was very moving, wasn't it, Father?' Beatrice said. 'Whitehall was crowded and as Big Ben struck eleven everyone fell silent.'

The next minute Vicky arrived. 'Sorry, Aunt Mabel,' she said. 'It was very busy on the wards this morning, and although it was my day off they asked me to work for a couple of hours. We're beginning to get more bronchitis cases again.'

Amy led Beth to the dining room, sitting beside her.

'I suppose you heard about your friend Max,' Ma said to Peter as the braised beef was served. 'I can't think why you encouraged him to settle here.'

Amy wished Ma had not mentioned Max in front of Vicky, who had gone pale.

'How do you think people felt when Miss Miller found his collection of passports and discovered he was really German?' Ma went on.

'The situation is much more complicated than you suppose,' Peter said calmly, 'though obviously I'm sorry about all the uproar that's been caused. Maxim comes from Alsace, just west of the Rhine. He was born in Strasbourg.'

'That's in Germany, isn't it?' demanded Ma.

'It's in France now,' Peter said. 'During the war there were sympathisers for both sides. The Germans were trying to hold Strasbourg and the French to win it back, for they'd held it till 1870.' He had a confident expression in his blue eyes, clear of his facts.

The others round the table exchanged glances in bewilderment.

'And by helping us in the war, Maxim has put himself in danger,' Peter went on. 'He deserves our help.'

Vicky held a handkerchief to her eyes as they filled with tears.

'You became a close friend of his, didn't you, Vicky?' Peter said. 'I'm sorry you didn't know all the facts. You should ask him to explain about Strasbourg.'

'I don't even see him anymore,' sobbed Vicky. 'He's gone to London.'

'Must you discuss this in the middle of lunch?' Ma asked angrily. 'See how you've upset Vicky.'

'Dearest, I believe it was you who first raised the subject,' Pa said gently.

She looked confused. The family fell quiet while they finished their main course in an awkward atmosphere. Beth wriggled and left half her food, while Vicky left most of hers.

As Cook cleared the plates, Vicky stood up. 'I'm sorry, Aunt; it was very kind of you to invite me to such a nice lunch, but I don't believe I can bear hearing any more discussion about Maxim.' She rose to her feet. 'I'm afraid I'm going to leave for Wealdham now. I'm sorry I haven't seen you for long, Peter.'

Amy got up. 'We can drive you back to the station, can't we, Edmond?' she said. 'Would you excuse us, Ma? Shall we leave Beth here while we see Vicky off?'

'I'll look after Beth!' cried Beatrice. 'Come and sit next to me, dear. I believe Cook has made one of her splendid syrup puddings.'

'Will Aunt Mabel forgive me for ruining her lunch?' asked Vicky as they set off.

'It was all very unfortunate,' Amy said. She wanted to tell the younger girl to take some notice of what Peter said, but she suspected that for today, at least, she was too upset, and in any case, the young man had left town.

They took Vicky to the station and waited with her.

'Amy, I'm really sorry that you lost your baby.' Vicky had written her a sympathetic letter at the time.

'I'm always thankful that I have such a lovely daughter, but I still can't stop thinking of the little one we lost,' Amy said.

'They're planning to open a maternity unit at Wealdham,' Vicky said. 'They want to improve the welfare of mothers and reduce infant mortality.'

'It's a fine plan.'

'One day I'm sure Amy and I will have another child,' Edmond said. 'There's no especial hurry.'

'Will you come to Roehampton one weekend to see us?' Amy asked Vicky.

'Yes – I'd like that.'

'We're on the telephone now,' Edmond said proudly, for they had decided that was a convenience they needed and could just about afford. 'You can ring us from the public call box by the hospital, can't you?' He wrote down their number and gave it to his cousin.

They waited with her until the Wealdham train steamed in and she boarded a second-class carriage.

Can anything be done about her and Max, Amy wondered, as the train pulled out of the station.

Chapter 13

Elsie Johnson sat in the pew beside her mother. Philip, now a robust toddler of seventeen months, wriggled on her lap. The church was chilly that November morning. The vicar was talking about the ceremonies held in London for Remembrance Day, earlier that week.

'So the Unknown Soldier was buried in Westminster Abbey,' he said. 'In this area alone several men have been lost, without us knowing where they fell.' He mentioned some of those who had fallen, and the name Henry Smith registered in Elsie's mind.

'And the King unveiled the Cenotaph in Whitehall,' the vicar continued. 'It will be a monument to commem-orate our courageous dead from the Great War. And of course our own monument here in Larchbury will soon be ready for its unveiling.'

Elsie seldom read newspapers and some of the facts were new to her. She remembered vaguely that the slab of carved stone in the village would bear the names of those who had died, and that some people had been disappointed that it was not, after all, completed yet.

Soon she was walking down the aisle at the end of the Sunday service, holding Philip's hand, and wishing Miss Miller, and some other members of the congregation, would stop staring at her. In her mind she was still turning over some of what she had heard.

'What did they say that tomb thing is called in London?' she asked her mother.

'The Cenotaph.'

'And Henry Smith is buried there?'

'No, dear, the Cenotaph is empty. The Unknown Soldier has been buried in Westminster Abbey.'

'So Henry is in Westminster Abbey?'

'No, Elsie, we don't know who's buried there. It's some soldier who died in the war, that's all we know.'

Her mother was soon talking to a neighbour. Elsie turned to talk to the schoolteacher, Miss Clifford, who was now married to the vicar's son. 'Is Henry Smith buried in the Ceno— Cenotaph?' she asked her.

'No, Elsie, the Cenotaph is an empty tomb, kind of symbolic.'

'Then Henry's buried in Westminster Abbey?'

'Well, some soldier is buried there, someone who died in the war, one of the young men whose final resting place is unknown. It could be Henry Smith.'

'Henry Smith is the soldier in Westminster Abbey!' Elsie cried. 'At last we know where he is! Philip, your father is buried in London, in Westminster Abbey! Mum, can we go to London one day and show Philip where his father is buried?'

Her mother turned around and listened to what she was saying.

'Elsie, are you telling us that Henry Smith is Philip's father?'

'Yes. He's buried in Westminster Abbey.'

'You're sure it's Henry who's his father?'

'Yes – I loved him ever so much.'

A small group of curious village folk was forming around Elsie. Miss Miller made her repeat what she had told the others.

When they finally reached home, her mother made her repeat it again. 'So Philip Brownlee isn't little Philip's father?'

'No, his father's Henry Smith. I just told you.'

'Then why did you ever say Philip Brownlee was his father?'

'He was such a handsome young man. He flew aeroplanes. I asked him to meet me one evening but he never turned up.'

—

On Fundraising Day at Wealdham Hospital Vicky was given the task of selling homemade baking on the cake stall.

'They've made a fine effort here,' Lavinia said when she arrived.

Vicky smiled at baby Christopher in his pram. 'We need the funds,' she said. 'During the war they built the nurses' hostel, but hardly any upkeep was done on the wards, and now they'd like to get an X-ray machine too.'

'We need a lift for patients going up to the first floor.'

'I didn't have time to make cakes or help with the knitting for the handicrafts stall,' Vicky said, 'but at least I can serve people as I'm not working this afternoon.' The goods for sale were displayed in the Outpatients Hall.

'Look, Amy's just arrived!' Lavinia waved to her.

She was hurrying to join them, with Beth and Edmond, and a young man in officer's uniform who Vicky did not recognise.

'I'm glad you managed to come,' Vicky said. She had asked them if they could support the event, but Edmond had been uncertain if they could find the time.

'This is Frank Bentley, my comrade from the trenches,' Edmond said. 'We both joined up at the same time and we've kept in touch ever since.'

'I suppose you're posted to the Rhine now,' Lavinia said.

'That's right.'

Beneath his cap Vicky could see he had red hair. He smiled at her.

'Will you show us around the stalls?' Amy asked her.

'They need me to cover this one for a while longer,' she said truthfully. The young man looked pleasant but he was not about to make her forget Max.

The others looked disappointed as they continued on their way, with Lavinia joining them.

A few months had passed since Vicky had seen Max, but to her it still felt as though at some time he must appear and recover his place in her life. She tried to concentrate on selling cakes and not become downhearted.

Lavinia returned half an hour later. 'They're not raising as much as I'd hoped,' she said.

Vicky had never quite believed they could get the amount they were aiming for, but it was still disappointing, after all their efforts.

'I'll go around and try to get some more bun pennies,' Lavinia said, propping the collecting box on the front of Christopher's pram.

Now Edmond and the others were heading in her direction again, just in time for Lavinia to confront them.

'We need your bun pennies!' she cried.

In the early years of Victoria's reign the queen had worn her hair in a bun, and this image of the young queen appeared on coins of that period. In later years there had been an image of the old queen with a veil upon her head. People still liked bun pennies and some collected them for good luck.

'Turn out your pockets!' Lavinia implored them. Edmond soon unearthed two of the sought-after coins, now a little thin and discoloured, and Amy and Frank each found one to add to the collection. 'You'll be surprised how much we can sometimes raise like this,' Lavinia said as she set off to continue through the hall.

'Can you leave your stall for long enough to have a cup of tea with us?' Amy asked Vicky.

She felt like taking a break.

'I can manage on my own for a while,' said Nora, the friend who was helping her. By now most of the cakes had been sold.

Vicky followed the others to the tea stall and sat down wearily.

It seemed that Edmond and Amy were spending the weekend at The Beeches and Frank Bentley was visiting from a nearby village.

'How much longer are you on leave?' Amy asked him.

'I've just got another three days with my parents, then I set off back to Cologne,' he said.

'You'll be relieved when you get discharged?' Edmond asked.

'Yes, though I'm not sure whether I shall be bored, going back to working as a clerk, like I did before the war.'

'Will you still play football?' Edmond said.

'It won't be easy, since I got shrapnel in my leg at Passchendaele – maybe the village team will consider me.'

Edmond was interested in his impressions of Germany.

'While I have the chance, I'm trying to spend short periods of leave looking around,' Frank said. 'The Rhine is very impressive. You should see how much river traffic there is.'

'Do the Germans still hate the occupation?' Edmond asked.

'Very much so. And recently they've been infuriated that the Rhine navigation is no longer controlled from Mannheim but from Strasbourg, especially as that town isn't even in Germany anymore but has been handed back to France.'

Vicky looked up from her cup of tea, suddenly interested. Wasn't that where Max was supposed to have come from, at least according to Peter?

'Have you visited Strasbourg?' she asked Frank curiously.

'Yes – it's a strange place. There's a fine cathedral there and other notable buildings, but there's an uneasy atmosphere.'

'Why's that?' asked Amy.

'Half the inhabitants resented the way the Germans seized it in 1870, and the other half can't bear that it's been handed back to the French now.'

Vicky was intrigued by his words. *Didn't Peter imply there was some such conflict there?* she thought. *Didn't Max claim to come from an area where there were opposing factions?* She would have liked to pump the newcomer for more information, but she did not know where to begin. *And originally Max said he came from Bar-le-Duc,* she recalled.

On Amy's lap Beth was wriggling. 'I'm afraid we should be leaving,' Amy said. 'I expect we'll see you at The Beeches before long.'

'It might be some time before I get there again,' Vicky said. 'At the moment we can't train in obstetrics at this hospital. They're sending Nora and me to a mothers' home in the East End for a few weeks for midwifery training.'

'That sounds like valuable experience.'

'Yes – on the whole I'm looking forward to it.' When she considered it seriously, it was daunting, the idea of actually delivering babies.

She said goodbye to the others and made her way back to the stall to relieve Nora. For a moment she had thought she was on the brink of understanding more of Max's background. *When I last saw Max why didn't I let him explain it all to me*, she thought. Now it was too late.

–

'I shall have to tell them tonight,' Peter said. 'I can't put it off any longer.'

He had managed to obtain leave again for Christmas, and the annual ball had taken place the night before. 'Now, between the dance and New Year's Eve, will be the time to make my explanations,' he told Edmond and Amy. 'It's not going to be an easy evening.'

He had made up his mind to return to India, where he had spent several years before the war.

'I wish Vicky had come to the party,' Amy said. 'She's been training in the East End of London and probably needs a break.'

'She's still sensitive to gossip about Max,' Edmond said.

The chief talking point at the ball had been Elsie's revelation that Henry Smith was the father of her baby, and her admission that she had not, after all, had a liaison with Philip Brownlee.

'Why couldn't she have said so in the first place?' Ma had demanded, scarcely lowering her voice when Mrs Johnson was within earshot.

'She's just a bit simple,' Amy told her. 'I'm glad the Smith family are going to give a home to her and little Philip.'

Edmond had urged Amy to slow down as she helped clear up after the party. 'The servants will do it for us,' he told her. 'You should take the opportunity to relax.'

'There aren't as many staff as there used to be,' she said. 'I've already had some days free of domestic chores over Christmas.' She joined him on the sofa. 'I'm glad they've given you the whole week off. You've been working very hard.'

'It's worthwhile,' he said, 'that's what matters.' He would set off for work eagerly every morning, looking forward to helping casualties with their recovery. When he returned in the early evening he often looked weary.

Soon after they had arrived in Larchbury they had visited the war memorial, which had been unveiled early in December. Amy had found Bertie's name, and had run her finger over the carved letters, with tears running down her face. 'I'll bring Beth to see it when she's a little older,' she said. 'She must understand what it signifies.'

There were other names to find as well, including John Spencer, from the inn.

–

Later that evening as they were in the dining room, finishing their dessert, Edmond exchanged glances with Amy. He waited tensely; would Peter broach the subject of his plans?

'When do you think they'll finally discharge you?' Ma asked. Now he could hardly avoid breaking his news.

'In a couple of months I should be free to leave my army duties,' Peter told them. He was impeccably dressed as usual, and his dark hair was precisely parted at the side and more thoroughly smoothed with brilliantine than Edmond's hair.

'That's capital!' exclaimed Pa. 'Why didn't you tell us sooner?'

'I've made plans,' he said awkwardly. 'I intend to return to India.'

'Oh, no, dear,' Ma's face lost its contented expression. 'Why must you go so far away again? It'll be worse than having you in France or occupied Germany.'

'Say you'll stay in England with us now!' Beatrice said.

'They've told me I can have my old position back.'

'But your father needs you to help him with the plantation! Tell him he must stay, Edmond,' said Ma.

The garlands from the pine trees seemed to be beckoning from their positions on the walls, reminding him of their presence.

'It's for Peter to decide, Ma.'

'Do you remember me talking of Patricia Fellowes who I used to spend time with out there?' Peter asked. 'I'm so looking forward to being with her again.'

'But you haven't seen her for years!' Ma objected. 'She's probably married by now.'

'I happen to know she isn't. We've corresponded regularly while I've been in Europe.' A hush fell as they realised he was determined. 'I'm sorry to disappoint you all.'

Ma seemed to shrivel into an older woman as she rose from the table. Beatrice got up and put her arm around her, and Amy followed them into the drawing room.

Edmond poured glasses of port for his father and Peter.

'I'm very sorry, Pa,' Peter said. 'It's been difficult to make plans during the war, but I've always meant to return there if at all possible.'

'You must do as you wish,' Pa said. 'I shouldn't stand in your way.'

Edmond detected a sadness in his voice. He recognised that his parents were growing older. Who could tell how much longer they would live? Ma had become more frail lately. What if Peter set off again for the east and never saw her again?

'You should consider taking on another forestry worker,' Peter said. He and Edmond always took an interest in the plantation when they were at The Beeches. 'Those two older men who helped out during the war have left now, so that just leaves you with Ross and three others, one of whom is approaching sixty years old.'

'I have George and Joe working on the gardens now,' he told them. 'I often send one of them up to the forest to help out. And there's not quite so much demand for timber now the war is over.'

'There's more call for Christmas trees now,' Edmond reminded him. Besides the giant one in the ballroom, this year there was a smaller one in the drawing room. 'You should consider getting more manpower.' He remembered his father toiling with his workers at busy times and did not want to see him getting worn out.

Pa topped up their glasses. 'Well now, Edmond, you've made a promising start with your career. Have you any other plans for the new year?'

'We want to go to France,' he told the others. 'We want to visit the grave of Bertie, Amy's brother who was killed on the Somme. They've notified the Fletchers now of its whereabouts in one of the cemeteries. Florence is planning to come too, as she was once engaged to him.'

What will it be like, going back there now, he wondered.

From Amy and Edmond's new home on the fringe of Roehampton there was a view of distant woodland. The houses mainly had bay windows, and were set a little apart, instead of in a terrace. Tall elm trees, bare of leaves, lined the nearby common, and Amy was content that a short walk took her across it to the village shop, the local church and a bus stop.

'It's a pretty area,' said Vicky, who had arrived that Friday afternoon to stay for the rest of the weekend. 'Have you made friends with any neighbours yet?'

'There's another family towards the end of the road,' Amy said. 'They've got a little girl a year older than Beth, and the two play together well.'

Beth kept her busy and wanted her attention a good deal in the daytime, but sometimes it seemed dull here when Edmond was at work. Her new friend had always lived quietly, enjoying domestic tasks. She regarded Amy as very adventurous, having worked as a wartime nurse.

'If only I still had Florence living nearby,' she said, for they had frequently met up in the late afternoon after her school day had finished. Her new neighbour was a suitable person to approach when she needed a recipe, but if she wanted to discuss women's rights, Amy could not expect much response.

Her memories of their old home in Cambridge were largely pleasant ones, but lately they had become tainted. She could not think of their bedroom there without recollecting that day in May when she had lost her baby. In some ways she had been ready for a fresh start.

'Isn't it lovely here?' Vicky admired their parlour, which was a little larger than the one in their old house. It had been bright in the autumn afternoons, but now in winter the sun set in late afternoon. Amy drew her smart William Morris curtains which had originally come from The Beeches. She and Edmond had bought two landscapes for their room, and she had filled their vase with early daffodils, though it lacked the style of Beatrice's flower arrangements. She had lit the fire earlier in the afternoon and now the room was becoming cosy.

They went into the dining room and Amy fetched her best china plates: her Royal Albert Crown ones with a gold rim. The dinner service they had been given for their wedding had languished unused for years, before she and Edmond had finally had the chance to set up home together after the war. When he reached home that evening she would serve the chicken pie she had in the oven. She would let Beth stay up to eat with them before hurrying her to bed.

'Do you have many visitors?' Vicky asked.

'Edmond's friends from Cambridge have promised to come one weekend.' Dennis had now been discharged from the army and had returned to College that autumn, and Horace would come too. It would be a busy weekend for her, but it was important to Edmond to keep in touch with his old friends.

'How was your midwifery course?' she asked Vicky.

'Tiring. They'd wake us up in the middle of the night if a mother was reaching the final stages of labour. Can you believe it, if they wanted us to come on duty someone would run down the corridor banging on a coal scuttle. They'd wake up the nurse they wanted, and everyone else as well.'

'Goodness!'

Vicky placed glasses on the white, lacy cloth that Amy's mother had made them, and they helped Beth set out the cutlery.

'We learnt a lot there, but Nora and I both felt we needed longer.'

'So you're back at Wealdham Hospital now. Did they make much money from their Fundraising Day?'

'Better than I expected. We raised nearly enough for an X-ray machine, and a well-off patient has left a legacy, so they should be able to get it.'

'That's splendid news.'

Vicky had looked hesitant since she arrived, as though she had something else to tell her. 'I'm trying to make contact with Max again,' she blurted out, looking a little anxious as though Amy might query her wisdom.

'Oh – it must be months since you've seen him…'

'Yes. When I was working in the East End I kept wondering where he was. It was almost unbearable to think of him somewhere among all the masses of people in the city and wonder if he was missing me as much as I miss him. And that time Peter spoke so well of him, I realised that I never listened properly, when he finally offered to explain about his background. So I thought I should hear what he has to say, if he's still prepared to meet me. When I got back I went to see your uncle, Reverend Fletcher, and he passed on Max's address at a hotel in west London where he works. The vicar still keeps in touch with him. I've written to Max and asked how he's getting on, and whether he would still like to tell me about his background.'

'Have you heard anything?' Amy was not sure whether or not she should encourage Vicky.

'No, but I only wrote the day before yesterday. Perhaps there'll be a letter waiting when I get back to my hostel. Do you think I've been foolish?'

'I'm confused about Max. Like you, I wonder why he deceived us. But at the same time I respect Peter's judgement. I just don't know what to think.' She looked at Vicky's strained face. 'I remember how close you and he seemed, that time you both came to the Christmas ball. I can understand if you want to meet him again, but take things slowly, and see if his explanations really make sense.'

Am I giving her the right advice? she wondered. *I'd hate her to be hurt all over again.* Vicky's enthusiasm for Max's company had always reminded her of her own early weeks and months of meeting Edmond and falling in love with him. They had been determined to stay together, even when his mother and sister had at first opposed their marriage.

Chapter 14

Larchbury and Melbridge, March to June 1921

It was usually dark when Vicky finished work for the day. She was late again, so leaving on her own rather than in a group of women. As she came out she was vaguely aware of a figure to one side of the gate. She started as a young man stepped forward. 'Max!' she exclaimed. Her heart leapt, remembering that day, soon after they had first met, when he had unexpectedly greeted her outside the hospital.

'Vicky! It was a wonderful surprise, getting your letter.' He touched her arm gently, then stood a respectful distance from her. 'I want to tell you everything, as you suggested. Will you come with me to take a meal?'

'Yes.' She hoped she would not feel she had to rush away, like the last time.

'Let's go to *The Pigeons*,' he urged her. She walked beside him downhill, as they had walked that merry summer evening. There was no question of having a proper talk outdoors, at this time of year. She would give him the chance to tell her what he needed to about his past.

They reached the comfortable restaurant. Max asked the waiter if they might sit at a table in a quiet alcove and they were soon installed there. She was impressed once more with how good-looking he was, though his expression was more serious than when they had first met. He seemed to have gained confidence while he had been away, and his English was more fluent.

Absentmindedly she ordered the speciality of the day, which was coq-au-vin.

She had pulled off her nurse's cap and now she went to the ladies' room, took her hair out of its chignon and combed it.

Max looked at her admiringly as she returned. The waiter brought the wine he had ordered, and she let him pour her a glass, but barely sipped it.

'I need to tell you what it was like, living in Strasbourg,' he began.

'It's in Germany, isn't it?'

'Not anymore. Alsace has gone back to being French again now.'

His blue eyes fixed on hers, seeming to grasp how confusing it all was for her.

'The city lies just to the west of the Rhine, and through the ages it has changed hands several times between France and Germany. Most citizens understand both languages. Some speak a kind of dialect. It's fair to say that when I was born, Strasbourg belonged to Germany. But when my grandparents were born there, it was part of France! Even when Father was born it was French, but by a few years later the Germans had occupied it.'

It was still baffling for her, but so far as she could remember, it matched what Peter had told them.

'In 1870 the Germans seized Strasbourg, in the Franco-Prussian war. When my mother was born, in the early 1870s, it was German, and she was brought up as a

German. Father was taught at school to think of himself as German.'

He took a gulp of his wine. 'When I was young my mother was expecting another child, but she lost the baby. She bled a lot and remained very weak for two or three years. Her mother, my grandmother, used to take me to her house most days to care for me. My grandparents were among those who were shocked at the outcome of the war and still regarded themselves as French.'

He fell silent as the waiter brought their meals, then he continued. 'At school we were taught German, and learnt German history. I learnt to behave differently at my grandparents' house from how I did at school. As my mother recovered gradually, she and my father encouraged me to conform to the German outlook, but I was still close to my grandparents, and could not forget the French culture I had absorbed... Is your meal all right?'

'Yes, it's lovely.' She had been eating it, hardly aware of its taste. 'Did you always want to be a chef?'

'I learnt the violin for a while and briefly attended the conservatoire at Cologne,' he told her. 'That is very much German. But it was only a summer school, and although I considered applying for a scholarship, by that time the war was looming. I thought of attending university, but even in Strasbourg they would have encouraged a rigorously German outlook. I've always been interested in cooking, so I decided to study to become a chef. The French cuisine is prestigious, and there was the opportunity to concentrate on that. Soon after I started the course the war started and the French patriots in Strasbourg wanted to win Alsace back for France.'

'It must have been a nightmare, once the two countries were at war.'

'That's right. Men from Alsace were made to fight against France, but the military began to mistrust their loyalty and sent them to fight on the Eastern Front. They tried to ban the French language in the province. Some men deserted and went to fight in France. I bought a forged French passport. It gave my hometown as Bar-le-Duc, which is in eastern France. My French accent would sound suspicious for a Parisian, or a person from western France.'

'Did you actually fight for the French?'

'No, but I obtained information from sympathisers in Alsace and passed it to the French.'

Vicky set aside her knife and fork, before finishing her meal. Soon he set down his too. They did not order anything else, both too tense. Vicky tried to imagine herself living in a region where there were such conflicts of loyalty.

'What about that passport in the name of a German officer?' she asked.

'Early in the war they needed someone with the credentials of a German officer to help Allied soldiers stuck behind the lines in Flanders. They forged me a German passport in the name of Lieutenant Johann Bauer, a common name. There were two lieutenants with the name, one of them dead.'

'But I don't understand – those passports seemed very incriminating. Why did you bring them all with you to England?'

'I didn't want to reveal myself as German, so I needed the French one, which was one of the false ones. I kept the real one, too. Then there was the one claiming to be a German officer; after the end of the war I meant to get rid of it, but somehow I kept forgetting I still had it with me.'

Vicky drank a glass of water. His story was almost incredible. 'It's a miracle you survived the war.'

'Yes. After a while you've done so many devious things you almost forget who you are. And you get used to taking chances, like a gambler.'

He was looking directly at her, though with an uneasy manner. She felt sure he was telling the truth, though much of it was disturbing.

'Back in Alsace there are men who know or suspect some of what I did and would cheerfully murder me. Peter suggested I came to England to work. Alsace has become French again, though some residents would prefer to remain German. But it's actually true now that I come from France.'

The evening still had an air of unreality. 'What would you like for dessert?' Max asked.

'Just some fruit salad, thank you.'

Afterwards he asked for the bill. 'When you stopped seeing me I regretted not following my instincts to be open with you from the start,' he told her.

He paid their bill and they went outside into the smoky atmosphere, as the wind was blowing from the direction of the crowded houses and factories. Tentatively he took her gloved hand as they began to walk uphill towards her hostel.

'I'll understand if you don't want to see me anymore,' he told her. 'I've led a very deceitful life during the war, but I could not support the Germans.'

'Oh, Max!' she stopped by a lamppost and he held her close. 'I want to go on seeing you. When we were apart

I kept thinking there must be some innocent explanation for what had happened.'

He took hold of a lock of her hair and kissed it. 'I was wretched when I thought I had thrown away my chance of being with you.' For a few moments he held her close, stooping, his warm forehead against hers, then he led her back to her hostel.

'So you're living at the hotel in London where you work?' she asked, remembering his address. 'How long will it take you to get back there?'

'I should be able to catch the 9.30 and arrive at Victoria soon after 11 p.m.' He reached out and engulfed her in an embrace, then his warm lips came down on hers.

Before leaving he arranged another visit.

At the back of her mind she could anticipate hostility from Aunt Mabel, and almost certainly from her parents as well, because of his complicated past. *I need to be with him,* she thought. *That's all I can think about at the moment. I'm not going to worry about the future.*

–

'It's lovely, coming to visit you here,' Vicky said as she and Max arrived at the vicarage in time for Saturday lunch.

'Will you call in at The Beeches while you're in Larchbury?' the vicar asked them.

'I don't know – maybe briefly, before we catch our trains back. It's so tricky, because Aunt Mabel and Beatrice don't approve of Max.'

'Once they didn't approve of Amy,' Florence told her. 'Remember when you became bridesmaid for Amy at the last minute because Beatrice had refused to attend her?'

'Goodness, yes! But Aunt Mabel wrote and told my parents about the reputation Max was getting, and it's made everything very difficult for me.'

They went and joined the others around the lunch table and the vicar's wife began serving her pork casserole.

'You didn't come to the Christmas ball at The Beeches,' James said. 'We went and as usual it was a fine occasion.'

'I was still trying to decide whether or not to contact Max,' Vicky said. 'I was unwilling to attract local gossip. Besides, I'd have needed to be allowed time off from my course in London.' Babies did not delay arriving to suit seasonal celebrations.

'We're glad to see you together again,' James said.

'Once I used to be welcome at The Beeches,' Max said. 'I remember when I played my violin there. Then there was the ball I went to in 1919. The war seemed to be in the past, and I relaxed my guard and drank a little more than usual. That was when I started making stupid mistakes, like clicking my heels, and I believe I recommended the wrong type of wine.'

'On New Year's Day there was another party at Amy's parents' house, for Beth's third birthday,' Florence said. 'That was lovely too.'

The days were rushing by. Already Easter had passed and it was the first week of April.

James's mother brought in the rhubarb pie. 'It's wonderful that they've ended the rationing,' she said. 'We can get all the sugar we want now.'

It was a bright, mild afternoon and the young couple decided to take a walk down to the brook. 'It must be about a year since I came here with Emil, that young German who the vicar invited,' Max said. 'Then, soon afterwards, one of the pastors recognised me and my extra passports came to light. That was when it all went wrong.'

'We wasted a year, not seeing each other,' Vicky complained as they walked by the trailing willows. It was almost as bad as the separation Edmond and Amy had suffered. 'And now we live nearly forty miles apart.'

He took her in his arms. 'It's unbearable to face all these problems. I want to be with you, Vicky. I want to marry you. But perhaps that's not fair of me – I'm a few years older than you.'

'I want to be with you all the time,' she told him resolutely. Often when she was alone her thoughts pursued that idea. Now she was overwhelmed that he felt the same.

He kissed her tenderly. 'I don't suppose you imagined marrying a suspicious foreign character like me. And when I carried out those clandestine activities I couldn't look far ahead, and I didn't imagine it might cause a barrier between me and the girl I would come to love.'

'What are we going to do, Max? You're working in London now, and I'm at the hospital in Wealdham.'

'I don't know. I daresay I can move again, but it will look better if I stay in the same job for a while first.'

She leant her head against his shoulder. 'You must come and visit my family soon,' she said.

–

Edmond, Amy and Beth joined Florence in the vicarage garden on Whit Sunday afternoon. 'So James and his father have a new interest,' Florence told them. The garden looked parched, for there had been little rain. 'They're becoming involved with the new British Legion organisation.'

Amy remembered Uncle speaking of it in his morning service. It was being formed by the combination of three other organisations for servicemen from the war. 'I'm glad there'll be an overall body to provide support for veterans,' she said. There must be hundreds of thousands who had been badly injured, like Edmond and Charles, and most of them would not have well-off families who could help support them.

'They'll support the dependants as well,' Florence said. Beneath her straw hat she looked a little weary. She passed Amy and Edmond cups of tea, and Beth a drink of lemonade. There was some of Aunt Sophie's seedcake, too. 'If there's any local branch, James might be able to work there.' He was still looking for steady employment.

Amy leant back in her deck chair. She and Edmond were staying at The Beeches for Whit weekend. The previous day they, along with the other Derwents, had seen off Peter on the train on the first stage of his journey back to India. Ma was particularly downcast at saying farewell for what was likely to prove a long parting.

'Now then. About our trip to France…' Amy said to Florence. She and Edmond had been choosing dates and deciding the best route to take to the Somme area to visit the cemetery where Bertie was buried. *What'll it be like, travelling through areas of northern France in peacetime,* she wondered. *I can't imagine some areas ever returning to normal.* 'If we go at the end of July, you'll have finished school for the year by then, won't you? I expect James will come too?'

Florence shuffled in her deck chair. 'I've been meaning to talk to you about that. There's a complication now and I won't be able to go with you.'

'Why not?' Bertie had once been Florence's fiancé, and Amy was disappointed that her friend would not join her to pay her respects.

'Can't you guess? It's really very good news…'

'You mean…'

'Yes! I'm expecting a baby! To be honest, I've been a little reluctant to tell you, because of your disappointment last year.'

Amy got up and hugged her. 'You know I've always been eager for you to have a child,' she assured her friend.

'He or she should be here by December. Isn't it marvellous? Though in some ways I'd prefer James to be more settled in employment. Anyway, I'm afraid it means I need to be careful, and I'd better not travel with you this summer.'

'Oh, but I understand completely!'

'I'm determined to visit Bertie's grave sometime in the future.'

'Will you go on living here?'

'If only James can get steady work we'd like to find our own house. Just a small one will do.'

So another of Amy's friends was expecting a child, and there still was no brother or sister for three-year-old Beth. But she had the opportunity to visit Bertie's grave before she found herself expecting again.

'Will you drive around France? You won't take Edmond's motorbike, will you?' Florence looked dubious.

'It's tempting,' Edmond said mischievously. 'But no, we can't stay there for very long, and we want to go as far as Liège, in Belgium, to see Madame Rousseau. It'll be much easier if we take the car with us across the Channel.'

The sun was beating down fiercely and presently Amy got up to leave. 'We'd better get back to The Beeches.

Now Peter has left, Ma is horribly depressed, and Beatrice is miserable. Pa is making a valiant effort to remain cheerful, but I can tell he's badly affected too.'

–

'This is Max. It's high time you met him.' Vicky's parents had seemed reluctant. When she had suggested it earlier in the spring they had told her they had friends visiting that weekend, and put off the meeting. They had agreed that she might bring him for the day on Whit Monday. He had gone directly from London to Melbridge station, not far from Croydon, and waited for her to arrive from Wealdham.

As she had led him through the streets her misgivings had returned. The previous year, when she had stopped seeing Max, she had simply told her parents that they were no longer friends, but Aunt Mabel had written and told them about his suspicious behaviour.

If only they don't interrogate him about what he was doing in France during the war, she thought. *I don't want him to tell falsehoods again, but what he actually did sounds so implausible.*

Soon they reached the severe-looking, detached house of grey stone where she had been brought up.

During lunch her parents were polite to Max, but mostly asked her for news of her nursing work. She had been taught a good deal about infectious diseases lately, but that was not what she had come to discuss.

'It's hot again this afternoon,' Father said afterwards. 'Let's stay indoors.' Mother was apt to feel unwell in extreme temperatures.

They sat in the easy chairs in the dim parlour. Around her were the familiar lacy antimacassars and old-fashioned portraits.

'Where did you say you come from?' Father asked Max.

'Strasbourg.'

'That's in Germany!' He sounded disgusted.

Max's accent had improved a good deal since he had first arrived in Larchbury, but it was still noticeable that he was not British. Her father looked at him with the kind of distrustful stare that the most hostile villagers bestowed.

'Not anymore. It's been returned to France, under the Treaty of Versailles. We were part of France until 1870, and many of us have always regarded ourselves as French.'

'But what you're really saying is that you were brought up German,' Father said.

Mother's jaw dropped open.

'Not from choice. My grandparents remained loyal to the French.'

'Max wants to put all the international quarrels behind him,' Vicky put in quickly. 'That's why he's moved to England. He's doing very well as a chef.'

Her father's face formed a disagreeable expression. 'My sister Mabel wrote and told me a lot about you, young man,' he said. 'Some story about you having fictitious passports…'

'I assure you, in the war I was working for the Allies.' His blue eyes were wide open and convincing.

'Peter's told us that he was bringing valuable information from the Germans,' Vicky said.

'I hear you passed yourself off as French from the day you arrived in Larchbury,' Father said.

Mother was looking nervous.

'We don't want anyone like you visiting us,' Father said. 'Don't bring him here again, Victoria.'

'Father, please! The war's been over for more than two years now!'

'My friend's son was lost on the Somme. And have you forgotten what the Huns did to Edmond?'

'Edmond likes Max. Father, Mother, we want to get married!'

'The very idea! We won't allow it!' Father declared.

Tears poured down Vicky's face. 'I'll marry him anyway!' she cried.

Max went and put his arm around Vicky. 'I'll wait for your daughter, if I have to.'

Vicky felt queasy. She hated the idea of defying her parents, especially her mother who was delicate, but she could not give up Max.

'I can wait until I'm of age,' she told them. 'I reach twenty-one in November.'

'If you marry without our consent, don't expect a penny from us!' Her father was red in the face now.

She wanted to beg him to reconsider, but when Father spoke in that tone of voice it was useless trying to reason with him. She picked up her bag. There was no point in staying any longer. 'Sorry, Mother,' she said, trying not to cry. 'Thank you for giving us lunch.'

–

'Will your American be coming on leave soon?' Caroline was curious when Beatrice visited the hat shop.

'Caleb's planning to come this summer,' she said. They wrote regularly; they still declared their love, but weeks and months had passed without them seeing each other.

With Peter sailing away, to India rather than just to the Continent, her circle had closed still further. 'Sometimes I wonder if I'm being punished,' she confessed to Caroline.

'Why should you be?' her friend looked mystified.

'I let Charles Shenwood release me from my engagement to him when he was badly injured. Lots of people said at the time that I was heartless.' Sometimes afterwards she had felt ashamed of her behaviour.

'Do you wish now you'd married him?'

'No – I don't believe I was as in love as I supposed when I became engaged. He's doing very well, I hear, from Edmond who's still a good friend of his. He's married Lavinia Westholme, and they've got a son now, and seem very happy. I wish them well. But my prospects look bleak.'

–

Beatrice was pleased to have visitors. In mid-June Edmond and Amy were at The Beeches again. He had taken Friday afternoon off, so they could spend a whole leisurely weekend there. Beatrice was glad he realised it was especially important to visit now that his family were upset about Peter's return to India.

The weather was stuffy and they soon went indoors.

'I wish you hadn't turned Vicky's parents against Max,' Edmond told his mother once they had finished their dinner and settled in the drawing room. 'Now they're trying to prevent her from marrying him. She came to visit us last week and she was desperately upset that they're not prepared to accept him.'

'I only told them the truth, about his passports,' Ma said angrily. From outside there was a faint, distant thunderclap.

'You didn't say anything about his courageous actions, bringing the Allies information.'

'He studied music in Cologne,' Beatrice reminded them. 'Why did he choose to go there instead of finding somewhere in France, or at least in that area on the border where he says he comes from?'

'Vicky wants to marry him anyway,' Amy said. 'She'll only need to wait till November, when she's twenty-one.'

'But her father won't give her any money, and the young man has only poorly paid work,' said Pa.

'There are a few more months till Vicky is of age – time for her to see reason,' said Ma. 'I still mistrust anyone from Germany.'

'So do I,' said Beatrice. 'How can you forgive them, Edmond? You barely survived your wounds.'

The argument reverberated around the room. Amy and Edmond went to bed and the others soon did the same, out of sorts.

For a while Beatrice tried to fall asleep. *Why do I resent Vicky*, she asked herself. *Perhaps because she's determined to marry whom she chooses, whatever the consequences, and she'll probably be wed before me. Sometimes my own plans seem unrealistic. Will Vicky come to regret her decision?*

At last it was fully dark, but there was the occasional thunderclap, one of them loud enough to reverberate for a while, and still she could not sleep. She paced her room, the Turkish carpet soft beneath her bare feet. *I too must marry whom I choose, regardless of my husband's position in life, or what anyone thinks, she resolved.* She opened the curtain and gazed across the parched lawn, sloping down towards Larchbury. Light spread across it – moonlight, she supposed, coming from behind the house. Yet there was a curious effect of the light, as though it was flickering. She looked at it in puzzlement, as the impression increased. With sudden concern, she seized her wrap and hurried out of her room and into the unoccupied guest room opposite, where there was a table almost overflowing with the hats she was making.

The windows faced the forest, and ahead of her, up the slope, the trees were alight.

Chapter 15

Larchbury, June 1921

Edmond was woken by Beatrice's voice screaming along the landing. 'Wake up, everyone! Come quickly – the forest is on fire!'

Amy awoke at the same time and the two of them dashed into Peter's empty room opposite and stared through the window at the flames consuming the pine trees they could see ahead. 'Quick!' cried Edmond. 'We must get dressed and help Pa deal with this.'

A sleepy-headed Beth opened the nursery door; she had outgrown her cot and slept in a bed now. 'Go back to sleep, darling,' cried Amy. 'There's been thunder, but everything's all right.' She took the child's hand and led her back into her room.

'I've tucked her up with her toy rabbit,' Amy told Edmond soon afterwards. 'I believe she'll go back to sleep.'

'Pa will be phoning the fire brigade,' he told her, as they pulled on their nearest clothes. 'He's always had a plan for dealing with a fire, if it happened.' *Though I don't believe he expected to discover one this well-established*, he thought.

Downstairs a white-faced Pa was hovering by the hall telephone, while Beatrice, still in her nightdress and wrap, passed him sheets of paper with phone numbers written on them. Ma, draped in a shawl, was trembling and reaching for her smelling salts.

'What can I do, Pa?' Edmond cried when he stopped between calls. 'Shall I head uphill to help tackle the flames?'

'You'll do no such thing, with your poor lungs. Take over here while I go up there. Amy, go and fetch Cook's first aid kit and stand by in case there are any casualties.'

'Yes, of course, Pa.' Her blonde hair was still tousled about her shoulders.

Only Cook and Chambers still lived on the premises, and both soon appeared. Pa and Chambers were loading barrels and pails onto a wagon and filling them with water. Then they harnessed the largest horses to drag them up the hill.

'Pa...' Edmond seized his arm. 'Please don't take any chances.'

'Don't worry about me, Son. Send the workers up to me as they arrive. And we can use water from the tower.' He set off on the wagon.

'There are always some barrels of water kept up in the forest,' Edmond said, 'and some wooden beaters to put out flames. We've had the occasional summer fire before, but never anything on this scale.'

Amy was trying to pacify Ma, but she looked terrified.

'It's a question of trying to call in the workers,' Edmond went on. 'So many aren't on the phone. I had to call the vicarage three times before I could rouse your uncle, but now James is on his way and the vicar is going around with his pony and trap to rouse our forestry workers and any strong young men who might be prepared to help. We've got the water tower up there, remember.'

'Oh, yes.' It was in an elevated position in the forest.

'I'll run to fetch Ross,' Cook said, for he lived in a nearby cottage. She ran off, showing more speed than he expected.

There was a sound of a motor vehicle and loud bells, and the fire engine could be seen coming up the drive in the flickering light. He watched as it continued up the hill. Soon the men began directing water at the flames. They went to draw some from the water tower, under pressure.

Stepping out through the veranda and staring uphill, it was easy for Edmond to see that the fire had grown considerably since they had first noticed it, and their efforts were having little effect. Beatrice joined him. The light was brighter and there was a rushing noise, and the crackling of burning branches. Sometimes they saw a whole tree collapse, or burning branches falling to one side to ignite a fresh area. Their forest, the source of the Derwent income, was being devoured in front of their eyes. They exchanged glances, unable to find anything reassuring to say.

Edmond found himself swaying, caught in a wave of tiredness and anxiety. Then Amy came around with a tray of cups of tea.

She squeezed his arm but said nothing. *She knows the forest is being destroyed*, he thought. There was a distant rumble of thunder. *If only we could have some proper rain.*

Beatrice had found time to get dressed. Even her hair looked well brushed. Ross and the other forestry workers began rushing into their grounds, along with George and Joe Smith. As young men arrived, Beatrice smiled at them in an encouraging way and sent them uphill to help. James and other men arrived. They prepared another wagon with more barrels of water.

Edmond followed Beatrice indoors. She fetched a thicker shawl than Ma had chosen, and arranged it around her mother's shoulders, while the bewildered woman shuffled around, asking everyone how such a misfortune could happen.

Amy went to check on Beth and reported that she was fast asleep.

Edmond went outside again, scarcely able to keep his eyes from the conflagration. In the distance he could now see human figures, silhouetted against the flames as they rushed around. The wind was blowing acrid smoke in their direction and he began coughing, feeling the irritation in his damaged lung. Amy put her arm around him. 'For goodness' sake, Edmond! Come inside!'

'Are they making any progress? Any impression on it at all? I can't bear just sitting here.'

Chambers stumbled into the house, looking exhausted. *He's extremely loyal, but he's too old to be helping with this*, Edmond thought. 'How is it going?' he asked him desperately.

'The firemen are managing to stop it spreading. Listen, Mr Edmond, I've got young Joe on the wagon – he's got his arm burnt. He's too impetuous for his own good. He's weak with the pain. Cook, will you help me bring him inside, then Mrs Amy can take a look at it.'

Soon she had a pale, trembling patient sitting in the kitchen, and Beatrice was phoning for the doctor. Edmond watched, alarmed, as Amy examined his burn, looking frightened. She dabbed water around the outer edge to cool it, but did not dare touch the area in the centre, where the skin was broken. They were relieved when the doctor arrived. Doctor Stanhope, who had treated Ma when she had had the flu, had resumed his retirement now younger doctors were no longer needed at the Front. Doctor Heath, a man in his forties, had taken his place. He confirmed Amy's opinion that Joe needed to go to the hospital. 'I'll drive him to Wealdham,' the doctor said, to their relief.

As they saw them off, the sky was beginning to lighten towards the north-east. Turning towards the blaze he noticed that it was dying back a little: he had hardly dared to hope they would manage to check it.

'It looks as though they'll actually save part of it!' Amy cried.

'I think the main firebreak through the centre has saved the eastern area,' he said, 'providing a strong wind doesn't spring up.' Pa had always insisted the wide gap was left to act as a barrier if ever there was a fire. *Thank God he did so*, Edmond thought. But the view was sickening. Flames still attacked some of the trees, while others were blackened heaps of debris. Smoke continued to blow down the hill and Amy hurried him back inside.

Beatrice looked at them anxiously. 'They're bringing it under control!' Edmond told her. He looked at his wife and sister. 'When they're able to stop briefly we should offer drinks to the workers. Chambers, can you help me bring up a beer barrel from the cellar?'

'Very good, Mr Edmond. But the barrels are heavy to bring up. You're not very strong and shouldn't be straining yourself.'

In the end Amy went down with them and the three of them began manoeuvring the heavy barrel up the stone steps. Even Beatrice edged down the steps to help them. They rolled the barrel into the kitchen and set beer glasses on the table.

'Would you mind going back up there, Chambers? I think they're making more impression on the blaze now. Get them to take a break in twos and threes. They can come down on a wagon and we can send it back up with some more water. Cook, can you set out some bread and cheese and make tea for anyone who'd like some.'

Beatrice laid her hand on his arm. 'Edmond, thank goodness you're here to help!'

The first smoke-streaked workers soon arrived in the kitchen. Beatrice and Amy served them food and drink and thanked them for their contribution. But Edmond struggled to maintain a confident appearance.

One of the other men had a small burn and one had a graze, so Amy's skills were needed again.

The work continued for another hour, as daylight arrived and the sun edged over the horizon. Weary figures wandered up and down the hill.

Finally Chambers brought Pa into the kitchen, ash lodged in his hair. His face was still white and drawn. 'With respect, Sir, you need to take some rest.'

Edmond made him sit in the kitchen and Amy brought him food and drink. Beatrice brought Ma in to see him. 'How exhausted you look!' she cried.

'Chambers, see that some of the freshest men remain up there this morning,' Pa said. 'We have to keep alert in case the flames break out again.'

'Mamma!' cried a shrill voice, and Beth came running into the kitchen in her nightdress, looking about her in astonishment at the crowd of smoky young men loitering there.

'It's all right, sweetie,' Amy said, taking their daughter in her arms and fetching her a drink of water. Edmond joined his wife in reassuring the little girl, though it was hard to conceal that something was gravely amiss. *We've lost half the forest,* he thought. *It's like losing a member of the family.*

Everyone was exhausted that morning, and they took it in turns to try to catch up with their sleep, though it was hard to overcome the shock at what had taken place. Amy was occupied with trying to divert Beth. She did not want to take her outside where she would see the devastation. Edmond had gone back to their room.

Telephone calls kept coming from friends and acquaintances. Amy's parents were among the first to express their concern. Pa would take the calls and they would hear him making light of their problems, until at last he nodded off in an armchair. Amy helped Beatrice take the calls. 'Don't tell anyone how much of the forest we've lost!' she told Amy, though anyone who walked nearby would soon see the extent. 'Pa has his pride. He doesn't want people speculating on how our business may have suffered.'

At last Mrs Johnson offered to look after Beth so Amy could take a rest. Edmond had managed to fall asleep, but Amy did not suppose she would be able to slumber in broad daylight. She lay down beside him, and felt weariness come over her. The next thing she knew, it was early afternoon.

This was not turning out to be the relaxing weekend they had planned. Edmond and Amy joined Pa and Beatrice as they went to inspect the stricken plantation. Amy felt sick at heart as the stench of burnt wood assailed them as they neared the top of the hill. Ross and two of his assistants were piling burnt branches into heaps. Some of the undergrowth was still damp from all the water that had been directed at the blaze. The western section of the forest had huge gaps where the sky and crown of the hill were visible. The flourishing trees, which had brought the family prosperity, and which she had always taken for granted, were reduced to charcoal and ashes.

'There hasn't been any further outbreak, Mr Derwent,' Ross told him.

Pa expressed his relief, but his shoulders stooped in an unfamiliar attitude of dejection. How he had toiled, all through the war, to maintain the supply of timber. As for Edmond, she had seldom seen him so sombre.

The only glimmer of encouragement came from the fact that the eastern section, beyond the broad firebreak, showed little damage apart from scorch marks.

'Let's get the debris piled up as compactly as possible,' Pa told Ross. 'I believe the *Wealdham Gazette* is sending a reporter and photographer. I don't want them to see a shambles. They'll expect some damage, of course, but if we can get them to face towards the east we can make it obvious that much of our forest has survived.'

'Right, Sir.'

'We need to clear all this undergrowth,' he went on, 'so there's less chance of another fire breaking out while the drought lasts. Then I must decide which areas of the remaining forest can be cut down to fulfil our orders, and which will be available in the autumn when people start needing firewood.'

He began to plan restocking the stricken area. 'I'll start to draw up a schedule for you on Monday.'

'Yes, Sir. The Christmas trees have become very popular lately.'

'Poor Pa!' Edmond said to Amy when they were alone. 'He needs to plan for the future to convince himself the forest will recover. But I can tell he's so tired he can scarcely think what he's saying.'

–

On the Sunday they seized time, after lunch and before setting off home, to visit Joe in the hospital at Wealdham. Edmond drove them there in the car, while Amy's mother welcomed Beth for the afternoon.

When they reached the hospital ward they found Vicky was one of the nurses on duty.

'I gather you had quite a blaze,' she said. 'Joe told me about it and a sister who lives in Alderbank said they could see it from there, very early on Saturday morning.'

Amy exchanged glances with Edmond. Pa was still dismayed that the reporter from the *Wealdham Gazette* had spent a whole hour questioning him about the losses he had suffered.

'Try not to spread the story around too much,' Edmond told her.

They went to see Joe, whose arm was heavily bandaged.

'How are you doing?' Amy asked him. 'You were very brave yesterday.'

'I feel better now, Mrs Derwent. When I think what my brothers went through in the war I know I shouldn't complain at having to fight a fire. Henry died out there in France.'

They'll be giving Joe pain relief, she thought.

'Mr Derwent wants you to know he'll pay any charges for your treatment,' she told him.

They followed Vicky out of the ward. 'I did the best I could,' Amy told her guiltily, 'but it was a worse burn than I'd had to deal with before.'

'The doctor and sister had to treat it,' she told them. 'They say he should make a good recovery, especially as he's young, but it'll take several weeks at least before he's fit to work again.'

The hospital was not particularly busy that afternoon and they had time to talk. 'Are you still seeing Max regularly?' Amy asked.

'We often can't get the same day off,' Vicky said. 'Sometimes we go two or three weeks without meeting, but we're determined we'll be together one day soon.'

Amy squeezed her arm. 'Stick to your convictions,' she said. 'It worked out for Edmond and me.'

Chapter 16

'I'm worried about Pa,' Edmond said, so they visited The Beeches again on the first Saturday of July.

Morale was low, they could see that. Ma and Beatrice looked pale and edgy, but Pa, who had kept their spirits high throughout the war, looked hunched and even seemed to have lost weight.

'I want to see what progress you've made up at the forest,' Edmond insisted, so they set off up the hill. They had prepared Beth for the change in its appearance. Ross and one of the other men were there, loading burnt trunks and branches on to a wagon for disposal.

'It rained the day after you were last here,' Pa said. 'Proper rain at last, ending the drought. It eased my mind a little to know that fire was less likely to break out again.'

He pointed out where they had cleared some of the burnt area ready to plant replacement trees. 'We'll start with some that are suitable for Christmas trees,' he said. 'They'll have a few months to grow before December.'

After lunch they gathered on the veranda to drink coffee. The weather was cooler now, more refreshing. Even so, the family were ill at ease.

'How long will it take you to restock the forest?' Edmond asked Pa.

'Years. I'll need to buy the saplings first, but not all at once, because of having to find the money. We'll plant them, but they'll take years to grow. And all the while we must keep a good supply of timber from the established part of the forest, to try to keep a steady income.'

Amy looked at the dismay on Edmond's face. They both recognised that the recovery would be tough for his father, but it was only now that they understood the extent of the problem. She wished Peter was not so far away in India. Edmond had written to him, telling him what had happened, without sparing him the details, as Pa would probably do. She wondered if Edmond would ever contemplate helping Pa run the forest after all. *He shouldn't do that*, she thought, *not when he's completed his degree and settled in his chosen career. I'd understand, but I simply don't believe it'd be right for him to make the change now.*

'We'll have to draw on all our reserves,' Pa said. 'I'm afraid life won't be so easy, for the next few years.' He looked around at his wife and daughter. 'I'd hoped we could afford some good holidays, and weekends in London to visit the theatre, but those are the kind of luxuries we must do without for a while.'

'You're being harsh with us,' Ma said. 'After all the privations of the war years we deserve a few little treats.'

'I believe Pa knows best in this respect,' Beatrice said, to Amy's surprise.

Beth wriggled on Amy's lap. She was beginning to grow out of her afternoon nap. *In a minute I'll have to take her for a walk*, she thought.

'People think of us as well off and have come to expect us to entertain,' Pa went on. 'They count on us to hold the fête at the end of each summer, and it's not all that costly – we have the land available. The Christmas ball is expensive, though.'

'Perhaps you should discontinue it, Pa,' Edmond said, though his wife and sister looked displeased.

Pa was about to say something, but fell quiet as Daisy came to collect their coffee cups.

When she had left he continued. 'We may have to cut back on staff. We might need to manage without one of them, either Daisy or Mrs Johnson.'

'But I can't cope without either!' Ma exclaimed. 'Do you remember how I struggled at the end of the war? Can't you cut back on forestry staff?'

'Not now I'm trying to get the forest cleared and restocked,' he explained patiently.

'Listen, Pa, one thing is clear,' Edmond said. 'Amy and I can manage on less. I'm earning a proper income at last. We're extremely grateful that you've helped support us so much for years, but now please cut back on our allowance.'

'Yes, please do as Edmond suggests,' Amy said. They had discussed the possibility on the way there, and she knew it was the right thing to do. All the same, the thought of managing on less money made her anxious.

'I wonder if I should sell the car and get a cheaper model?' Pa said. 'It's far from new, though, and I can't make do with a smaller one, because there are often visitors who need driving somewhere.'

'Somehow we'll manage,' Beatrice asserted.

'Listen,' Pa said, 'there's one important thing I have to say. What happened was dreadful, but you all rallied around and helped in the emergency. I'll always remember that.'

They exchanged glances. It was not strictly true that Ma had helped, but Amy recognised how she and Edmond and Beatrice had all done their best.

'The servants all worked flat out, even though it was the middle of the night,' Edmond said.

'I know – I've been thanking them too. Your loyalty, and that of the staff, is what heartens me, and gives me hope for the future,' Pa said.

–

'We will still be able to go to France, won't we?' Amy asked Edmond when they got home. There were only four weeks to go till they set off. Her parents were looking forward to caring for Beth while they were away.

'Yes, definitely. I've already booked the ferry.'

For a moment she caught her breath. 'Listen, Edmond, are you sure you'll be all right going back there? You used to have nightmares about the battles.'

'A long time has passed since then. I'll be all right, especially with you beside me.'

She was reassured. 'Will we be able to go to Belgium as well? Madame Rousseau has been begging me to visit her.'

'While we're on the Continent I believe we should go there too. We can use our savings for the trip.'

She was uneasy. There would be little left for autumn expenses. She needed new shoes and Edmond's overcoat was worn. Beth grew out of her clothes very rapidly.

It's up to me to make the economies, she thought. *Edmond hasn't grown up accustomed to being thrifty, like I have.*

She began to spend less on food and prepare economical, if time-consuming dishes. She sowed lettuces in their garden and waited impatiently for them to grow.

'Might I have a word, Mrs Derwent?' asked Rose, her maid, one day. She was seventeen, thin but healthy-looking, with freckles.

'Yes, of course.'

'I wondered if I might come here to work just one day a week instead of two. My Mam's been ill and wants me to help more at home, with the laundry and looking after my little brothers.'

It'll suit me fine, Amy thought. 'Yes, Rose, I understand.' They agreed that the girl need not work on Tuesdays.

'Shall I see if one of my friends could oblige?'

'Not for the moment, thanks, Rose. I'll see if I can manage without you that day.'

Two weeks earlier, Dennis and Horace had come from Cambridge to stay for the weekend. She and Edmond had been delighted to see them again and exchange news.

All the same, by the Sunday she had been tired, and was relieved when they set off back. Edmond had taken her in his arms. 'Thank you for making them so welcome, darling!' he had said. His appreciation gave her a warm glow and made her feel her efforts were worthwhile.

Now she was thankful that their visit had taken place while Rose had still been working there for two days each week.

Reducing her maid's hours saved them some money each week, but when Tuesday came Beth was being demanding and Amy only finished the ironing just before Edmond reached home.

They went and put Beth to bed, then Amy served the shepherd's pie. She yawned as she sat down at the table.

'You look exhausted, darling,' Edmond said. 'Are you all right?'

'Yes, fine, but it's hot again. We'll be on holiday soon, though.'

–

Beatrice arranged the latest hat she had made on the stand in the front of Miss Parsons's window, and repositioned some of the other smart items of millinery. The elder Miss Parsons had retired now, and Caroline had mentioned to Beatrice that another assistant was required for two days a week.

She imagined that Caroline had guessed that the forest fire had upset the Derwents' finances. It was hard to prevent such speculation when the news had been on the front page of the *Wealdham Gazette*, along with a picture of the ravaged plantation.

Her father had groaned at the unfortunate publicity. 'People know anyway,' Beatrice had told him gently. 'Many of them were woken up in the middle of the night. They heard the commotion as the fire engine set out. They saw the fire burning on the hill – in fact, people in Alderbank could see it too. And they have only to walk along the path outside our grounds to see the devastation for themselves.' She saw the look of anguish on his face. 'I'm sorry, Pa, but we can't pretend people don't know about it.'

She applied for the work in the millinery shop. 'Beatrice is gifted at making and decorating hats, too,' Caroline told Miss Parsons helpfully.

Ma had still not forgiven her for taking paid work.

'But it's an answer to our problems,' Beatrice told her parents, when she was officially employed serving in the shop. 'Pa needs us to make economies. I can manage without my allowance. It's decent, feminine work – you could regard it as artistic.'

It was a Saturday, when the shop was busy, and both she and Caroline were helping Miss Parsons. For a while she felt elated at making a fresh start, in a pastime which interested her. The hat she had made was one of the handsomest in the window.

She stood attaching a label to another new hat. She had been delighted that morning when a letter had arrived from Caleb in Germany. He sounded eager to see her when he was granted leave, as he should be in the near future. But she could not ignore the fresh difficulties relating to her interest in him. Everything was conspiring against her. Her brother had gone back to India, making it harder to even contemplate leaving her parents for America with Caleb. And the setback with the forest, and her father's loss of fortune, made it even less reasonable for her to occasion them fresh worry.

She was aroused from her daydream by the jangling of the doorbell. She looked around and saw Harriet Patterson, or rather Harriet Fairlawn as she now was, walking elegantly into their shop. Beatrice blushed with embarrassment. For one thing, she was uneasy about Harriet seeing her working there – she was the kind of woman who would not understand why she had chosen this course in her family predicament. Besides that, Harriet was now married to Wilfrid, and Beatrice was still traumatised by the memory of him molesting her in a taxi.

'Hello, Caroline, hello Beatrice,' said Harriet. For a moment Beatrice thought she saw a flicker of embarrassment on her face. 'I was very sorry to hear about the fire damage to your forest,' she told Beatrice, apparently sincere.

Miss Parsons left her and Caroline to serve the customer, seeing she was obviously a friend.

Caroline stepped forward to show the smart customer their newest creations. Harriet took off the flowered hat she was wearing and picked up another one to try on her glossy black hair.

'Is your husband still serving in Germany?' Caroline asked her.

'Yes,' she said shortly. Beatrice wondered if Harriet was no longer entirely happy with Wilfrid, but there was no way she could decently ask her former friend.

'And you've got a baby now?'

'Yes, little Cynthia.'

Caroline continued to show Harriet more of their hats which she thought might suit her. At one stage she toyed with the one Beatrice had made, though Caroline had not mentioned it was her design. Eventually Harriet chose a different one, though the style was similar. Caroline went to the other side of the shop to find a suitable box.

'Beatrice, I owe you an apology,' Harriet said suddenly, lowering her voice. 'You told me what Wilfrid is like, but I didn't believe you.'

'He was well-respected because of his war record,' Beatrice said, remembering the time she had been unwilling to believe Amy's warning about Wilfrid's conduct. Suddenly she was anxious to restore good relations.

'He has been convicted of assaulting women,' she said, wringing her hands. 'I keep hoping he will reform but he finds it hard to keep his hands off our maids. I have my little girl now and I don't want the scandal of a divorce. While he's in Germany I stay in London or with my parents near Wealdham, and have some respite.'

Beatrice felt sorry for her now.

'When he returns we will see how he behaves,' Harriet said. 'Perhaps I should take up an occupation, like you and Caroline.'

The latter returned with a smart hatbox and packed Harriet's purchase. 'It's been lovely seeing both of you again,' Harriet said as she left.

Chapter 17

France, summer 1921

Edmond and Amy drove to Larchbury on the last Friday of July. They spent two nights at The Beeches and took Beth to Amy's parents' house. She was looking forward to spending time with them.

On the Sunday they drove to Dover and crossed to France, thankful that the Channel was no longer mined, and drove south the following day. By late afternoon they saw a sign for Béthune, the attractive town where they had seized a weekend together in 1917. 'Shall we stop here and see if the same hotel has a room?' he asked.

'The place is in a bad state now, from what I've heard… But yes, let's stay here again.' Beth was likely to have been conceived there in the Easter of 1917.

As they approached, the road was in poor condition, almost as though they were still in the middle of a war zone. They bumped along its uneven surface.

'I didn't realise it was so bad here,' Amy said, half afraid she would feel sick like Florence had done on her trip to France.

'Around here it was bombarded in 1918, after we both came home,' Edmond reminded her. He was beginning to look anxious. 'I think there's something seriously wrong with our tyres.'

There was another signpost, for they were approaching the town. As they drove in, Amy's eyes opened wide at the devastation: little was recognisable of the Flemish town they had known. The famous belfry, from the top of which they had been able to see as far as Belgium, was still being repaired. Amy wiped a tear from her eye, while reminding herself that the human loss was what mattered most.

'We need to have the tyres checked,' Edmond said. He stopped and enquired of a passer-by. He had forgotten that the dialect was hard to understand in this part of Flanders, but eventually he was directed to a fairly basic garage where he might have his wheels examined. Soon two men, probably in their forties, were looking over the car with some interest, as though they seldom now had one like it to repair. There was a good deal of shrugging at the state of the tyres.

'We'll need to get it repaired ready for tomorrow morning,' Edmond said.

Amy boldly asked after the hotel they remembered and was told it was likely to have vacancies. They told the men of their wartime visit to the town. They looked down-hearted; it had been almost flattened by the bombardment in 1918, one of them said, and many of its citizens had been killed, along with German troops.

Two of the tyres needed changing, and suitable ones would have to be fetched from a different town the following morning. They left the car there and set off towards the square, still recognisable, where the top of the belfry was being reconstructed. From there they headed for the hotel. There were few young men to be seen in the streets, though some were toiling on rebuilding projects.

Older folk trudged through the streets, often in sabots, calling at the rundown market.

At last they reached the hotel, where Amy could even remember the middle-aged waiter who had served them in 1917. Before long he was shaking their hands as they were booked into it once more.

In the cool of the evening they waited downstairs in the hotel for a simple meal to be prepared. The dining room needed a fresh coat of paint, but there were still curtains of Flemish lace, and they had acquired mussels from the coast that day.

'I'm sorry that you have lost so many people and had your town damaged,' Amy said as the waiter served them local cider.

Soon he was telling them of the reconstruction plans. 'There is a scheme to rebuild the centre, with wide streets and modern sewage. Yet they are instructed to retain the pre-war layout, so that the Boches have not destroyed our traditional town – what a challenge for us to achieve!'

Soon they were enjoying the mussels. 'If only I'd fitted some new tyres before we came!' Edmond said. 'I'm sorry, darling, I should have taken more care and expected the roads might be in poor condition.'

'I'm still pleased to be passing through here again,' she said, though they were facing extra expense and a longer journey.

Next morning they had to wait while new tyres were fetched for them. They sat in the sunshine outside the remaining café, glancing from time to time at the work on the belfry. The church they had visited at Easter 1917 had also been damaged.

Eventually, in early afternoon, they set off again along the same route south, just west of Arras, which had been familiar while Amy had been nursing. The road was still in a poor state from being churned up by heavy army vehicles and occasionally hit by artillery.

They stopped outside Amy's hospital, which had been housed in a converted chateau. It did not look busy now, but there was still an ambulance outside, so it must have been providing some medical service, maybe for long-term war-wounded Frenchmen. They continued on their way, through farmland, where there were occasional craters.

'Years ago, before the war, you came to Europe on holiday,' she reminded him. 'Did you come through this area then?'

'Only briefly, on the way to Paris – and I wasn't especially curious about the region. But I believe it was pleasant and pastoral. How long will it take them to restore it to that state, I wonder?'

It was mid-afternoon. 'We've plenty of time to reach Amiens,' he said.

They carried on, passing a sign to Bapaume. 'Remember our outings when we had leave!' Edmond said. How they had longed for those snatched moments together.

A convent bell was sounding as Edmond drove into Amiens in early evening. 'Do you know where to find the hotel you remember from the war?' Amy asked, anxious that he must be growing tired.

'Yes, providing it's still standing,' he said. 'They fought over Amiens fiercely towards the end of the war, but by then we were winning.'

She was relieved when they reached the hotel. The manager seemed pleased to receive British visitors and found them a room. There was already a map in the lobby showing the whereabouts of allied war cemeteries. As they studied it, the manager, a trim middle-aged man, returned to talk to them in accented English.

'You fought near here?' he asked.

Edmond told him where he had fought in the great battles of summer 1916. 'We're here to visit the grave of my wife's brother, near Morval,' he said.

The Frenchman was sympathetic. 'My nephews fought at Verdun in the same year,' he told them. 'One died there. The other is back on his parents' farm, some ten kilometres from here.'

'I'm glad he's safe now,' Amy said.

'No one's really safe around here. They keep finding unexploded ordnance in the soil. A young man was blown up recently while he was tilling the ground.'

Amy murmured her regrets. Here she was again, back in the land where these horrors had taken place.

—

When Edmond woke up at first light a clock was striking five. The previous day they had passed an inconspicuous sign for Pozières and now he could not stop thinking of his terror the day he and Frank had had to lead their men into the attack near there. Soon after dawn they had surged up a stepladder and across No-Man's Land, with shells whistling past. How could he ever have expected to simply forget such memories?

But this time he had Amy beside him. He looked at her sweet face and blonde hair on the pillow beside him – how fortunate he was. She stretched for a moment and then fell asleep again.

He tried to concentrate on her beloved form, but his mind would not allow him peace. Near here both of

George's comrades had been killed on the same day, and later Bertie had died.

At the back of his mind an even more unspeakable shadow was trying to engulf him. There was that day the following year, much further north, near Ypres, when pieces of debris from a shell had pierced his right lung and nearly killed him. He began to tremble.

'Edmond, are you all right, darling?' Amy's arm came around him.

'Yes – I remembered going into battle when I was here before…'

She was kissing him and stroking his arm. 'Tell me about it.'

How could he do that? It might make her imagine what it was like for Bertie. He told her how the days had dragged on as they longed to make a significant advance, and of the casualties staggering back. She listened for a while, holding him in the cool dawn. He wished they had not come.

'Let's get up,' he said, for neither of them would sleep now.

At breakfast he looked around the dining room, wondering if some other guests had come to visit the cemetery, but if they had it might not be appropriate to intrude on their grief.

They set off in the car along the road through farmland. Occasionally a sign alerted them to the British cemetery ahead. The sunshine seemed inappropriate.

'Do your parents ever think of visiting?' he asked Amy.

'They're still trying to decide. Father is keen but Mother isn't sure she could bear it. They've neither of them been abroad before, and can speak very little French.'

At last they reached the great wrought iron gate and parked outside. As they approached he was transfixed by the rows of white gravestones he could see ahead. Hundreds or thousands of them, there must be.

–

Amy stopped by the flower seller and bought two bunches of red roses. Then they went inside. She noticed the chapel, and the lines of rosebushes between the rows of graves.

Her parents had been sent sheets of information about the cemetery. She had marked Bertie's details, and now she read out the row where his grave was to be found.

Edmond seized her hand and they walked along the pathway around the edge. Each gravestone was almost identical, simply stating the man's name, rank, regiment, date of death and age. Underneath was a simple cross carved into the white stone. In the distance, where the ground began to rise, was a partially completed line of headstones, with room for more beyond.

Ahead they could see a middle-aged couple bending in front of one of the memorials. There was also a gardener, busily trimming the nearby bushes. The area was calm, with just the sound of birdsong.

Amy squeezed his hand as she located the right row. They moved along, between the headstones, stopping in front of the one for Second Lieutenant Albert Fletcher. She bent down to lay the bunches of flowers on his grave: one from her, and one Florence had asked her to place there.

Looking at the pristine white headstone, she felt giddy. How could this be all that was left of Bertie? Sometimes, back in Larchbury, she still seemed to sense his presence as she walked into her parents' house, and hear his laughter. She remembered him as a boy, fishing in the brook and arriving home with a jam jar full of tiddlers. As they had grown up, he had been kind and supportive, when her parents had been dubious about her interest in the Suffragettes. And she recalled his merry courtship of Florence that last summer. That had been five years ago, and now she thought about it, by then he had been apt to fall quiet and anxious, having seen action in France.

Edmond put his arms about her as she began to shed tears, and pressed her to his chest. 'He was just a year older than me,' he said.

'He was nearly twenty-three when he died.' Once more she felt the raw, powerless feeling of despair at losing him.

'I can't tell you why it was decreed that Bertie should die so young, while I survived.' Edmond's face looked haggard.

Amy slipped away from him and stepped back from the grave. 'Look at that one,' she said, pointing to the neighbouring headstone. '*A soldier of the Great War*,' it proclaimed, '*known unto God*.' When they looked there were many more headstones with that inscription.

She lingered there for a while, committing the details to memory, so she could describe the scene to her parents and Florence. They walked back to the entrance. 'I think that middle-aged couple are staying in our hotel,' Amy said.

'I thought they looked familiar.'

'Thank you for taking me,' she said as they got back into the car. 'At least now I've paid my respects and seen what a peaceful place they've found for him.'

'I know what my task is now,' Edmond said. 'I must make sure Bertie and the other unfortunates like him are never forgotten.'

—

That evening in the hotel, Amy saw the couple they had noticed in the graveyard. The woman smiled at her and the pair came to their table, introducing themselves as Mr and Mrs Swan. 'Our son was lost on the first day of the fighting on the Somme,' they said.

They went on to tell Amy and Edmond of their struggles to reach their son's grave. 'We've never been abroad before, and we don't speak the language,' Mr Swan said. 'It was a huge effort to find our way here on the trains, and to find somewhere to stay. Then we had to make our way to the cemetery by taxi.'

Amy wished they had introduced themselves earlier. They might have driven the couple to the cemetery. They all agreed that the peaceful atmosphere had been comforting.

'Can I help you in any way?' Edmond asked them. 'I can speak reasonable French.' He went through the menu with them and ordered their evening meal.

Their new acquaintances were setting off back the following day.

—

Next morning Edmond drove them to the station and helped them buy tickets to the port.

'People like them need suitable assistance to visit their relatives,' Amy said, when the older couple had left. 'There should be an organisation to arrange their travel. I'm going to mention it to Uncle Arthur and James.'

They got back into the car. 'Mind if we go to another cemetery today?' Edmond asked her. They drove elsewhere in the Somme area and briefly visited the resting place of the two Larchbury boys who had been George's comrades.

In late afternoon they took a short walk around Amiens.

'The manager told me the cathedral has been left as it was just after the 1918 offensive,' said Edmond. They found the windows were still boarded up. At one time it had not been expected to survive the German onslaught, but the enemy had been sent into retreat. They stared up at the cracked glass, wondering when it might be repaired.

In some areas of the town the damage was not too noticeable. They sat down at a bar on the pavement of one of the main streets, and Edmond ordered a beer and some cider for her. As a couple sat down at a nearby table, he caught a snatch of conversation and exchanged glances with Amy.

'That's German,' he whispered.

'I thought it was.' Without making any serious progress while she had been nursing in France, her French had improved a little and she had picked up a very few words of German.

'Are there German cemeteries near here as well?' she asked. 'I suppose there must be.'

'Yes, though I expect they try to keep British and German visitors from staying in the same hotels.'

As the German couple went on talking she thought she heard the word 'Albrecht.'

'The Germans have come to visit the grave of someone called Albrecht,' Edmond whispered.

'I'm sure that's the German equivalent of Albert!' she exclaimed. She had to force herself not to begin crying. They hurried to finish their drinks and he paid and took her hand as they left.

'Is that too much for you, discovering the family of his German opposite number?' he asked her.

'It underlines the futility of it all,' she said. As she thought about it some more she felt only sympathy for the German family.

The following day they returned to the cemetery for one more visit to Bertie's grave. This time they went to the chapel and said a prayer for him. Then they prepared to set off back north, heading for Belgium. Now it was Amy's turn to worry whether the return to the Ypres area would be traumatic for Edmond.

'Can we bypass Ypres?' she asked, as they waited to be served lunch in a café. She was unwilling to risk them seeing the hospital where he had nearly died.

He spread out the map on the café table, and ran his finger along a route north-east. 'It's more direct to go south of Wipers, towards Cambrai, and carry on to the Belgian border in that direction.'

She got up and followed his finger as he indicated his preferred route. 'Yes – that way's far shorter.'

A sudden memory taunted him. 'Confounded Wilfrid Fairlawn molested you in Ypres, didn't he?'

Just hearing his name made her feel shaky. 'That's another reason to avoid Ypres.'

Chapter 18

France and Belgium, summer 1921

On the way to Cambrai they could see stretches of land still covered with trees reduced to stumps, some weirdly sprouting with fresh growth. They reached the Belgian border many miles south of Ypres but it was unsettling even to see it signposted.

'Are you all right, darling?' Amy asked him.

'Yes,' he said, but he clung to the steering wheel, anxious he might veer off the road as memories overtook him. There was Charles's account of men drowning in the mud, besides his own recollection of being hit by the shell.

The early evening sunshine was bright as he drove cautiously along the route to Mons. Edmond had never been to the town, but knew that a battle had taken place there at the start of the war, and the final shot had been fired there too, when the Canadians had liberated it. It was largely brick-built and they were relieved that it was not as badly damaged as Ypres. They found a small hotel to spend the night, and the following morning Edmond continued eastwards. With occasional glimpses of the Sambre river they drove on, Amy following the map to keep to the route south of Brussels. The signs changed from Flemish to French as they headed towards Namur.

'It's exhausting for you,' Amy said as they stopped for lunch nearby. 'I should learn to drive.' She had tried it once and the demand for unfamiliar skills had made her nervous.

'We should have allowed longer for the trip,' he said.

'I don't like leaving Beth so long. She loves Mother and Father, and they're devoted to her, but by now she might be missing us, and tiring them out. And I so miss seeing her.'

'Yes, me too.'

Every day she kept wondering what her daughter was doing. She had sent a letter to her parents, with a message for Beth, but it might take a few days to reach them.

At last they found themselves heading towards the Ardennes hills and Liège.

He was weary as they drove through the outskirts, and then the broad streets of the centre and over the bridge across the wide Meuse river. As he drove she read out the directions Madame Rousseau had sent them, driving up a steep street and then turning off and stopping outside a stone cottage.

They got out and Amy knocked at the door. It opened, and there stood her Belgian friend with a broad smile. 'Welcome to Liège!' she exclaimed, ushering them inside. 'How is your little one? And how is dear Florence?'

They followed her into a small sitting room at the back of the house, with attractive lace curtains. Their hostess fetched them some coffee. 'How far did you come today?'

They told her.

'That was a long journey for you. Yolande works in a shop now, but she will be home soon and we will take a meal. You must meet my father, too. He has been gardening and has gone to wash before he comes to meet you.'

There was suddenly a commotion at the back of the house, and through the curtains he could see the outline of a train passing.

A stooped, grey-haired man of about seventy came in.

'Meet Fernand Renard, my papa,' Madame Rousseau said. 'We moved in with him after my husband fell ill and died in 1910.'

'I not have much English,' he said.

'I am pleased to meet you,' Edmond said.

As her father was eager to talk to them, Madame Rousseau sometimes translated his French, but they could understand some words and he could follow some English.

'I've often wondered what it was like for you to leave your country,' Amy said to Madame Rousseau.

'Some of the Germans were violating women, including girls as young as Yolande was then,' she said. 'I felt we should leave. It was very strange to start with, trying to settle in a new country, but I still believe we did the right thing. Do you remember where we stayed at first, Amy, in that large house in Wealdham? We must have had six families or more, all crammed in.'

Edmond wanted to know what it was like for her father, living under German occupation.

'Did you know we tried to halt their advance?' Papa said, a faraway look in his eyes. He was speaking in French now and Madame Rousseau had to translate for them. 'We held the forts on the Meuse. I had just retired from working on the railway, and sometimes at night I helped the others sabotage the rails so the Boches could not advance. Then they succeeded in bringing their Big Bertha gun this far. They aimed it at the forts to demolish them – at one we lost two hundred and fifty men, buried in the rubble.' His daughter looked dismayed as a tear trickled from his eye. 'I lost a lot of friends that day. We were all stunned. After that we could not hold back the Germans.'

'We heard about you in England,' Edmond said. 'You delayed the German advance for long enough to allow the British and French to mobilise.'

At this point they heard the front door opening and soon a young woman hurried into the room and greeted them in English. Edmond had not met Yolande before. He supposed she was around the same age as Vicky. She had long black hair and lively dark eyes.

'You've grown up since we last met,' Amy said, embracing her.

Soon Madame Rousseau and Yolande went into their kitchen to prepare a meal. Amy followed them to help.

'We never gave up here, you know,' Papa told Edmond, struggling to speak in English. 'You don't know what it is like to be invaded, you others. But our king stayed on a small section of the coast, between the sea, the Yser river and the flooded Nieuwpoort sluices. There was always a – what you say – corner of free Belgium.'

It became harder to talk while a heavy goods train passed at the end of their short garden. Edmond was tired from all the driving and was finding it difficult to concentrate on his host's memories.

'We did our best to help the British and French,' he went on, with a mischievous grin. 'I was one of those who watched the traffic going by on the railway, the main line from the German border to Brussels, and passed on information about troop movements and other important concerns.'

Suddenly Edmond became wide awake, remembering what Peter had told him. 'My brother worked for High Command,' he said. 'He told me they were getting important information from sympathisers in Belgium.'

Yolande came in and began setting the table.

'We often sent information by pigeon at first,' Papa said. 'As the Germans became suspicious it was much harder.' As he struggled with words Yolande helped him. 'We had to travel to pass on the information, and we had to memorise it, or write it in some disguised form so the Germans could not tell what we were doing. I had already attracted attention, for the Boches had heard that my family had left for England. I had to maintain the appearance of an old man who pays little attention to what is going on around him.'

Edmond was curious and would like to have learnt more, but Madame Rousseau was bringing in a platter of cold meat and portions of pâté. Amy followed with a large bowl of salad. Soon they were sitting around the table.

'Help yourselves to our Ardennes ham and boar pâté,' Madame Rousseau said. Talk of the war was interrupted while they ate, and fatigue overcame him once more.

'I believe we should go to bed soon,' Amy said. 'Edmond is much fitter now, but he still tires easily, and it's been a long day.'

Soon they were lying close together beneath the sloping ceiling in the spare room in the attic. Edmond was thankful the noisy trains were becoming less frequent.

'Papa told me about his wartime activities,' he told Amy, for he was still full of admiration for the old man's bravery. He began to tell her about the information he and his friends had passed on.

'I seem to remember Madame Rousseau saying that she could imagine her father watching the trains go by and giving information to the allies,' she said.

As they talked he was finding it hard to keep his eyes open. The next thing he knew it was morning, and another train was passing the little house.

—

When he got up there was a strong smell of coffee. Since arriving on the Continent he had been reminded how strong it was often served on this side of the Channel, and its strength was consistent now, whereas sometimes in the war it had been weaker.

It was Sunday and they accompanied Madame Rousseau and her family to the local church. 'It will be a Catholic service, of course,' their hostess advised them.

'We worship the same God,' Amy told her. 'We went to the Easter service in Béthune when we were there in 1917.'

A young man greeted Yolande when they arrived at the church, and after the service he accompanied them back to their house.

'This is Marcel,' Yolande told them. He was dark with a broad face, and walked with a slight limp. He seemed very attached to Yolande, and Edmond thought Marcel might be three or four years older than she was.

'I understand you were injured at Ypres,' Marcel asked him. His English was good as he was studying the language at university.

'Edmond nearly died,' Amy said hastily. She was very protective of his feelings when someone raised the subject.

'I was more fortunate than some of my comrades,' he told the Belgian. 'I took a long while to recover, but now I'm in good shape.'

What had Marcel done in the war, Edmond wondered, as they all sat in the tiny living room.

The Belgian seemed to guess his thoughts. 'When the Boches invaded I escaped to Holland,' he told them. 'I was able to reach France and fight alongside the French.'

Papa Renard looked at him approvingly. 'Marcel took a great risk. If he had been discovered trying to escape, the Boches could have shot him.'

'I was fortunate to have found an escape line to join.'

Yolande and Amy joined Madame as she prepared lunch. Edmond was intrigued to hear Marcel's account of the fighting around Verdun, where he had sustained a relatively minor injury to his leg.

At length, lunch was served. Madame brought them glasses of beer to drink with their veal in white sauce. 'We don't grow grapes for wine in Belgium,' she explained, 'but we have many famous beers, often produced in the monasteries.'

Edmond drank the brew appreciatively, but Amy was sipping dubiously from her glass, unaccustomed to drinking beer.

The conversation drifted back to the war. Edmond was curious about Marcel's escape from Belgium. 'We would be furnished with false passports, saying we were Dutch. I speak French, and Walloon, the dialect around here, but I can also speak Flemish, and most Germans can't tell it from Dutch. We would have some kind of cover story for why we happened to be in Belgium.'

'It sounds very dangerous,' Edmond said with admiration. He was reminded of the risks Peter had taken, even travelling across the front line to Belgium through a tunnel to gather information.

'I wasn't one of the first to leave, and as we waited to set off, the Germans were becoming increasingly suspicious.'

Edmond could barely concentrate on his meal as he listened to Marcel's account. 'We were lucky to have a young man travelling in the same train carriage who was posing as a German officer, though he was a sympathiser. I heard he carried out a few trips, and if there was any trouble he would tell the Germans that he had the authority to check papers and arrest anyone suspect. He played the part very well and the Boches allowed him to vouch for the travellers. They stopped me and my companion Antoine as we approached the Dutch border and I was terrified we'd be captured, or shot outright. The phoney officer was so convincingly German I was afraid he would suddenly betray us.'

'Who was he really?'

'He claimed to be Leutnant Bauer. Among those of us who escaped there was a lot of curiosity about him. One of the Belgian officers had got to know him better than the rest of us, and called him Johann. He spoke German like a native. The rumour was that he came from Alsace, that area on the border which has changed sides between the French and Germans several times.'

Something in the story sounded familiar, but Edmond could not fathom what it was.

'It was a very dangerous life they led, men like him,' Papa Renard said.

'Yes, I remember now, something terrifying happened as we made our escape,' Marcel said. 'We had just left the train and were crossing the border into Holland, followed by Johann, the supposed German officer. Holland was neutral, so anyone could travel there. My comrade Antoine is a hothead. As he stepped on to Dutch territory he sang a line of the Brabançonne, our national anthem, and stuck out his tongue to some Germans who had been in our carriage.'

Edmond listened, fascinated.

'It must have been a shock to them to realise we were not the Dutchmen they supposed us to be,' Marcel went on. 'One of them suspected suddenly that Johann was not who he claimed to be, and screamed at him and fired his gun. Then another German joined in. Johann started running, but they hit him in the arm. They began firing on us too, so we dashed off as fast as we could. We managed to get away from the border, well into Holland, but I never knew for certain if Johann was all right, or got the chance to thank him.'

Amy had looked up from her lunch, gripped by his story.

'I don't often talk of that time,' Marcel said. 'It makes me nervous even to think of it, and sometimes I have nightmares afterwards. Antoine nearly had us both shot. He was a complete imbecile. I had as little as possible to do with him afterwards.'

Marcel was happier telling them of his joyful return to his home country after the war. He was glad to talk to them to improve his English.

Edmond's new glimpses of life on the Continent during the war were stimulating, but soon Marcel was wanting to hear what was happening in England.

Madame Rousseau began to suggest what Edmond and Amy might do the following day.

'I should like to buy a present for Beth,' Amy said. 'Then we shall have to leave early on Tuesday. I'd like to stay longer, but we need to get back to her – I'm longing to see her again.'

–

Madame Rousseau accompanied Amy to a smart shop to buy a doll in a pretty lace dress. 'Beth will love it,' she said.

The following day they avoided Ypres again and crossed into France near Lille, before heading north-west towards the coast. It was another long drive and Amy persuaded Edmond to let her take the wheel for a while on a quiet stretch of road. She tried to conceal what a strain it was for her, concentrating hard to maintain a smooth path on the right-hand side of the road. She was relieved when they changed places again. The late afternoon was hot as they drove into Calais.

'We probably won't get a ferry this late,' he said. 'We'll need to find a hotel.'

They parked near the sea and got out to walk along a quiet stretch of the front, enjoying the sea breeze and view of the peaceful pale blue Channel.

'I'm so glad we came,' she said. Apart from visiting Bertie's grave, the continental countries had worked their charm, even so soon after the war.

Edmond was growing tired and they sat down on a bench. 'I've been thinking about what Marcel told us on Sunday,' he said.

'How brave some men were!'

'He mentioned someone called Leutnant Bauer, posing as a German officer. Does that remind you of anyone?'

She racked her brain unsuccessfully for a moment or two.

'I was thinking of Max,' he said. 'He had a passport claiming he was a German officer. Can you recall the name he used? I seem to remember he was supposed to be Johann Bauer.'

She gasped. 'I believe you may be right! Do you think he was helping men to escape from Belgium?'

'That's what I was wondering. It's very brave of him if that was his mission there.'

'James might know – he and Uncle Arthur have kept in touch with him – and Vicky, of course. We must ask them.'

'Charles has a friend who escaped from Belgium early in the war,' he said, his eyes lighting up. 'He even knew Nurse Cavell – she helped arrange his escape from a hospital. I believe he mentioned a man posing as a German officer.'

She was thrilled at the thought that Max might have been involved in such an enterprise.

'It's astonishing what people did,' he said. 'You should hear what Peter got up to.'

'I'd love to hear, but you won't tell me.'

'Not just yet. It's still secret.'

Soon they got up and walked back to the car, to find a hotel.

'We must come back again for another holiday,' he said. 'The reconstruction will go on and the towns will get more like they were before the war.'

'Yes,' she agreed. Their memories were very mixed, and sometimes horrific, yet there was much that was memorable or even inspiring. 'I want to remember our meetings, when we'd make the most of a weekend together, or even a few hours.'

'You'd ride on the back of my motorbike!'

She had scandalised Sister Reed with her unladylike behaviour, but it had all been worth it.

How soon could they come this side of the Channel again? She could not give up the idea that it was time to have another child, if they were fortunate in her next pregnancy. With a baby, as well as an older child, it would be harder to travel. It was high time Beth had a brother or sister.

Back then, in the turmoil of war, she had been unable to see their way ahead. Even now, in these more secure times, she could not be certain what lay in the future.

Chapter 19

Larchbury, August 1921

'So, at least Bertie's last resting place is calm and dignified,' Amy told Florence.

'One day I'll go and visit the cemetery, I promise.' They were lounging in the vicarage garden, while Beth, just collected from her grandparents' house, examined the flowerbeds. With Aunt Sophie's permission she began picking marigolds.

Florence was growing larger as her pregnancy advanced, and had given up her job at the end of term.

'I hope to take up teaching again one day,' she said, 'though they don't normally employ married women, now men are returning from the war. Do you think they'll take us back one day? I'd like to continue in my profession.'

'They should see it'll be a waste of your training if they don't allow it.'

'I saw Lavinia the other day. She's happy to be wife to Charles and mother of Christopher, but I can tell she's frustrated at spending so much time at home on domestic tasks.'

Amy told Florence more about her trip. 'We met another couple, visiting their son's grave. They didn't speak much French and were having trouble finding their way around, till Edmond helped them. There should be some provision for families visiting the cemeteries – people advising them how to travel to the area, making bookings for them and so on. Have James and Uncle ever thought of helping with an enterprise like that?'

'I don't know – I'll ask them. But they really need tour guides to conduct groups of relatives there, don't they?'

'Perhaps someone could teach them basic French before they go, enough to make themselves understood with the essentials.'

'Most people won't just launch themselves there like I did in my school holidays!' Florence blushed a little. 'I can hardly believe how rashly I set off there in 1918 to see James while he was convalescing. And I nearly ruined the whole trip by being sick when I had to travel on Lavinia's motorbike.'

When they had finished laughing at her exploits, Amy went on to tell her about their visit to Belgium. Florence was pleased to hear that Madame Rousseau and Yolande were happily restored to their homeland.

'We heard a very interesting story about a young Belgian chap who escaped the country via Holland,' Amy told her next. 'He was helped by someone posing as a German officer. He said the man was from Alsace, claiming to be a Leutnant Bauer.'

'People had some extraordinary experiences, didn't they?' Florence did not grasp the reason for her particular interest.

'Remember how Max had a passport under a false name, identifying him as a German officer?'

'Oh, yes, I believe he did. Could he have been involved in an undertaking like that?'

'Can you remember the name on his passport? We thought it might have been Bauer.'

'Goodness, could that have been him? I can't honestly remember the name he used, but James or his father might remember.'

James was out, for he now worked for the British Legion, which had a branch in Wealdham. Amy and Florence went into the vicarage, dim after the bright sunshine, with Beth following. Aunt Sophie poured the little girl some lemonade. Amy and Florence went and knocked on the door of her uncle's study. He summoned them inside and looked up from a book, pleased to see them.

Amy asked him about Max. He was still in touch with the young man.

'Yes – I believe you're right – it could well be him.'

'Can you remember the first name that was on his passport?'

'It was Johann, I think.'

'I always found it hard to believe he was our enemy,' Amy said. 'But what a complicated life he must have led, during the war!'

'That's my impression. With so much deception behind him it must be hard to resume a normal life.'

–

Mr Derwent stared uphill from his garden at the remains of his forest, silhouetted against another blue sky. He had got up late after spending the previous night up there, then snatching a few hours' sleep. Soon he must return there.

When he went indoors for lunch his wife looked in distaste at his ancient plus-fours. 'Must you really go back to work?' she complained.

'It's very unfortunate that Ross is injured, just when I need him most,' he said, suppressing a yawn.

Ross, his best worker, had fallen over a tree root and sprained his ankle. He was not expected to return to work for several days.

Just as they finished lunch, a visitor arrived. Mr Derwent looked up in surprise at the tall young man in American uniform. It was Beatrice's friend.

'Good day, Caleb. How are you? Would you care for some lunch?' There would be leftovers from the cold meat and salad Cook had served them.

'Thank you, Mr Derwent, but I've just eaten at the inn.'

'Then join us in the drawing room for coffee.' He rang the bell to ask Cook for an extra cup.

His wife was staring at the young man. *Are we supposed to be expecting him*, Mr Derwent wondered as they all settled in the easy chairs. He did not remember Beatrice mentioning a visit from her admirer.

'How are you getting on in the Rhineland?'

'It's quite tedious, Sir, but sometimes we can make a trip to a different area, like the towns along the Mosel.'

'I'm afraid Beatrice isn't here this afternoon. Have you heard she's serving in the hat shop in the village?'

'Is that so? No, she wrote in a letter that she was making and decorating hats, but I didn't know she was working in the shop.'

'She didn't tell us you might be coming,' said his wife.

'I wrote her that I had leave – didn't she say?'

'I don't remember there being any recent mail from Germany,' he said.

Cook came and poured them coffee.

'It's those confounded Huns!' Caleb cried. 'They resent the occupation and seize opportunities for sabotage.

We don't generally let them handle our mail, but if they get half a chance some of them will interfere with it.'

'Did Beatrice tell you about the fire?' Pa asked. 'Our circumstances have changed somewhat since you last came.'

'Yes, Sir. I heard it was severe, but I hadn't grasped the extent till just now. As I was coming up the drive I could see how much the forest has been affected. It must have been very frightening and upsetting. My uncle manages a small forest near where I live, and I've worked there a couple of times in my school holidays.'

Mr Derwent knew his wife did not approve of Caleb, but he was growing to like and respect him. 'I'm afraid Beatrice won't be back till about six,' he said, 'but you're welcome to dine with us this evening. You might want to go back to the inn until later. I'm afraid I need to go up to the forest, as I'm short of workers just now.'

Caleb seemed to hesitate.

'You could come up there and look around, if you'd like to,' he suggested.

'Thank you, Mr Derwent. I might be able to give you a hand.'

'I don't expect you to work!'

'I'd be happy to help. I've done forestry before.'

If the young chap is willing I'll gladly find him a suitable task, he thought. 'Your uniform looks quite new – better change into some old clothes. I'll see what's left in Peter's room, he's about your size.'

When Caleb was suitably dressed they climbed the hill; the smell of scorched wood was still noticeable.

As they approached the forest his workers touched their caps before continuing with their work. They had cleared much of the burnt side of the forest, but some blackened wood remained. From the summit there was a view downhill towards Alderbank, and Wealdham beyond, which had not been visible before.

'I'm doing my best to carry on as normal with the eastern area,' Mr Derwent said. 'As you see, we've also begun to replant the western side, but the trees there are little more than saplings. We're hoping some will be ready to sell by December, for Christmas trees. Do you have Christmas trees in America?'

'Yes, we do – some Americans have German origins and they first introduced them.'

'Here people stopped buying them during the war, but they're gradually becoming popular again.'

He checked that his workers were continuing with their tasks from the previous day. They paused as he introduced the American soldier. 'I'm showing him around the plantation,' he said. 'What's left of it, that is.'

The men went back to work.

'Two of them are cutting down some of the remaining trees for timber, as you see.' Those nearest the blaze were singed on one side and their branches drooped where they had been exposed to the heat.

'The other chaps are keeping the firebreak clear, and making a new one to divide the remaining trees,' he told his visitor. 'Now the weather is dry again I'm terrified of another fire breaking out.'

'It must be very worrying while the drought lasts.'

'The forest is our source of income,' he admitted. 'Just when I've so much to do to replant it, Ross, my most experienced worker is injured. And Joe, who splits his work between the garden and the forest, is recovering from a bad burn from the night we were fighting the blaze.

He's made progress – they've released him from hospital – but he's not quite fit enough to return to work yet.'

'Listen, Mr Derwent, I'll be very glad to help.'

He looked once again at the young soldier. The army life would have kept him fit, he supposed. 'If you're sure, you could help George and Bill clearing the fresh growth along the firebreak.'

'Sure.'

'If you get tired you must stop. I don't normally make my guests work!'

'It'll be a pleasure.'

For a while he watched his new helper swinging an axe confidently to hack back the new growth. Then he went on to join the other men in their efforts.

–

Beatrice arrived home around ten past six, a little tired, for the shop had been busy, but glad that she had sold one of her own hats.

'That soldier friend of yours is here,' her mother told her.

'Caleb? I didn't even know he had leave!' If only he had told her she might have been able to take a day off work.

'He's waiting for you on the veranda.'

She went to her room to comb her hair, then hurried down.

'What a lovely surprise!' she exclaimed, rushing on to the veranda, which was warm in the late afternoon sun.

He stood up, caught her hands in his and kissed her respectfully on the cheek. 'I've been longing to see you.'

He explained that he had written but the letter seemed to have gone missing in the post.

'I'd have been here if I'd known you were coming,' she said, sitting down in one of the wicker chairs. He sat beside her. On the glass-topped table was a half-full teacup.

'I'm glad they're looking after you. How long have you been here?'

'Since around one o'clock. I've been helping your father in the forest.'

'Really? You've been helping with the plantation?' She was quite shocked at the idea of him working there.

'If your father works there why shouldn't I? I've done similar work occasionally for my uncle. I can see how concerned your father is.'

'So, you didn't find the work too hard? I'm sure Pa was very grateful.'

Cook bustled out with a fresh pot of tea and poured a cup for Beatrice. 'Are you ready for another cup, Sir?'

'Just top this one up, would you? Thank you.'

'I stayed up there till about five,' he told Beatrice, 'then I came down to wash and change before you arrived home. I didn't know you were actually serving in the hat shop. Do you enjoy the work?'

'Yes, I do. I'm not used to working, I have to say, but when I think what some women did during the war, it's very light work and I'm interested in fashion, and millinery in particular.'

'It sounds like a very refined kind of work. I imagine you're good at it.'

She touched his arm lightly. 'Listen, Caleb, I don't know if you realise, but we're less well-off now we've lost half the forest. I know Pa is desperately worried, though he won't admit it, and Ma expects to enjoy all the advantages she's used to. It was an easy decision for me to apply for the vacancy in the shop. It means I don't need an allowance from Pa anymore for clothes, outings and such like.'

Until recently she could not have imagined working, but now she was proud of her progress. She felt a warm glow as he seemed impressed.

'Your father told me he goes up to the forest at night, to watch over it.'

'I'm worried about him – he's exhausting himself. If only my brother Peter hadn't been determined to return to India. Pa is terrified of there being another fire. There's a water tower up there, but when the fire broke out that night it was well established before anyone realised what was happening. There was a lightning strike which set it off, without any rain to quench it. He couldn't bear it if it happened again – neither could I. So he'll go and sit up there all night, until the men arrive for work in the morning.'

'Good heavens, he must be wearing himself out.'

'George and one of the others have done the occasional night – so did Ross, before his fall. But Pa is up there several times a week, and wants to carry on until there's a good rainfall.'

'Well, he won't be setting out to do it tonight,' Caleb asserted. 'I'll go up there and do it for him.'

'Would you?' Relief swept over her. 'I'd be so grateful if you would. He won't want to impose on you, but I'll back you up and so will Ma, I'm sure.'

Pa was reluctant to take advantage of his visitor.

'I'm used to doing guard duty at night,' Caleb insisted.

'I dare say, but you're on leave now.'

'You've made me welcome here several times. I'd like to help.'

'Very well. I'd certainly appreciate a night off. Cook will have some leftover soup for you to take in a thermos flask. And if it rains a significant amount, you can come back to the house, as the danger will be over for the night.'

–

Beatrice awoke, refreshed, to thin sunshine, just after six in the morning. She wondered what kind of night Caleb had spent up at the forest.

Her window was open and she could hear the birds singing. She got up, slipped into some clothes and went to the kitchen, which was empty. She prepared some coffee and took some rolls from the larder. Slipping into a lightweight jacket she set off up the hill. By now Caleb would be glad of some breakfast.

The morning was fresh and invigorating, so she was only a little out of breath as she approached the treeline and saw Caleb sitting on a bench facing the forest. As he heard her approach he looked around and broke into a smile.

'Hello, darling,' he said, catching her in his arms and kissing her on the mouth. They lingered for a while in the embrace, welcoming the privacy of their early morning encounter. Then they sat together on the bench and enjoyed breakfast.

'It was an uneventful night, I'm glad to say,' he told her.

'Pa said you were a great help in the forest yesterday.'

'I'd like to help him some more while I'm here.'

'How long are you staying?'

'Only a week, I'm afraid.' He put his arm around her and directed the gaze from his light blue eyes towards her. 'I long to spend more time with you. There's talk that we may be allowed to apply for discharge fairly soon. We're to hand over our occupation area to the French in two years' time.'

'Oh – what will you do then?' She hardly dared look at him, afraid he would talk of returning to his family in America. Would he ask her to go with him, and would she want to take the drastic step of leaving her family? It would be hard for all of them. When Peter had just left for a far continent, how could she distress her parents further by leaving for another distant destination?

'I don't know,' he said. 'I just know I want us to have a future together.'

'So do I!' She nestled into his shoulder, until from the corner of her eye she noticed a distant movement. George was arriving for work. 'We can go back to the house now and you can catch up on your sleep.'

Chapter 20

Wealdham, Larchbury and Alderbank, late summer 1921

'Max! I didn't expect to see you!' Vicky found him waiting outside the hospital when she came off duty. They did not manage to meet every week, now he worked so far away, but did their best. She hugged him quickly, hoping none of the sisters was watching.

'I've some good news.' His face was suntanned as it usually was in summer. He kissed her lightly on the cheek, then took her arm and linked it through his. 'Let's go and eat. Would you mind going to that place near the station?'

'No, fine.' He could not afford to take her to The Pigeons every time they met. They set off downhill through the mild evening. It was August, and in three months she would be twenty-one, old enough to marry without her parents' consent. He still seemed as eager as she that it would happen. 'What have you got to tell me?'

'Let's sit down and order our meal first.'

Impatiently she preceded him into the little café and they ordered a chicken dish from its limited menu.

'Let's have a bottle of wine,' he said, ordering a modest white.

He leant across their table and took her hand. 'What do you think? They're taking on another chef at The Pigeons, and I applied for the position. I came to see the manager this afternoon, but I didn't want to raise your hopes in case they had other, better, applicants. Anyway, I have succeeded in getting the job!'

'Oh, darling, that's simply wonderful!' Unexpected joy coursed through her. 'So we'll be living in the same town at last.' She knew that he had used his time wisely at the hotel in London, gaining experience of new dishes.

'In November we can get married,' he said. 'You do still want to, don't you, darling?'

'Of course I do!'

'I haven't much to offer – you could find a husband with a good income and a conventional British background...'

'It's you I want.'

'Just as well,' he said, taking a small box from his pocket and passing it to her.

Breathlessly she opened it. Inside was a dainty ring with tiny amethysts. 'It's lovely!' she gasped.

He eased it on to her finger.

'It's a good fit as well,' she approved.

'I wish I could have bought you something more valuable, with larger stones,' he said, 'but this second-hand one was all I can afford, for now at least.'

'It's perfect. At last it seems real that we'll actually be married in the autumn!'

The waiter was hovering with their bottle of wine, smiling for he had realised it was their special moment. After Max had approved it, he poured it for them.

They chinked glasses.

'We'll need to find somewhere to live,' she said, 'lodgings in Wealdham.' *Somewhere we can afford*, she thought anxiously. *We'll both be working... both with difficult hours.* 'We'll be together, that's what matters.'

'Your parents still don't approve of me?'

She had tried to persuade them of his merits, and the importance of his wartime work, shrouded with subterfuge as it was. 'I'm afraid I haven't persuaded them,' she said. *It would be so simple if I could marry from my parents' house, like a normal bride.*

'Are you a Catholic?' she asked, suddenly worried there might be another complication.

'No, I've been brought up Protestant. As you can imagine, in a city like Strasbourg we have both faiths represented. The cathedral has been both Catholic and Protestant over the centuries – these days it's Catholic.'

'At least there'll be no difficulty about us worshipping together!'

As their meal arrived, she reviewed what was needed. 'Should we marry in Larchbury?' she asked.

'Yes, let's do that. The vicar and James have been kind to me, so understanding.'

'I need someone to give me away. I don't know if Uncle Hugh will be prepared to take on the role, as my parents oppose the wedding. But I think Edmond would be happy to do it. What about your family? Will any of them come from Strasbourg?'

'I doubt it. I thought we might travel there for our honeymoon. The situation there is still confused, I understand, but you should meet my family.'

'Of course. That would be wonderful.' Travelling to his hometown on the Continent would be exciting, though from what she had heard there were still political tensions there.

And I need a bridesmaid, she thought – *no, I'll ask Amy to be matron of honour. Perhaps Beth could be a tiny bridesmaid, too. And I need a dress, and somewhere to set out from, other than my home. If we're not careful this wedding will be a travesty. Will there be any guests, even?*

But in the end, that's not what matters, she concluded.

She looked up, catching the longing expression in his deep blue eyes. We'll be together, at last.

—

'I must thank you for making me so welcome,' Caleb said to Mr Derwent as they and Beatrice sat on the veranda on the final day before he had to return to the Rhineland. Ma was taking her afternoon nap, which had become a regular occurrence.

'On the contrary, you've given me some invaluable help.'

Instead of staying at the inn, Caleb had moved to The Beeches and stayed in Peter's room, so he was able to help Pa, including watching the forest at night once more. After a few days there had been a heavy rainstorm, and the danger of fire had passed.

Pa got up and went back into the house.

'However long will it be till I see you again?' Beatrice asked Caleb.

'I'll get my discharge as soon as I can.'

'Listen, Pa was talking to me a few evenings ago, when you spent the night in the forest. He said when you're discharged, if you ever wanted to work for him in the plantation he'd be happy to take you on – in a managerial position as you clearly know what you're doing and can give guidance to the others. He didn't know whether to suggest it to you, or if you'd feel it wasn't a suitable job for you.'

He took her hand. 'Beatrice, I was just wishing for the same thing. I had thought once I should try going to university and bettering myself, but I think I might be happier in an outdoor, physical job. The army prepares you for that kind of life… but above all, it would give me the ideal chance to be here with you. And I've dealt with vehicles in the army – I can keep your father's car in good order.'

'Edmond is the one who could do with some help, I think. He bought that scruffy car because it was cheap.'

'Next time he and I are both here, I'll certainly look it over and see what attention it needs.'

'What about America? Would you want to go back?'

'For visits, of course, to see my folks – but I've come to enjoy being in Europe.'

'Caleb, Pa knows we want to be together. I'm sure he'd accept you as a son-in-law. Even Ma might come around to the idea eventually.'

'I've felt that they might think of me as a fortune-seeker.'

'Caleb, we aren't wealthy anymore!'

'Look, I sure am sorry about what happened to your plantation, but it makes it less embarrassing for me to ask for your hand.'

'There's something else, that Pa hasn't mentioned yet. He used to hope that Peter or Edmond would want to take charge of the forest when he's ready to retire. It's been a great disappointment that neither of them wants to do that. I think, if we were married, he might consider you for the position. He hasn't said anything to me about it – he'd first want to make very sure that you've got the abilities required. I think you could do it.'

'That would be wonderful, Beatrice, but I mustn't presume. I'll speak to your father tonight about my plans. Darling, will you marry me?'

'Yes, Caleb – I've never felt the same about anyone else.' As he enclosed her in his arms and kissed her tenderly, she was engulfed by the bliss that had eluded her for so long.

–

'So there's no fête this year?' Edmond asked when he, Amy and Beth spent a weekend at The Beeches in early September.

'We couldn't hold it here this year,' Ma said. 'We always provided some free refreshments, and this year we're short of money, and staff.' They were relaxing on the veranda after lunch. Beth had gone to the kitchen with Cook, who had offered to let her help make a cake.

'I couldn't face welcoming the public to our garden, when the forest is still looking so ravaged,' Pa said. 'Even the gardens are unkempt, for I've needed George and Joe to help in the forest.'

'I'm glad he's recovered now,' Amy said. Joe had recently returned to work. When they had arrived the previous evening he had been leaving, and she had examined his arm and told them that it had healed well.

'The vicar held a small fête in the vicarage garden last week,' Ma told them. 'Even that aroused controversy. First of all he wanted to raise funds for his project of reconciliation with Germany, but it became clear that there would be a shortage of supporters.'

'Then he proposed splitting it between funds for the church and to help restore our forest,' Pa said. 'I had to object to that. Our forestry is commercial, and we could never ask the public to subsidise us.'

'The idea is mortifying,' Beatrice agreed.

'So in the end they raised funds for the new British Legion,' Pa said. 'Everyone agreed that was a worthwhile cause.'

'At least there's some good family news,' Edmond said, looking at his sister, who seemed more content than he could remember. 'Have you any idea when you'll be getting married?' He could not help noticing the flicker of distaste on his mother's face.

'Some time next year, if Caleb's discharge is approved. It won't be a smart event.'

'It won't be shabby, I assure you!' asserted Pa.

'And now there's Vicky's wedding to plan for,' Edmond broached nervously. 'Would you allow her to hold the reception here, I wonder?'

'Certainly not!' Ma said. 'I'll never approve of her marrying that German.'

'I don't know how you can forgive them for nearly killing you,' Beatrice told her brother, 'and wounding Charles so disastrously.'

'Max was actually helping our side in the war,' Edmond told her once more. 'Peter vouched for him, remember.'

'It's out of the question,' Ma said.

'I believe Uncle Arthur has offered to let them use the large reception room in the vicarage,' Amy told them. 'It's not much used but a good size.'

Edmond remembered the room. Its décor remained noticeably Victorian. It lacked the distinction of the ball-room and other sizeable reception room at The Beeches, but he suspected Vicky and Max would be content with it. They were not expecting there to be many guests.

'How did Ma take the idea of you marrying Caleb?' Edmond could not resist asking Beatrice when his parents had gone indoors.

'Not well,' she admitted. 'She said she was growing resigned to none of her children considering her feelings anymore. She only began to forgive me when I made her a stunning new hat.'

'Will you be going to Vicky's wedding?' he asked her.

'I feel the same as Ma about her marrying a German. I kept hoping she would decide it was a mistake.'

'Max comes from Alsace, where many of the people regard themselves as French. In fact, it's part of France again now.'

She winced. 'I'd better stay away. Vicky is defying public opinion by making such a controversial choice of husband.'

'What if they think the same about you and Caleb?' he pursued.

She was silent, considering what he had said. 'Sometimes I'm surprised at myself,' she owned at last. 'He's not the kind of man I imagined myself marrying. But once we met, we were drawn together. For a long while I couldn't see how we could become husband and wife, but the idea of losing him was unbearable. Now we're officially together we simply couldn't be happier!'

–

The following afternoon, Edmond and Amy drove to see Charles and Lavinia at Appletrees. They had a visitor staying, Captain Turnbull, Charles's army comrade who Edmond remembered meeting at Charles's wedding.

Beth had come with them, and she was soon following Christopher as he toddled around the room. When he fell over once she helped him up gently. *She's ready for a brother or sister*, Amy thought.

Before long Lavinia rang a bell for a young woman called Lucy, who proved to be a nanny. She carried the little boy off to the nursery and Beth went too.

'My father has been talking about giving Christopher toy soldiers to play with,' Charles said. 'There are my old ones, in uniforms from Victorian battles in Africa. He suggested buying some more with up-to-date uniforms. I've told him Chris is much too young for us to start thinking of that, but I'm not sure I want him to have soldiers at all.'

'That's tricky,' Edmond said. 'We need to respect all the fighting men, without making the conflict seem like an exciting adventure.'

'I'm determined to spend a good deal of each day with little Chris,' Lavinia told them, 'but I confess it's a relief to have a break from him now and then. I want to take up my painting again, and some activity to stretch the mind – I've taken a place on the committee supporting the hospital in Wealdham.'

'I knew you'd get involved in something like that,' Amy approved.

She and her friend were soon busily chatting about raising funds to help the poor to receive medical care, and becoming involved in the new scheme pioneered by Marie Stopes to bring birth control to women. 'Think how it could ease the life of the poor, by helping them limit their family size,' Lavinia said.

After lunch Edmond sat in a wicker chair in the garden with Charles and Captain Turnbull. The young women wandered around the garden before settling in a shadier area.

'Are you still serving in the Army of Occupation?' Edmond asked the captain.

'Yes – we're based near Cologne. The Huns hate us, of course.'

'Turnbull's regular army,' Charles reminded him.

'Yes,' his friend said, 'I went all through the war. I was relatively fortunate, for though my shoulder was injured in 1914 and my foot in 1917, I didn't sustain much permanent damage. I'm still serving. I was relieved my unit didn't get sent to Ireland.'

The Irish war of Independence had recently come to an end with a truce.

'Are you the chap who escaped from Belgium early in the war?' Edmond asked, remembering hearing some such story when they had met before.

'That's correct. I was injured in the early fighting around Mons and wound up in a hospital near Brussels, the one where Nurse Cavell was serving. She passed me on to an escape line for men fleeing to neutral Holland. The journey involved hiding in safe houses and travelling on false papers for two days, with another British soldier who was on the run, but we made it. I'm still terrified when I think about it.'

'Have you heard of a man posing as a German officer, helping men reach Holland?'

'Yes, when we went by train there was a German officer in the same carriage and if anyone queried who we were he took over – he had an air of authority and would convince them he knew how to check our credentials. He was a tremendous chap – we wouldn't have made it without his help. He wasn't really an officer, and he was from somewhere near the border – he didn't regard himself as genuinely German.'

'I don't suppose you remember his name?'

'No – it was a common German name, I might recognise it if I heard it.'

'Was the surname Bauer?'

'I believe it was!'

'Do you think his Christian name might have been Johann?'

'That sounds familiar too.'

'My cousin is planning to marry a young man from the Continent who carried out some kind of clandestine work during the war. He says he's from Strasbourg.'

'Could he be the same man?' asked Charles.

'Yes, Strasbourg – that's it!' said Captain Turnbull. 'I remember now, that's where he was from.'

'What did he look like?' asked Edmond.

'Tall, but not as tall as me – slightly olive skin, but blue eyes…'

'He sounds just like my cousin's fiancé, who now calls himself Max,' Edmond said as the captain described him.

'So you know him? It's unfortunate that I have to leave for Germany tomorrow. I'd have liked to meet him again, to thank him.'

Amy hurried across the garden. 'We'd better be going,' she said. 'We've got to get back to Roehampton.'

Edmond agreed; it was time to leave. Reluctantly they fetched Beth from the nursery and said their goodbyes.

'You're right,' Edmond told Amy as he drove off. 'The man who posed as a German officer sounds just like Max.'

Chapter 21

Amy, Beth and Edmond went back to The Beeches for a weekend the following month. 'I must see how the preparations are going for Vicky's wedding,' Amy explained to the Derwents over dinner on Friday evening. 'Vicky isn't working tomorrow and she and Max will be meeting me at the vicarage tomorrow morning.' She was shocked that the bride's parents were refusing to have any part in the ceremony.

Meanwhile, Edmond's parents had heard from Peter in India. 'He was horrified to hear what had happened to the forest, of course,' Pa told them. 'He sent me some money – he's anxious to forward some each month to help us restore the plantation. It's noble of him, but I hate the idea of him feeling he has to help support us. I was tempted to send his money straight back.'

'Peter made the point that if Pa wouldn't take the money for himself he should use it to make sure Ma and I didn't go short of anything as a result of the setback,' Beatrice said, smiling. 'He's offered it so cleverly – he presented Pa with a situation where he could hardly refuse!'

'So we're getting Mrs Johnson back!' Ma exclaimed triumphantly. Pa had made them manage without her since the loss of half the forest had reduced their income. 'Luckily she hadn't taken on any permanent work for anyone else on the days she was used to coming here.'

'I'm very grateful Peter's so generous,' Edmond said.

–

Next morning Amy set out with Beth, walking through the October sunshine to the vicarage.

Florence greeted her, moving slowly, for she was nearly seven months pregnant. 'I've some tremendous news,' she told Amy. 'We've found a little house, in Alma Road. James is very proud that he earns enough now for us to start buying our own home.'

'Splendid!' Amy said. That street was very near where her parents lived. 'When are you likely to move in?'

'Before the baby comes, I hope.'

'You must take the greatest care not to overdo things!' Amy cried, remembering her own loss.

'I know. James's parents are anxious to help us prepare everything. Even my parents have promised to help, and to lend us their maid for a few weeks.'

'They were slow to approve of James – I'm glad they're being kind.'

'They've come to like and respect him, and they're especially thrilled that there'll be another grandchild.'

They joined Aunt Sophie to discuss the arrangements for Vicky's wedding.

'Will you need extra chairs for the reception?' Amy asked, wondering if some rustic ones from the church hall would look too shabby.

'It's hard to tell,' her aunt said. 'I'm not sure that there'll be many guests.'

They debated what flowers they would be able to pick from the garden for the occasion, and then moved on to planning the catering. Edmond's father was going to attend the wedding, along with Beatrice, who had had a change of heart, but they were not participating much, out of sensitivity to Ma's feelings. Pa had quietly presented Aunt Sophie with a cheque to cover some of the expenses, however.

Soon Max and Vicky arrived from Wealdham. Max had taken up his new position at *The Pigeons*, and was living in one of the rooms there, but he and Vicky had just that week found lodgings for when they were married. She was bright-eyed as she described the modest two-room accommodation in a house conveniently placed in Wealdham. Amy was thankful it was well away from the smoky industrial area near the river.

'It's not a smart place,' Max told her, 'but I hope to better myself. The manager at *The Pigeons* has promised to raise my salary if I prove sufficiently competent.' He turned to James, who had come to greet them. 'Thank you so much for being best man.'

'I'm looking forward to the occasion.'

'And you must pass on my thanks to Edmond,' Vicky said. 'It's so important to have someone from my family to give me away.'

They left Max with Uncle Arthur and James, who was eager to tell him about his work for the British Legion. Vicky accompanied Amy to her parents' home in Sebastopol Terrace. 'It's marvellous that your mother has offered to make my wedding dress as well as the outfits for you and Beth,' Vicky said. At first Amy had offered her own wedding dress to Vicky, and the girl had been enthusiastic until she had tried it on and found that it was too tight, with her not being quite as slim as Amy.

'Mother's still grateful for the way you stepped in at my wedding when Beatrice refused to be bridesmaid,' Amy said.

'I didn't even have a proper bridesmaid's dress!' Vicky said, smiling, as they walked up the path to Amy's parents' front door.

Soon Vicky was trying on the ivory-coloured gown that Amy's mother was making her. 'It's beautiful,' she said. 'That lace trimming is exactly right – pretty but not too elaborate.' Mother put in pins where slight adjustments were needed.

'What about a veil?' Amy asked suddenly. 'You can wear mine, if you like.'

'Beatrice is making me one,' Vicky said, to her surprise. 'The last time I visited The Beeches she offered to design one for me. I don't think her mother knows about it. Apparently she's thinking of making veils to sell in her shop.'

'Oh – how lovely. I'm sure she'll create something very stylish.'

Then Amy and Beth tried on their light blue dresses. 'You've grown again, sweetheart,' Mother told Beth. 'I'll need to let down the hem.' Beth wriggled out of the dress, impatient to return to the rocking horse her grandparents had bought her.

They walked back to the vicarage for lunch. 'What are you wearing to go away?' Amy asked Vicky.

'I bought a decent suit, when I got paid,' she said. 'I haven't got many smart clothes, because I wear uniform most days. At least I've got one pretty blouse to wear with the suit.'

'Are many of your friends coming to the wedding?' Amy asked her nervously.

'Nora and another of my nursing friends, and a waiter friend of Max's,' she said. 'I invited some of my old friends from Melbridge, too, but only one of them is coming. I'm afraid they've listened to my parents, who've persuaded them the wedding is a ghastly mistake.'

'I'm sorry.'

'It's understandable that Max won't have relatives there, but I'm miserable that so few of my family will be attending.'

At first Amy had wondered if the room at the vicarage would be large enough for the reception, but now she was becoming concerned that it would be half empty.

'Have you invited Lavinia and her husband? She's been very interested to hear about your wedding.'

'I thought of inviting her but it's awkward – she was senior to me at the hospital.'

'I'm sure she'd love to come.'

'Then I'll send her an invitation.'

'It's bound to be a wonderful day.'

'I'm so excited I can hardly think of anything else! Max and I have both arranged leave from work for the entire week after the wedding, so we can go to Strasbourg afterwards and see his parents.'

Her excitement was infectious. *They're devoted to each other*, Amy thought. *Vicky and Max will overcome their difficulties, the way Edmond and I have done.*

–

One afternoon when Vicky was coming off duty at the hospital, she saw Lavinia coming out of the room where they held the fundraising committee. She was dressed in a smart hat, a tweed jacket and a slightly eccentric-looking divided skirt.

'Hello, Vicky,' the older woman said. 'Thank you for the invitation to your wedding. I've put our acceptance in the post. Are your preparations going well?'

'Yes,' she said optimistically, as they walked down the corridor with its yellow tiles. 'I'll be one of the few nurses not living in the hostel.' She told Lavinia about their flat. 'In fact, I was worried last week, because one of the sisters told me that nurses weren't supposed to go on working after they were married. But Amy did, didn't she? I looked in my contract and I couldn't see that restriction written down anywhere.'

'Let's see, when did you start? It was soon after the war, wasn't it?'

'Yes, spring 1919.'

'They needed nurses so much then, they didn't usually make any conditions about marriage. Even after the war there were many injured men still, and the flu epidemic went on for a few months more.'

Vicky was relieved that there should not be any problem. They went through the main entrance, to the area outside where people left cars and bikes.

'I hear they're planning to start a birth control clinic,' Vicky went on. Some women would be embarrassed even to talk of such a project, but she knew Lavinia had a no-nonsense approach.

'That's right. They're opening it next week.'

'It should be very worthwhile.'

'I think so.' Lavinia went to unpadlock her bicycle. They said goodbye and she rode off.

One day Vicky and Max would be ready to welcome children, but not just yet. She needed to finish her training, and Max to progress in his career, so that he could support her and a child or two. Then they would be ready for a family.

–

The next time Edmond drove them to The Beeches it was on a Friday, a week before Max and Vicky's wedding. Edmond took the afternoon off work and they travelled to Larchbury then, so they would arrive in good time. Amy planned that she and Beth would stay for the whole week, so she could help Vicky and Aunt Sophie with the preparations.

'James will be pleased,' Edmond said as they drove through Wealdham. 'Poppy Day has clearly been a great success.'

It was the third anniversary of the Armistice, and the newly founded British Legion was selling artificial poppies made of cotton or silk, for people to buy and wear to commemorate the fallen, besides raising money for ex-servicemen. Edmond and Amy had bought their cotton ones before leaving Roehampton, and were wearing them proudly. As they had passed through towns on their way they had seen volunteers selling them in the streets, and in Wealdham there was the same enthusiasm.

'They're made in France by a widow who's raising money for war orphans,' Amy told Edmond, 'but James says there are plans to found a factory in Britain, staffed by ex-servicemen, to make them next year.'

Over dinner that night Beatrice mentioned Vicky's wedding, and the veil she had made for her. She soon stopped talking about it as Ma was unwilling to hear about the subject.

Next morning dawned frosty but bright. 'Let's go and look at the forest,' Amy suggested. She made sure Beth was warmly dressed.

'I'd like to ride up there on Wanderer,' Edmond said, so they went to the stables. Beth patted the aged, chestnut horse as Edmond mounted him. They set off up the hill, Wanderer making slow progress. Ahead they could see the stark gap in the forest, although there had been some replanting and fresh growth. Pa was there with some of his workers, for the younger ones worked on Saturdays. In the distance they heard a sound which Amy had heard occasionally before while she had lived at The Beeches, the toot of a hunting horn.

'Let's go and look at the young trees,' Edmond said to Beth. 'Let's see if we'll have plenty of Christmas trees next month.' In the shade of the forest the ground was still frosty.

'I want to ride Wanderer!' Beth said.

'Perhaps when you're older,' Edmond told her.

Amy recalled that he had first ridden the horse as a schoolboy, and it seemed unlikely that the animal would survive long enough to be a suitable mount for Beth.

'In a few years we might ask Grandpa if we can get a pony for you and keep it here,' she said.

As they approached the treeline the horn sounded again – *why is it so near*? Amy wondered. They reached the newly planted saplings. 'They're doing well,' Amy said. 'I think they've grown since we last saw them.'

Pa was hurrying across to greet them. The hunting horn sounded from nearby. Amy could hear the sound of voices now, dogs barking and thudding horses' hooves.

Then a streak of rust-coloured fur shot past, and Beth pointed to the fox rushing downhill.

Now there was pandemonium as hounds dashed after their prey, and the huntsmen, clad in their distinctive red jackets, and mounted on thoroughbreds, began to appear through the gap in the forest. 'How dare they ride across our land without permission!' Edmond cried angrily.

His father came rushing to where they were standing. 'I've heard the Alderbank hunt are a rabble but this is completely unacceptable.'

Amy was nervous as the horses galloped swiftly towards them. She held Beth close to her. Then she saw suddenly that the leading huntsman was Wilfrid Fairlawn, with a determined look on his face as the hunt surged through the forest. He and his fellow huntsmen headed remorselessly towards them.

Amy thought she heard someone further back shouting at them to take care. Horses thudded towards them as she shrank back with Beth.

Edmond was holding Wanderer's reins tensely. 'Go back!' he was crying impotently to the huntsmen. 'Go back at once!'

As he approached, Wilfrid seemed to notice them, and his expression changed to one of distaste as he recognised them. The last time they had seen him had been two years before, in the restaurant in Cambridge where they had had the confrontation. A sneer came across Wilfrid's face as he charged towards Amy and Beth as though they were his prey, only swerving out of their way at the last minute.

'Stop! For God's sake, stop!' Edmond cried. He launched his horse towards Wilfrid's superior animal as other hunters rode towards them, one following Wilfrid's wild path and narrowly missing Amy and Beth.

The situation was becoming very confused. A few of the huntsmen continued downhill with the hounds, in pursuit of the fox. One rider stopped, concerned. 'Have a care, Fairlawn!' he exclaimed in a disgusted tone.

Pa was hurrying towards the riders, and from slightly to one side, in the forest, George and Ross were running. Beth was beginning to cry. Wilfrid Fairlawn, on his bay mount, had slowed down, but he was galloping in an adversarial fashion towards Edmond astride Wanderer.

'How dare you ride like that towards my wife and daughter!' Edmond seemed incensed, unaware of danger, as his old horse continued a little faster towards the prime animal that Wilfrid was riding. The huntsman glowered and sped up once more. While Amy watched helplessly, Wanderer shied at the last minute and slipped and fell. Edmond was thrown and landed heavily. She screamed in panic. Wanderer moved as though to try to get up, and then fell back.

Amy was overcome with terror as Edmond remained motionless. She wanted to help him but was unable to let go of Beth.

Wilfrid seemed suddenly to become aware of the situation. He reined hard and galloped away downhill, other riders following him, keeping a sensible distance.

Pa and the other forestry workers arrived. Pa bent and examined Edmond's prone body, beside the crippled horse. 'He's in a bad way!' he exclaimed. 'George, bring the wagon to take Edmond back to the house.'

One of the huntsmen remained, an appalled expression on his face. 'What can I say?' he uttered. 'Nothing excuses the way Fairlawn behaved, and some of the others aren't much better.'

Pa put his arms around Amy and Beth. 'If you want to help,' he told the huntsman, 'ride down to the house and tell them to send for the doctor.'

'Yes, right away.' He set off at a gallop.

Beth was still crying as her grandfather took her into his arms. Amy sobbed as she bent over Edmond. He was unconscious, and his breathing was uneven, as it had been when he had been injured in Flanders. He had fallen on his right side, where he had been injured before, and he must have hit his head as well. Not far away the grass was churned up from the riders.

As they brought up the wagon she was terrified that moving Edmond would worsen his injuries, but clearly he could not stay where he had fallen. She made them support him as best they could and place him very carefully on some sacking in the back of the wagon. Wanderer lay groaning where he had fallen, only making the occasional unsuccessful attempt to get up.

Amy climbed in with Edmond while Beth sat at the front beside her grandfather as he guided the forestry horses back towards The Beeches.

Amy examined Edmond. She undid his jacket and between her tears she could see blood seeping through his waistcoat. There was also a swelling appearing on the side of his head. She shuddered; this kind of accident could kill or badly disable a healthy man, and Edmond had not been fully fit since he had been wounded near Ypres.

They reached the house and saw the huntsman's horse tied up outside. Beatrice greeted them in tears while Ma made use of her smelling salts. Pa took Beth to see Cook, who would look after her and comfort her as best she could.

Soon afterwards Dr Heath arrived. He examined Edmond while he was still lying in the wagon. Amy watched as he gently undid Edmond's waistcoat and pulled up his shirt and vest. She reminded the doctor about his war wound. Besides the old scars from Flanders there was fresh blood and a protruding rib.

'He'll need an operation,' he said tersely. 'I'll phone for an ambulance to take him to Wealdham Hospital.'

She rearranged his clothes to keep him warm.

'I was a nurse during the war,' she told him when he returned from using the phone in the hall. 'I'm worried about his breathing, and the fact that he's still unconscious.'

'We need to operate promptly to clear any debris in the lung. Then I hope he'll recover consciousness, but I can't promise, especially in view of his history.'

'Can Mr Westholme operate?' she asked desperately. 'Perhaps he's at his house in Alderbank as it's the weekend.'

He looked at her critically, for asking for a particular surgeon.

'Mr Westholme pulled him round in Flanders,' she explained. 'And I'm a friend of his daughter, Lavinia.' Somehow she must get Edmond the best attention.

'I'll see what I can do.'

The huntsman emerged from the house. Amy had the feeling she had seen him before. Probably he was a friend of Charles who she had met at his wedding to Lavinia.

He held out his hand. 'I'm Hector Anderson. I've told your father-in-law that Fairlawn's behaviour was completely unacceptable,' he said. 'I'm prepared to say so in court. And I'm determined to have him thrown out of the Alderbank hunt.'

'Thank you,' she said. She had almost forgotten that Wilfrid Fairlawn was once more the cause of disaster to the family. What appalling luck it was that he had been on leave from the army this very weekend.

'Your husband was determined to keep Fairlawn off his family's land,' Mr Anderson said. 'He was brave to stand up to the man. He approached Fairlawn as though he was taking part in a medieval joust. But the horse lacked the youth and strength to face Fairlawn's beast.'

She bent over Edmond once more. He was still unconscious and his breathing ragged. 'Get better for me, darling!' she said to him, stroking his cheek. 'You've done it once and Beth and I need you to do it again.' There was no response.

At last the ambulance arrived. 'I'm going with Daddy to the hospital,' she told Beth.

'I want to go too!'

'No darling, you can't at the moment. Perhaps when he's getting better you can visit him.'

They moved Edmond as carefully as possible into the ambulance and she climbed in too as they set off. *They probably don't even allow children to visit the hospital, she thought.*

Chapter 22

Wealdham, November 1921

Amy leant her head against the wall as she sat impotently in the small side ward, waiting for Edmond to be brought back from the operating theatre. She was worried beyond measure, only having been comforted a little by seeing Mr Westholme arrive to examine him before he operated, and watching the staff rush to prepare Edmond for prompt treatment. Now she recalled the few times she had helped in theatre, while nursing as a member of the Voluntary Aid Detachment during the war. She was confident in Mr Westholme's ability, but could not avoid remembering the traumatic sights she had seen, and the men they had been unable to save.

Hector Anderson had likened Edmond's confrontation with Wilfrid to a joust from the Middle Ages. Amy remembered her husband's horror at hearing how Wilfrid had molested her in Ypres. It seemed unlikely Edmond could ever forgive him for what had happened that night. Seeing the man galloping wildly towards his wife and daughter had provoked Edmond to confront him.

She looked up as someone stepped lightly into the ward. It was Vicky, her face alarmed. 'I heard there'd been a hunting accident,' she said. 'I was horrified when I found out it was Edmond who was injured.'

Amy could not bring herself to discuss the details of the 'accident'. She told Vicky about Edmond's injuries, finding some relief in confiding in another nurse. The girl had worked at the hospital for over two years now, but she went pale at hearing the details.

'I need to return to my ward,' she said, 'but I'll come back in my meal break to see how he's doing.'

But it's the wedding on Friday! Amy realised suddenly after Vicky had left. *Edmond is supposed to be giving Vicky away in church. He won't be fit to carry out that role. What is Vicky to do?*

Soon they wheeled Edmond in, still unconscious, and laid him in his bed. She thought his breathing was a little easier now.

'He should come round within the next hour,' said Sister Green, who was in charge of this ward and the larger one alongside. 'I can't promise he'll do so, as he was concussed to start with. You can try talking to him if he's slow coming round.' She looked thoughtfully at Amy. 'You were a nurse in the war, I gather?'

'Yes, Sister.'

'We're quite busy at the moment. The air quality is poor around the factories again, and we've got a lot of patients. I need to return to the main ward for a while, but if there's any change in Lieutenant Derwent's condition, come and fetch me at once.'

The lump on the right-hand side of Edmond's head had swollen larger than before. Amy undid the jacket buttons on the hospital pyjamas they had found for him. Once more he had a large dressing above his right lung.

The door opened again and this time it was Mr West-holme. 'I've dealt with the damage to Edmond's chest,' he told her, wearing the reassuring smile that he bestowed on patients and their relatives even when he knew the outcome was grim. 'I've cleared out the debris from a broken rib, and stitched up a tear in his lung.'

During the war Edmond had already lost ribs and lung tissue, and acquired substantial scarring. 'How well will he recover?' she faltered.

'He managed to largely overcome his injuries before, didn't he?' the surgeon said brightly. 'I'm concerned about the concussion. If he doesn't come round normally, try speaking to him.'

'Yes, I will. Thank you so much.' She remembered once more that besides tending to Edmond after he was wounded near Ypres, after the Armistice Mr Westholme had reset her injured ankle and aligned the bones successfully.

Edmond lay there, his breathing still less regular than usual. He showed no sign of regaining consciousness. 'Come on, Edmond, darling! Wake up!' she urged him at intervals. The afternoon wore on and his condition seemed unchanged. The sister came back and looked concerned, but refused to discuss his prognosis with her, in spite of her nursing background.

'Your family phoned and I told them the operation seemed successful though he's still concussed,' she said. Amy imagined them all, anxious for news. 'A visit is out of the question, at least for today.' She bustled off.

A nurse brought her a cup of tea. Amy continued to speak to Edmond at intervals. It was growing dark, so she turned on the light.

'Edmond, dearest – wake up! It's me, Amy.' For a moment she thought she saw his eyelids flutter. She spoke to him again, and this time nothing happened – had she imagined it before?

Vicky returned about six. 'Still the same? Oh, good-ness. How long do you plan to stay?'

'All night. I want to keep talking to him. I thought I saw his eyelids flutter once.'

They both spoke to him but he lay still, slumped in the position he had been placed when they had brought him back from theatre.

'I'll go and ask the canteen to make you a sandwich,' Vicky said.

'What'll you do about the wedding?' Amy asked her when she returned with the snack. 'I can't see Edmond being fit by Friday. You're short of someone to give you away now.'

'Goodness knows how I'll manage. Don't worry about it, Amy. But I think we should go ahead with the cere-mony, now Max and I have both arranged leave.'

'Yes, you should,' Amy agreed, remembering the exasperating delays before she had been able to marry Edmond. 'Are you going to your hostel now? You look weary.'

'I suppose I'd better leave. I'm not on duty tomorrow, and Max is taking me to *The Crown* for a meal to celebrate my twenty-first birthday. We can't eat at *The Pigeons* now he works there.'

'Have a lovely time!'

'We're choosing cheaper items from the menu to keep the cost down. After all, Friday will be the big occasion. I wish now we weren't celebrating my birthday while Edmond is ill again. Sometime in the day I'll call in to check on his progress.' She still looked anxious as she left.

If Edmond wakes up now he'll be in a lot of pain, Amy thought. *But if he stays in a coma that's dangerous too.* She went on speaking to him at intervals, and once more she saw his eyelids flutter momentarily and struggled to convince herself he was making headway.

Sister Green tried to persuade her to catch an evening train to Larchbury, but Amy was determined to stay. She turned off the light, though a faint glow came from the corridor outside. She dozed off and then awoke, slumped uncomfortably in her chair, with the conviction that she was in the hospital in Ypres and Edmond was fighting for his life.

She poured herself a glass of water. When she spoke to Edmond he was unresponsive. In her next dream she was running through the rubble in an Ypres street, while Wilfrid Fairlawn pursued her. It must be over a year since that nightmare had last plagued her. Between dreams she continued to talk to Edmond to try to stimulate some response.

–

As it grew light next morning, Edmond seemed much the same. The night sister brought Amy some tea and a bowl of porridge before going off duty.

'Any change?' Sister Green asked.

'Occasionally his eyelids flutter,' she said.

'That's a good sign, but I'm surprised the pain hasn't roused him. They'll have injected medication to suppress the feeling, but it must be wearing off by now. It's bad for the patient to be lying motionless for so long.' She hurried back to her main ward.

Just after nine the little ward suddenly became full: Ma, Pa, Beatrice and Beth all rushed in.

'Keep quiet!' Amy begged them, looking firmly at Beth. 'Patients aren't supposed to have this many visitors!

Did you ask if it was all right for Edmond to receive visits now?'

'We just got in the car and came,' Pa admitted.

He was afraid Sister would refuse, she thought, *so he brought them without asking*.

'He looks peaceful now,' said Beatrice.

'I believe the operation went well,' Amy told the others.

Beth tried to climb on the bed. 'Daddy!' she cried.

'Shush, darling! And stay still.'

'Why doesn't he wake up?' Ma asked.

'He hasn't come round yet,' Amy explained. 'It might happen soon, though.'

'Can't you let him sleep a while longer?' Beatrice asked. 'He'll be in pain if he wakes up, won't he?'

'Yes, but it's not good for him to remain in a coma,' Amy explained. 'If he stays lying down for a long time he might catch pneumonia. With his damaged lung you can imagine how dangerous that would be.'

Beatrice looked horrified and Ma opened her bag to find her smelling salts.

The door opened and Sister Green swept in. 'What in the world is going on here?' The noise had alerted her to their presence, as Amy had feared. 'What's that child doing in here? We don't allow children to visit. And only two visitors are allowed at a time.'

'I'm sorry they all arrived at once, Sister. I was about to organise them so that only two are here at any time.'

'But visiting hour is in the afternoon, between three and four. I must insist you all leave.'

'Listen, Sister, it's important to stimulate the patient, as you know, so he regains consciousness. I believe in my husband's case it's vital he hears his family talking around him. We found in the hospitals in Flanders that seriously ill men were more likely to recover if close relatives were able to visit.'

Amy was afraid she might have further antagonised the sister, but she could tell from the woman's expression that she recognised the truth of what she had said.

'Very well,' she said. 'But keep the noise down. No more than two of you in here at once. And someone take the little girl outside – this isn't a suitable place for her to visit.'

They decided that Ma and Beatrice would stay with Edmond for a while. 'Talk to him,' Amy urged them. 'If his eyelids flutter that's a good sign that he's aware of people around him.'

She and Pa took Beth for a walk around the frosty hospital grounds.

She knew there were matters they should be discussing, but it was difficult with Beth there. Amy took them to the little café near the hospital where they managed to buy warm drinks. Then it was time to go back to the ward.

Ma and Beatrice looked despondent. 'We did try to talk to him,' Beatrice said.

Amy and Pa went to take their place. 'But I want to see Daddy!' Beth said.

'Later,' Amy told her. They could at least give her a brief chance to speak to him before they left.

Amy and Pa tried briefly to communicate with Edmond, but there were no signs that he was aware of them.

'I've reported Fairlawn's behaviour to the police,' Pa said grimly. 'That chap who helped us yesterday is prepared to back me up. But the last I heard, yesterday evening, was that Fairlawn has left his family home in

Alderbank for some other house, or possibly a hotel in London, to try and evade being questioned.'

Amy shuddered. While she was so worried about Edmond she had not spent long considering how to make Wilfrid responsible for his actions. Now she thought about it she was concerned that his pompous father would protect him again and he would get away with what he had done.

'And I'm afraid we had to have poor Wanderer put down,' Pa added. 'He was a reasonable age for a horse, but Edmond will be upset when he hears.'

'How did the huntsmen get on to the forestry land? I suppose their horses must have leapt the fence.'

'Yes – though their riders should have reined them in. The hounds probably squeezed under a gate.'

There was another matter she had to raise with Pa. 'It's Vicky's wedding on Friday,' she reminded him. 'Edmond was to give her away. Would you be able to do it instead?'

Pa sighed. 'It's extremely awkward. Ma is still very much against the wedding. She's dismayed that Beatrice and I have accepted invitations. There's been a lot to distress her this year, with Peter returning to India, and the fire in the forest, and Beatrice determined to marry Caleb. She's become very depressed and I don't want to risk upsetting her further.'

'I understand,' Amy said reluctantly. She could only think of asking her own father to perform the task. He liked Vicky and she felt sure he would be willing to take on the role, but the bride would be disappointed that no member of her own family was prepared to take part in the ceremony.

They turned their attention to Edmond again. How could she bear it if he continued to lie there, motionless?

She held his limp hand and they began speaking to him, calling his name and begging him to reply. Once they both saw his eyelids flutter.

Soon there was a commotion outside and Beth rushed in again, followed by Beatrice and Ma.

'I suppose we should go back,' Pa said. 'We can come again tomorrow.'

'I want to talk to Daddy!' Beth said, trying to climb on to the bed.

'I've got a better idea,' Beatrice said. 'Let's sing him a song.' She seized his other hand and began singing '*Ride a Cock-horse to Banbury Cross*' with Beth joining in. Amy added her voice to theirs.

Inevitably Sister Green burst into the room. 'How dare you!' she cried.

'Look at your patient!' Amy said.

Suddenly Edmond's eyes were open. He looked at his daughter and then looked around the room, bemused.

'Good heavens!' cried the sister. 'At last he's come round.'

Amy remembered Edmond telling her that the song had been his favourite nursery rhyme as a child. Even Ma was beaming.

'My chest is bad again,' Edmond said. 'Am I back in Wipers?'

'No, you're in Wealdham,' Amy told him, 'and you're going to get better for all of us.'

But he still looked perplexed. He tried to raise himself a little in the bed and collapsed back down again.

'He's definitely improving,' the sister said, 'but he still needs rest. You may stay, if you wish, Mrs Derwent, but I must ask all the rest of you to leave.'

After they had gone, Edmond began to talk to Amy, to her relief. He could not remember how he had come to be injured. She explained that he had fallen from Wanderer in an accident, without reminding him of the cause, or telling him the fate of his horse.

'My head hurts,' he complained. The bump on his forehead was as large as ever and had turned purple with bruising.

Then Mr Westholme arrived and examined his wound. Amy saw that it was minor compared with the one in Ypres, and looked clean and free of infection. He shrugged off her thanks.

When he had gone, Edmond yawned. He still seemed very frail and Sister Green had given him another injection of painkiller. Soon he was asleep, though he was shifting position occasionally and she was satisfied he was no longer concussed.

She went out and bought a pasty with mashed potato in the little café. She felt tired and still anxious as she rushed back to the ward.

He was sleeping calmly, but soon stirred and was ready to talk again.

'Was Beth here earlier?' he asked. 'And Beatrice?'

'Yes. We're all anxious for you to get well quickly.'

He remembered now that he was in Wealdham, but he needed reminding about the accident. She repeated the brief details she had given him before.

'What day is it?'

'Sunday.'

Just then Vicky arrived. 'Oh, Edmond you're better – I'm so glad. I'm going to meet Max soon, but I came to check on you first.'

'Oh. Have I been asleep a long time?'

'Yes, but now you're going to get well again.'

'Oh yes, I will. I did after I was injured at Wipers, didn't I?' For a moment his eyes lit up and his winning smile returned to his face.

He should be all right, Amy thought. Edmond had always been resilient. But how could a thug like Wilfrid Fairlawn put his health at risk again?

'I must tell you how he regained consciousness,' Amy said to Vicky. 'It was Beatrice's doing. She sang to him, and Beth and I joined in.'

He seized her hand. 'Amy, Beth and Beatrice,' he said, 'my three best girls.'

Before long he was yawning again.

'I'd almost forgotten, it's your twenty-first birthday,' Amy said to Vicky. 'I've bought you a present, but of course it isn't here. I'll try to get it to you in a day or two.'

'Don't worry – just look after Edmond,' Vicky said, before going off to join Max.

'I'd better go back to The Beeches,' Amy said to Edmond, 'but I promise I'll come to see you again tomorrow.'

I must phone Roehampton hospital and tell them what's happened to him, she thought. I don't know how soon he'll be able to get back.

She intended at first to walk to the station and take the train to Larchbury, but now she realised how tired she was after her disturbed night. She made a call to The Beeches from a telephone box and waited in the hospital entrance for Pa to collect her in the car.

–

Pa was desperately anxious about Edmond's condition. Amy visited the hospital on the Monday, keeping to the visiting hour, and told him that Edmond's progress was very slow. His memory was still poor and he seemed weak and tired, but he had got up in the afternoon and sat in the chair by his bed.

On the Tuesday Pa took time off from tending the forest to visit Edmond himself. He drove Amy to Wealdham and the two of them went to the ward. Sister Green looked in on them and told them the wound was healing well but Edmond tired quickly if he walked around.

'Was the hunt there on Saturday, when I got injured?' Edmond asked them suddenly.

'Yes.'

'I remember now, they all surged through that gap in the forest, with their red jackets and squealing hounds.'

Pa waited anxiously for more questions relating to Wilfrid Fairlawn. Amy looked nervous at the thought of Edmond growing angry if he recalled further details, but soon his attention wandered.

Just then another visitor arrived. It was Edmond's old friend, Charles Shenwood, walking a little awkwardly on his appliances.

'Charles! Good to see you.'

'I'll leave you two to talk to Edmond,' Amy said. As she left the side ward, Pa thought she looked weary.

He was content to share the remains of visiting time with Charles. He had always liked the young man, who he had once regarded as a future son-in-law, until Beatrice had found herself unable to face his injuries. Pa hoped Charles would not mention Fairlawn, but on the whole he trusted him to behave sensitively, having spent several months in hospitals.

'That's a nasty lump on your forehead,' Charles said to Edmond.

'It was much worse earlier in the week,' Pa told him.

'Your cousin Vicky marries Max soon, doesn't she?'

'Yes,' Edmond said. 'Let's see, is it taking place this Friday?'

'Yes,' said Pa, 'but Vicky knows you're here and won't be able to attend. Did she call into the ward to see you today?'

'Yes – oh, Pa, what am I going to do?' Realisation seemed to strike him suddenly. 'I'm supposed to be giving Vicky away. Do you suppose I might be fit enough by Friday?'

'No – we'll find someone else.' He looked sternly at Charles to discourage him from pursuing the subject.

'Do you remember what we spoke about last time you and Amy visited us at Appletrees?' Charles asked. 'Captain Turnbull was there and told us about his escape from Belgium. We think Max was involved.'

'I remember now,' Edmond said, 'but I don't think I got around to telling Pa the story.'

'I remember you telling me about an officer who escaped from behind German lines in Belgium,' Pa said.

'Someone who sounds just like Max was posing as a German lieutenant and travelling in the same carriage when Turnbull and his comrade went by train, so he could take over if anyone questioned their credentials,' Charles explained. 'He was instrumental in their escape.'

'Why does he think it was Max?' Pa asked.

'The name on the passport Max had. Bauer, wasn't it, Edmond?'

He seemed to be having trouble concentrating. 'Yes, I think so.'

'We decided it was almost certainly Max,' Charles said. 'Turnbull described the German officer and it sounded just like him.'

'Really?' Pa was impressed. There had been much controversy about the young man, but Peter had always vouched for him.

Soon visiting time was over, and Amy joined them to say goodbye to Edmond.

'He's much better than earlier in the week,' she told Charles, 'but he still tires easily.'

Charles made slow progress as they walked down the corridor. 'How are you getting back to Alderbank?' Pa asked.

'I'll walk down to the station and take a train, then at Alderbank I'll phone for Lavinia to collect me. I'm largely managing with my appliances but I'm not yet willing to try driving.'

'I'll drive you home,' Pa said.

'It's quite all right. A little exercise is good for me.'

'Nonsense. Your house is practically on our way.'

They got into his car. 'I gather Max may have been helping men escape from Belgium at the start of the war,' Pa said to Amy.

'We think so. When we went to Liège we met a young Belgian who escaped to Holland thanks to someone who sounded just like Max.'

He dropped Charles at Appletrees, then drove thoughtfully on towards Larchbury. 'I believe I should offer to give Vicky away, so she has the support of someone in her family,' he said. 'Mabel will be dismayed – you'll support me when I explain to her, won't you?'

'Of course I will. I'm so glad you're going to do that for her, Pa. And Edmond will stop worrying about not being fit enough to do it.'

–

Vicky called in to see Edmond on the Thursday, while Amy was with him.

'I was so relieved when I heard you're still getting better,' she said.

He was sitting in the chair by his bed, and for a moment he looked regretful. 'I was hoping I'd be out of here in time for your wedding,' he told Vicky, 'but they won't let me leave yet.' The swelling on his forehead had gone down a little but his breathing was still not quite normal.

'Pa is giving Vicky away now,' Amy told him. 'It's all arranged and he's proud to do it.'

'I'm extremely grateful to him,' Vicky said. She was a little subdued when they discussed it, hurt that her parents were still refusing to attend her wedding.

'I've remembered to bring your birthday present at last,' Amy said. She handed Vicky the soft parcel and watched as she excitedly unwrapped it. Beneath the layers of tissue paper there was a beautiful, cream-coloured, crêpe de chine blouse.

'Oh, Amy – it's gorgeous!'

'I thought you should have another pretty blouse for your honeymoon.'

'It looks quite expensive.'

'It was your twenty-first. I enjoyed choosing it for you.'

'I'd better get back to the ward in a minute. The other nurses will be envious when they see this.'

'Beth and I will be at the wedding of course,' Amy said to Edmond. 'It's at eleven o'clock, and I'll try to leave the reception in time to get a taxicab here for visiting hour to see you and tell you all about it.' If she was late she would try to sneak in to see him anyway, she had decided.

'I'll miss watching the ceremony,' he objected. 'And I won't be able to see you all in your fine clothes.'

'Pa has engaged a photographer,' Amy told him.

'Then I can only wish you all the best, Vicky,' he said reluctantly, drawing his cousin towards him and kissing her. 'I'm sure you'll look lovely.'

Chapter 23

'Sometimes I thought this day would never come,' Vicky said as Amy's mother helped them dress in Amy's old room in Sebastopol Terrace.

'I thought the same, back in 1915,' Amy said. She was happy for Edmond's cousin but there was a bleak feeling that would not go away, knowing he was lying in hospital, his health impaired once more.

The ivory wedding dress skimmed Vicky's body attractively. Mother had retrieved the ivory velvet cape Amy had worn for her own wedding and made matching ones for Vicky and Beth.

Amy helped Vicky position her veil over her gleaming auburn hair. At the back it reached down to her waist.

'Isn't it elegant?' Vicky said. 'Beatrice is very gifted.'

As Amy had expected, her sister-in-law had created a beautiful confection, trimmed with satin ribbon formed into rosebuds.

'She's got plans to make more like it, to sell in the milliner's where she works,' Amy told her, 'but there won't be one exactly like yours. She plans to make each one unique.'

Her mother was doing up Beth's dress. 'Stay still, darling, please!' she begged.

'Promise me you'll be quiet and stay still in church,' Amy told her daughter, 'otherwise I shall have to ask someone to take you outside.'

Mother fitted the headband with tiny artificial flowers on Beth's head. 'With her blonde curls she looks so like you as a girl,' Mother said, though Amy fancied her daughter was a little plumper.

When Amy and Edmond had finally married it had been November, but it had been a brighter day. This time, as they set out in Mr Derwent's car, the early morning fog was just lifting enough to allow thin sunshine through.

They arrived a little early and hovered outside the church, Beth impatiently hopping from one foot to another. Villagers were standing around in the street, curious as ever to see the wedding, and some of them went on into the church. Despite their efforts, the suspicions about Max had not entirely died down. Miss Miller watched the guests arrive with a sour expression on her face.

Amy's parents arrived in their best clothes, having walked to the church, and went inside. Vicky tucked her arm into her uncle's, ready for him to lead her inside, and Amy took Beth's hand, eager to follow behind.

At that moment a taxicab came along the road and drew up outside. For a moment Amy's heart jolted, as she remembered the disruption of her own first attempt to get married. But surely nothing like that could possibly happen this time?

She relaxed when she saw a slim, smartly dressed woman stepping out of the taxi. She had seen her before, but where?

'Mother!' gasped Vicky, letting go of Edmond's father and rushing towards the newcomer. 'Oh, Mother, it's so lovely to see you!'

Her mother seized her hands and look her up and down. 'Don't you look beautiful!'

'I thought you weren't coming.'

'I decided I couldn't miss seeing you married. Your father still refused to come, I'm afraid, so I took the train and then a cab to St Stephen's.'

The clock on the church tower chimed eleven. 'I'm glad to see you, Agnes,' Pa said. 'If you go inside you'll see Beatrice in the front pew – why don't you join her? Now, Vicky, we'd better not keep Max waiting.'

Vicky's mother went ahead of them and then they processed up the aisle as the organist played the 'Wedding March'. Max was standing at the front, next to James, while Uncle Arthur waited to begin the service.

Amy held on to Beth as they passed the guests, seeing little but their back views. At the front, Vicky passed Amy her bouquet of rosebuds. Then Uncle Arthur stepped forward and the service began. Vicky made her responses loudly and confidently, and Max did much the same, though his slight accent was evident.

In a quiet moment Amy could not resist looking around. Florence, whose child was due in a month, was wearing a voluminous woollen cape over her dress.

After the service Amy joined the bridal couple in the vestry, where they signed the register. Max looked proud and Vicky radiant. Amy signed the document as a witness.

They processed back down the church, past Beatrice, who was gorgeously arrayed in her autumn suit and a splendid new hat with artificial flowers that she had made herself. She smiled at them graciously.

It was a short walk to the vicarage. The best room was decked with flowers, mainly chrysanthemums, in shades of russet and gold. At one end there was a large table, laden with dishes, though the hot food was still being prepared.

Pa escorted Vicky's mother to a chair.

Beatrice was looking a little confused. 'This is awkward,' she whispered to Amy. 'I haven't been able to avoid Charles completely since I broke off our engagement – I've come across him occasionally in the street in Larchbury or Wealdham, and he's greeted me politely, with no hard feelings. But we haven't attended the same social event together since we were engaged. When I realised he was coming I planned to go home immediately after the service, but now that Aunt Agnes is here I feel I should stay and talk to her. I haven't seen her since she came to Beth's christening.'

'I'm sure it will work out all right,' Amy said.

Sure enough, Lavinia and Charles came to greet her, and after brief comments about the happy couple they passed on. Charles and Beatrice were both committed elsewhere now.

The large room was gradually filling with people. It stretched from the back to the front of the house. Amy let go of Beth at last, thankful that she had behaved so far, and allowed her to join Mother and Father.

Amy experienced a bleak moment as she thought of Edmond, still in hospital. Guests kept approaching her and asking after him, and she related the improvement they had seen in him. *But how long will it take him to regain his usual health*, she could not help wondering. *He's spent years recovering from his war wound, only to be injured again.*

The newlyweds settled at the large central table at the opposite end of the room from the buffet table, and Amy joined them.

'We still haven't bought your wedding present, thanks to Edmond's injury,' she said. 'But I promise we'll get it soon!' They would be buying a set of serving dishes for the pair's new home.

Vicky assured them there was no immediate hurry. 'Only imagine Mother arriving!' she went on. 'She's always had poor health and seldom goes out, and hardly ever alone. She's made her way here, in spite of having to change trains.'

'She was very determined not to miss the occasion,' Amy said. She asked the pair about their honeymoon in Strasbourg. 'How long will you be there?'

'Only a few days,' Vicky said. 'Max could only get just over a week off. I wish we were staying longer.'

They were sitting by a window with a view of the road outside the vicarage. As Amy watched a vehicle approached.

'Another taxi!' Max exclaimed. 'Do you think it's your father this time, darling?'

The cab door opened and Amy gasped as Edmond stepped out, in the same old clothes he had been wearing the previous Saturday, when he had set out for the forest.

'Oh, my goodness – he's got here!' Vicky cried.

He walked slowly but confidently up the front path.

Amy found herself by the vicarage front door, without quite knowing how she had reached there. She opened the door and Edmond walked in.

'Hello, darling,' he said, smiling. 'I'm sorry to have missed the service, but at least I've made it to the reception!'

Pa appeared in the hall. 'Are you really well enough to be here?' he asked sternly.

'Yes, of course! Listen, Pa, this is embarrassing, but can you pay the cabbie? He's still waiting outside. I haven't enough cash on me. I'll pay you back later.'

Pa went outside to deal with the matter.

'Why aren't you in the hospital?' Amy demanded.

'I couldn't bear to miss the occasion.'

Vicky rushed into the hall, followed by Max. 'Oh, Edmond, I'm so glad you could come!'

'I was determined to see you on your wedding day. You look lovely in that gown. I'm sorry I couldn't get here in time for the service. And I must apologise for the way I look – I didn't want to lose time by going to The Beeches to get changed.' He had only left off the waistcoat. His shirt must be bloodstained too, but his jacket concealed that.

Vicky took his hand. 'Come inside and sit down,' she said.

Amy followed as they went into the reception room, Edmond walking slowly but confidently. He sat down at the large table with Vicky and Max. Beatrice rushed over to be reassured he was better.

'What did you tell them at the hospital?' Amy demanded.

'Well, er, soon after eleven o'clock Mr Westholme's deputy came and examined me, and he's very pleased with the way the wound is healing. He told Sister Green that I was making excellent progress. Then, after he had left, I – well, I just decided I should come to join everyone here.'

'You mean you sneaked out without telling anyone?'

'Yes – do you think I should phone them and tell them where I am, and apologise?'

'Yes – do it at once!'

He went off to use Uncle Arthur's telephone.

'He's quite incorrigible!' Amy complained to Vicky.

'But it shows he's getting better, doesn't it? He's in high spirits again.'

'Yes.' She remembered other occasions when he had swiftly grown bored with behaving as an invalid.

Charles came over to speak to Max, who he had not formally met before. 'I believe we have an acquaintance in common,' he said. 'My army comrade, Captain Turnbull, remembers someone like you helping him escape from Belgium in 1914. Actually he was still a lieutenant then.'

Max looked interested. 'I may well have done. I'm afraid I can't remember all the men who we helped. They were travelling under different names on false papers.'

'Turnbull is a tall, thin chap.'

'I seem to remember someone like that being handed over to us from the hospital near Brussels where Nurse Cavell worked.'

'That's right! That's what happened to him.' Charles went on telling him how Turnbull had served later in the war.

Aunt Sophie and Mrs Johnson were bringing in hot dishes to set on the table, and Mother got up to help serve the meal. As guests went to the table, Vicky went to ask her mother what she should fetch her.

Edmond rejoined Amy. 'I don't think Sister Green will forgive me for a while,' he said.

'You've behaved very badly!'

'But as you see, I'm much better. I don't think I need to return to the hospital. After all, you're a nurse. You can call Doctor Heath and ask him to come and check me over in a few days.'

'We'll see,' she said. She suspected he would soon grow tired. *If that happens I'll ask Pa to drive him back to The Beeches,* she thought, *and if I have the slightest worry about his progress I'll make sure he returns to the hospital.*

'Listen, darling, do you remember — it's our own anniversary tomorrow!'

'So it is!' With all that had happened she had almost forgotten.

—

It was Sunday evening before the newlyweds reached Strasbourg. Vicky had a brand new passport in her married name of Duclos, handed to her by the vicar on her marriage. 'Can I remain British?' she had asked Max.

'Let's leave it that way!' he had agreed readily. There had been quite enough disputes in his life about nationality. He was travelling on his genuine original German passport which gave his birthplace as Strasbourg. She had persuaded him to destroy the others.

Vicky was overcome with all her new experiences, including the tender evenings with Max, first in a London hotel and then in Paris where they had made a brief stop. She had seen the extensive scar on his right arm, which she had glimpsed that time at the inn when she had bandaged the limb further down.

'Where did you really get that scar?' she asked him. At first, when they had regarded him as an ordinary Frenchman, he had implied he had acquired it in battle.

'It was when I was posing as a German officer, but actually helping allies escape Belgium into Holland,' he explained. 'I'd check their papers and let them through. But one of the men I helped attracted attention at the border and I came under suspicion and got fired at by real Germans.'

She stared at him. 'I don't know how you could live like that!'

'Neither do I, now! For most of the war I was trying to keep an appearance of normality while terrified something would go wrong. I was constantly on edge, rather like the men who get shell-shocked.'

She remembered Peter telling her that his wartime exploits had been very dangerous.

During their journey she had acquired confused memories of the tortured countryside near the Somme, the city of Amiens they had passed through, with its still damaged cathedral, and then the sophisticated French capital. Then they had spent another day travelling east to Strasbourg. On some signs it was still spelled Straßburg, she noticed.

There had been so many new experiences. At first she had asked Max if he had visited some of the towns, and what they had been like during the war, but he made short answers and had a distant expression on his face.

'Was it very awful for you?' she had asked.

'I thought I could face it again now a few years have passed,' he told her, 'but all the devious journeys I made under cover are coming back to mind.'

When they reached their destination the station smelled strongly of continental cigarettes. She was weary as they walked the short distance past half-timbered houses to the one where Max's parents occupied an apartment.

Dusk was falling as they reached the house. 'There were food shortages here in the war,' Max told her, 'worse than in Britain, I think. But according to Grandfather's letters, the situation has improved now.'

He rang the bell and a middle-aged woman in a woollen jacket and skirt opened the door and embraced him. She could tell from her face that she must be his mother. Vicky had only a little French, but she realised that Max was introducing her, and stepped forward to grasp the woman's hand.

'Willkommen,' said the woman, and Vicky realised with a shock that she was speaking German. Then 'Bienvenue,' she said, with an unfamiliar accent.

Why didn't I realise it would be like this? I should have done. He's told me often enough that the town has belonged to both France and Germany. In fact, I seem to remember it's only a few miles west of the Rhine. Vicky followed them up a staircase to their apartment, on the next floor.

There were more greetings from the two men seated at the table – his father and grandfather, she realised. The father greeted her in German, while the grandfather smiled as he welcomed her in good French. She was thankful she had studied French for a while at school.

Max's mother took her hat and coat graciously and showed her where she could wash her hands.

Max led her to the table. It seemed a meal was imminent.

'Father, you speak a little English,' Max said now. 'Please try to talk to Vicky in her own language.'

'I try,' he said.

It seemed the grandfather only spoke French, but his words were clear as he asked about their journey, and she had to ask Max to explain that it had taken longer than she had expected.

'I am so sorry about Grandma,' Max told his grandfather in French. He had been away for years and she had died during his absence.

Mutti, as he called his mother, now served them a meal of sliced pork, sausages and pickled cabbage: choucroute, she called it. Vicki was hungry and found it tasty.

'In your last letter you told me many people here remain sympathetic to the Germans,' Max said in English. 'Has that changed at all?'

His father replied with much shrugging and gesticulation. He was speaking in German, so she could not understand what he was saying, but he seemed dissatisfied with the situation.

The grandfather turned to her. She remembered Max explaining that his generation had often remained loyal to the French. He spoke slowly in French, so she could understand some of what he said.

'You see, soon after the Germans were defeated, French troops under General Gouraud entered the city triumphantly, and a cheering crowd gathered around the town hall. President Poincaré claimed that there was no need for a plebiscite to confirm that Strasbourg should be French again. Then, following the Treaty of Versailles, the American President allowed the city to be annexed by France without a referendum. Not everyone was happy with his decision.'

Max's father retorted angrily in German.

'Vater is saying that lots of people here believe the city would have stayed German if there had been a referendum,' Max said. His father nodded.

'Many Germans had moved here since the Franco-Prussian war in 1870,' Max told her. 'Germany is more popular in the city than in the rural areas of the region.'

Mutti shrugged as though such arguments were a regular occurrence.

When they had finished eating the family accepted that she and Max were very tired. They hurried to the spare room and she turned back the bedspread.

'I'm sorry it's been like this,' Max said. 'I was hoping people would be more harmonious now.'

'I should have realised there might still be discord,' Vicky said. It had been true what people said: Max was effectively German. He had been brought up as one, even though his loyalties lay with his French heritage. For a moment she imagined herself aligning with Britain's enemies.

But it's a divided region, she thought. There are divisions between areas, between families, even within families.

Max lay in bed, his eyes fixed on hers. She took off her last few clothes and climbed into bed with him. In the dim lamplight her skin was pale against his, as his warm arms came around her.

–

The following morning Max was relieved to find the atmosphere was calmer. His grandfather asked Vicky if she worked, and she told him she was a student nurse, which met with his approval. Then she mentioned that Amy, her cousin's wife, had nursed during the war, and there was a feeling of tension once more. Even his mother understood some English. Vicky made Max explain that Amy had nursed German casualties as well as British ones.

Soon Max's father left for his office job. Max took Vicky out to show her around some of the town. The day was dull, but not too cold. People were going about their normal business, but she looked bewildered by the snatches of different languages being spoken, generally German or a version of French that she would have found almost as impenetrable. She liked the cobbled streets and little waterways crossed by tiny bridges, and he explained there were different branches of the river Ill.

They took lunch at a small café, then he showed her a monument to the pioneer printer, Gutenberg, and they peeped inside the cathedral. As they strolled back there was a tempting smell of gingerbread and they stopped by a stall so he could buy her some. She found it delightfully spicy, and it was clear she was beginning to enjoy her visit. How pretty she looked, her light brown suit setting off her auburn hair.

Time's passing, he thought. *Surely people here can forget the conflicts between different factions, now the actual fighting is well behind us.*

They dawdled back as it was growing dark. Some young men were leaving work, and as they approached, two of them called out to him. He greeted them a little warily in German and they taunted him angrily, calling him a traitor. The old emptiness overcame him, the feeling that he was unwelcome in his own hometown. What must it seem like to Vicky, who had grown up in a sedate household in comfortable Britain? He hurried her away.

'People here can be very hostile,' he told her. 'Those are chaps I knew at school. They know or suspect I was passing information to the French and the British in the war.' He looked around to see if they were following him, but they were out of sight. 'That's why I felt I could not come back here.'

She looked disconsolate as they walked back to the house. 'You need to make a new life in England,' she urged him.

Back home, he told his family what had happened.

His father shrugged. 'I warned you.'

They settled down to another family meal.

Later in the evening there were voices in the street outside. Then suddenly a shower of pebbles hit their window and they all recoiled in fright. Vicky trembled, and Max felt himself go pale. There was the sound of laughter and footsteps running away.

His grandfather pulled back the curtain, revealing a crack in the glass. He peered into the street. 'They've gone away. I don't suppose they'll be back.'

'I thought it was safe to return, at least for a brief visit,' Max said, miserably.

'People still insult us about you,' his father told him.

'Then we must leave, first thing tomorrow morning,' he told them. 'I don't want to put you in danger, or Vicky. I'm sorry, darling, we need to pack.'

She stared at him, as though unable to believe how he was being treated, and then reluctantly followed him into their room to collect up their belongings. They piled them into his large suitcase with the reinforced corners.

Next morning they prepared to leave at first light. The blouse she had washed the previous morning was only just dry enough to wear.

'Even with Amy's gift I've hardly sufficient clothes,' she told him.

'I will keep writing,' his grandfather said. 'Sometime soon the majority of people here will be glad to be French again, I feel sure of it.'

'It's what I long for.' Now he had seen them again he was deeply hurt by the continuing friction.

'Then you can come again to see us.'

His parents said goodbye, embracing both of them, but Grandfather held Vicky close. 'I'm pleased to have met you,' he said.

Grandfather is old now, Max thought. *Will I ever see him again?*

At the station he bought tickets for Paris: there was not long to wait for the train. She still looked downcast.

'We'll be able to stay there for four nights before we go back,' he told her, smiling.

She brightened. 'It'll be wonderful, having time to see the city properly! Have you ever had the chance to explore it?'

'Once, for nearly a week. Happily it is south of the areas where there was fighting, so it hasn't suffered much. You'll love it!'

'Can we afford to stay there?'

Barely, he thought. 'We'll find a cheap *pension*.'

Perhaps visiting the capital would make up to her for the disturbing situation in Strasbourg.

Chapter 24

Larchbury, December 1921

'What a wonderful surprise!' Amy cried as Aunt Sophie let her into the neat little house in Alma Road. Florence's baby had arrived two weeks earlier than expected, at the beginning of December, when she and James had only just moved into their home.

'Baby Simon and Florence are both doing well,' Aunt Sophie said, leading her into the parlour, where her friend was sitting contentedly with her baby. Amy admired the sleepy little boy.

'It was an easy birth,' Florence told her. 'James is thrilled with his son.' He had had to go to work that morning.

'I expect your parents are delighted, too.'

'Yes, though they wanted me to have a girl, as Sarah has boys!'

Amy looked around Florence's house, which she had not visited before. The comfortable blue-grey parlour furniture looked new, but Amy recognised a bookcase from Florence's room in her parents' house.

'We haven't been able to buy much furniture of our own,' Florence said. 'Our dining table is the one James's parents used before they replaced it with a larger one.'

'It looks as though you have all you need,' Amy said, approving the cosy nursery they had arranged for Simon.

When Aunt Sophie had phoned Amy with the news of the baby, she had rushed out, leaving Beth with her parents at Sebastopol Terrace, and come straight on to Florence's house. 'It's perfect for me that Simon arrived early,' she said, 'because the day after tomorrow we're going back to Roehampton. Edmond is eager to get back to work before Christmas.'

'Is he well enough now?'

'He assures me he is,' she said dubiously. The accident had caused further damage to his lung. He still tired easily and she wondered how exhausted he might become when he completed a whole day at work.

There was a knock at the door and this time it was Lavinia, who had driven over from Alderbank to see the new arrival. She swept in merrily, and Aunt Sophie went to make them all tea.

'Goodness, there are only just enough seats for everyone,' Florence said.

'How's Christopher?' Amy asked Lavinia.

'He's doing very well.' Amy seldom saw Lavinia's little boy, for she often left him with the nanny so she could pursue her various interests.

'Are you all right, Amy?' Florence asked her. 'You don't look as bright as usual.'

She had been feeling tired. 'I can't stop worrying about Edmond,' she admitted. 'When he was wounded in the war he nearly died. Then, as he began to recover, there was that setback when his bad lung was affected by the fumes from the factories in Wealdham.' She broke off to gratefully accept her tea.

'After a year he was well enough to go back to university,' she went on, 'but he still tired easily to start with. Then when we moved and he began work he was impatient to prove his ability, but I could see him growing weary and had to insist he rested at weekends. Now he's had another setback.' *Will there ever be a time when I can stop worrying about his health*, she wondered.

'It's been tough for you,' Florence said.

'We've had good times, though.' She was always happy in his company.

'Something else bothers me,' she went on. 'Wilfrid Fairlawn has behaved abominably again, and I expect he'll go unpunished.' Lavinia knew all the problems he had caused before, though Florence was not aware of what had taken place in Ypres.

'I think he's back serving with the Army of Occupation again,' Amy said, 'and his father is bound to use his influence to support him. When Wilfrid was charging towards us in the hunt he could have killed one of us – in fact, it was thanks to him the horse had to be put down.' She found her fists clenching whenever she thought about that day. She still missed seeing Wanderer. They had told Beth he had gone to a home for old horses. Edmond had discovered the loss soon after discharging himself from hospital, and for a while he had been inconsolable. Even on their wedding anniversary his smile had occasionally faded.

'Fairlawn is a nightmare,' Lavinia agreed. 'He and his father are well-respected for their wartime service, of course, but his behaviour that day has caused a lot of unpleasant scandal for him in Alderbank, and he won't be allowed to ride with the hunt again.'

Amy felt a little relieved. 'All the same, he'll probably avoid being prosecuted. If you have a certain status you can get away with almost anything, it seems.'

'It's that kind of thing that makes me want to become more involved in politics,' Lavinia said. 'Now women can become councillors, I plan to stand for election.'

The others looked at her with admiration.

—

Edmond was cleaning his car. Soon they would be loading in their belongings ready to return to Roehampton.

'I hope you're not overdoing it, son.' Pa had come outside to check his progress. 'There's some coffee – time you took a break.'

Edmond was unwilling to admit that he felt weary.

'I'll get Chambers to help you finish the car,' Pa said as Edmond followed him indoors.

'I suppose I should accept some assistance,' he said, 'if only so Amy doesn't worry.'

Sometimes he caught her looking anxious. *Poor darling, she suffered a serious shock when I was felled by Wilfrid Fairlawn*, he thought. He blamed himself for reacting in such an extreme way when the major had led the huntsmen on to their land. *If I hadn't been so furious with Fairlawn he probably wouldn't have reacted so wildly and I wouldn't have got injured again. And Wanderer might still be here. I must calm down and give Amy an easier time. I shouldn't occasion her any more anxiety.*

'I don't want to hear that you're overdoing things at Roehampton,' Pa went on. Ma and Beatrice had gone shopping. 'You must take it easy at weekends.'

'I'll be careful,' he promised.

'Are you all right for money?' Pa asked. 'It's unfortunate you've had over three weeks off. I can spare some cash so you're not under any pressure.'

'But you've had money problems, Pa. It can't be easy.'

'I've been checking the forest, and we've got some flourishing small trees that'll be ideal for Christmas – people in the village keep enquiring about them. I can spare some cash.'

'Very well, Pa – I'm really grateful.' He was only accepting it because he wanted to get Amy something special for Christmas.

–

He drove them back to The Beeches for Christmas. As they walked into the hall Beth exclaimed in delight at the Christmas tree standing there, festooned with baubles.

'You found a fine specimen!' Edmond cried as Pa greeted them.

'Yes, we had dozens that were a suitable size to dig up,' he said, beaming, 'thanks to everyone who worked so hard after the fire. We sold our supply of trees in the market, just before Christmas, and we actually ran out. We had to take orders and dig up a few slightly smaller ones and deliver them to customers the following day.'

On the morning of Christmas Day, as they opened their presents, Amy looked weary lounging beside him on the sofa. *At least she'll have the chance to relax here, Edmond thought.*

'I couldn't bring your present, sweetheart,' he told her, when all the other gifts had been exchanged. 'I couldn't wrap it up or fit it in the car. But it'll be delivered when we get back to Roehampton.'

Her eyes widened. 'Whatever is it? Are you going to at least tell me what you've chosen for me?'

He put his arm around her. 'Remember the piano we saw in that shop in Roehampton?'

'Oh, yes! You made me go in and try it out, even though it was quite costly.'

'It'll fit very well into that alcove in our drawing room. I've measured it out.'

'You mean...' Her eyes widened.

'Yes – I had to buy it for you. You've wanted one for so long!'

'What's it like?' Beatrice asked eagerly, and he had to give her all the details.

Amy was still looking anxious. 'Edmond, that was the sweetest idea, but we can't possibly afford it!'

Earlier in the autumn he had thought his salary would be enough to cover it, but he had missed some weeks after his accident. He had been worried, concerned he might need to empty their bank account or ask for an advance on his salary, and either option would alarm Amy. 'It's all right,' he told her. 'I negotiated some discount!'

The shop was owned by a neighbour of theirs, who had become a close friend since discovering that Edmond had served in the same regiment as his son. 'When I told him that you were in France too, as a VAD nurse, he was determined I should be able to buy it for you and gave me a reduction.'

She melted into his arms. 'Darling, it's the most wonderful gift I've ever had!'

'I'm glad you'll have your own instrument,' Beatrice said.

'I'll never reach your standard of playing,' Amy told her, 'but I intend to practise every day!'

His parents had decided fairly late in December to hold the ball as usual, three days after Christmas, though the guest list was shorter than other years, and the food would be less elaborate.

'We can't spend so much as usual,' Pa said. 'And it's been a very trying year for Ma – I couldn't ask her to provide a huge spread of festive food.'

'People will understand,' Edmond said.

A few hours before the ball, Pa drove to the station to meet Vicky and Max.

'I'm glad you invited them,' Edmond said to Ma.

'I suppose I must get used to having a German in the family,' she said wearily. 'Even Agnes has accepted him now.' Vicky's father still shunned his new son-in-law.

Amy put Beth to bed in the early evening, then changed into her best dress in peach-coloured silk. Edmond was changing into evening dress.

'It's going to be one of those evenings when we leave the festivities early,' she said. 'Remember you've still not fully recovered from your accident.' He was just about coping with being at work again, but she was anxious he should not overexert himself.

'So long as we can dance together.' They had been falling in love at the 1914 ball, the first she had attended. He had missed the 1915 one as he could not get leave. Later there had been the year he was recovering from his wounds and she had had a damaged ankle and was also expecting Beth a few days later. They had insisted on making a short, sedate tour of the dance floor together.

'And you shouldn't overdo things tonight either!' he told her, with a loving smile. On Christmas Day, after he had told her of the stupendous gift he had bought her, she had been impatient to impart her news. That evening, in their room, as she lay in his arms, she had revealed what lay ahead, to his great joy.

Tonight they were soon greeting guests in the ballroom, where there was another Christmas tree. Caleb had managed to get leave from Germany, and Beatrice seldom left his side. People were becoming accustomed to seeing him with her.

In spite of the shortened guest list, Amy was happy to see her parents there.

'It's a little unreal this year,' Pa was saying to them. 'I wanted to invite my forestry men, as they've worked so hard clearing and replanting the stricken area.'

'You should have,' Edmond said. 'Remember what's happening in the war cemeteries – there's no distinction between ranks.'

'My wife couldn't imagine some of the ones from quite poor families fitting in,' Pa told Amy's parents.

'I can see it might be a problem,' Father said.

She was glad that Pa now regarded him as a friend and confidant.

'So in the end I invited them all, and their wives, in the case of those who are married, to a meal at the inn, just before Christmas.'

'I've heard people talking of it in the village,' Mother said. 'It sounds as though they all enjoyed the occasion.'

—

Later they moved into the large dining room for the buffet. It was less lavish than usual but Cook had provided platters of chicken and tongue, and a meat loaf. Florence and James were there, though they were planning to leave early; Florence had left little Simon in the care of Aunt Sophie, but she needed to return to feed him.

'Someone at work, who lives in Alderbank, has heard something about Wilfrid Fairlawn,' James told them.

Amy looked at him warily. She had been trying to forget the man's existence.

'He's being sent to join the troops in Ireland,' James said. 'They're setting up the Irish Free State, but there's still unrest out there. I gather it's an unpopular posting. I think someone very senior has heard of his latest behaviour.'

She was relieved that he would be far away, and no longer regarded as a distinguished officer.

Vicky and Max joined them. It was the first opportunity Edmond's cousin had had to tell them about their honeymoon. Amy was concerned to learn of the situation in Strasbourg.

'Max told us the position might still be volatile there,' Edmond said.

Vicky went on to tell them of their days in Paris, in the hilly area of Montmartre. She was animated as she described the bohemian atmosphere there.

'One day soon you must both come to visit us in Roehampton,' Edmond said.

'That would be very enjoyable,' Max said.

'I've had an idea,' Amy said. 'We could also invite Aunt Agnes to come over for a day. It's not far for her to travel from Melbridge – she might take a bus or a cab. She could meet you both at our house.'

Vicky hugged her. 'That would be simply lovely!'

After the meal they returned to the ballroom. The musical quartet were about to begin playing for the dancing. Before they began properly they played a loud chord so that Pa could make some announcements. The guests, now mellow with food and wine, stood curiously.

'First of all, I must thank you for all the sympathy and support you've given me since the fire,' Pa said. 'I'm happy to say that, thanks to the efforts of my workers, the regeneration is under way.'

His guests clapped. *Pa is popular*, Amy thought, *everyone respects him.*

'Next, some news from India,' he continued. 'We've heard from my elder son Peter, and he's become engaged out there to Miss Patricia Fellowes, who he has known for some years. They will be getting married in the spring.'

There was more excitement. Amy and Edmond had heard this news when they had arrived at The Beeches.

'In addition, I'm delighted to announce that my daughter, Beatrice, is to marry Warrant Officer Caleb Fawcett,' he said. A buzz of conversation broke out, as people exchanged glances. Amy could imagine that some of them were remembering the time, four years earlier, when her engagement to Charles had been announced. *At last she'll be able to wear that gorgeous wedding dress*, she thought.

'Warrant Officer Fawcett hopes to be discharged soon from the United States Army,' he went on, 'and then I shall be welcoming him to join my business.'

There were murmurs of congratulation. Amy and Edmond hurried to embrace Beatrice and welcome Caleb to the family. He seemed thankful for their support. 'We must find a ring for Beatrice before I return to Germany,' he said.

The band began playing and Pa took Ma in his arms for the first waltz. She was elegantly dressed, as usual, with much silver jewellery. She went around with him in a stately fashion.

Soon other couples were taking their places on the dance floor. Beatrice and Caleb were quickly followed by Vicky and Max. Amy's parents and Florence and James followed more sedately. Then Edmond took Amy into his arms, dancing enthusiastically, as though his recent injury had been imagined. She moved more closely into his arms.

After another few dances, Caleb asked Florence for a dance and she joined him briefly for a waltz.

'I'm still grateful to him,' she told Amy afterwards, 'for that time in France when he drove me to the coast in his ambulance. But now James and I must be going home.'

'Stay a few more minutes!' Amy begged. 'I believe there will be another announcement.'

'We should tell them our news too,' she whispered to Edmond a moment later.

'Are you sure? Isn't it too early?'

'No – I'm certain now.'

She hurried to impart their news to Ma and Pa, and then, while Pa spoke to the leader of the quartet, to her own parents. All of them looked thrilled.

The musicians played another chord.

'There's yet another announcement!' Pa said. 'Finally, I am very happy to tell you that my son Edmond and his wife Amy will be presenting us with another grandchild next summer.'

There was further clapping, and more smiles and congratulations.

Florence came over to Amy and embraced her. 'I'm so glad for you!' she said.

The band started their next tune and Edmond took Amy into his arms again.

'If only the baby is all right this time,' she whispered.

'Don't worry. We're together, and that's what matters.'

'We survived the terrifying war years,' she agreed. 'We've come so far, and we have years of happiness ahead.' *Whatever happens, even if he has further health problems we'll manage somehow.*

He led her on to the dance floor. As they waltzed among the happy couples, it was as though the years were swept away and they were enjoying the first raptures of their love.

A letter from Rosemary

It's wonderful to see *Until We Can Forgive* published. I'm thrilled to have the backing of Hera Books, and that you have chosen my historical romance to read.

I'm also delighted that my books are to be available in paperback.

My first two books in the series covered the experiences of Amy and Edmond as they met and fell in love during World War I. We saw how its horrors affected them and their friends. This book begins in 1919. Edmond was adjusting to his severe war wound, continuing his studies at Cambridge.

Peace had finally arrived, but much had changed since 1914, and my characters needed to adjust to a different world. Would it ever be possible to be reconciled with the Germans?

One positive change was the emancipation of women – after their efforts during the war they would now get the vote – at least when they reached thirty! Our former Suffragettes welcomed new opportunities, but their situations were often complicated by the demands of marriage and motherhood.

Edmond's cousin Vicky and sister Beatrice fell in love with men from abroad they would not have met in earlier years.

I hope you enjoyed their story. If you did, I would love to hear your impressions in a review. I welcome readers' feedback, and it helps others to discover my book.

If you would like to talk to me directly about *Until We Can Forgive*, you can find me on my social media pages:

Twitter:
@RoseGoodacre
Facebook:
Rosemary Goodacre Author
LinkedIn:
Rosemary Goodacre

Thank you again for choosing my book and for your support. It is lovely to receive your comments, and encourages me to write further stories.

Best wishes

Rosemary

Acknowledgments

I am very grateful to Keshini Naidoo and Lindsey Mooney at Hera Books, for giving me this wonderful opportunity and guiding me through the process of being published.

I have obtained valuable information for this book from *Bandages & Benevolence*, by John Weeks, (published by Maidstone & Tunbridge Wells NHS Trust, printed by PB Group, ISBN No. 978-0-9576847-0-6.) It is an account of Tunbridge Wells hospitals from the time in the nineteenth century when they developed from a dispensary, to the present day. It describes what hospitals were like around 1920, well before the arrival of the NHS.

I have a great respect for the Suffragettes, active in the period before World War I, and the suffragists, who were less militant. Many of them did valuable war work and helped women to be recognised as deserving the same rights as their menfolk. By 1918 women were granted the vote.

I must also mention the Romantic Novelists' Association, a valuable source of helpful advice and encouragement for novice writers. Formed to promote romantic fiction and encourage good writing, this year (2020) it celebrates its sixtieth birthday (with virtual meetings, naturally).

Sincere thanks to all who helped me in my path to becoming a published writer.